THE OLD VICARAGE

Daphne Neville

ISBN: 978-1-326-42128-1

PublishNation, London
www.publishnation.co.uk

Other Titles by this Author

The Ringing Bells Inn
Polquillick
Sea, Sun, Cads and Scallywags
Grave Allegations

1986

CHAPTER ONE

Molly Smith took her thick winter coat from a brass peg tucked beneath the stairs in the hallway and carried it into the sitting room where she draped it across the back of the settee. From the rug in front of the hearth she picked up her fleecy lined bootees and slipped her feet into each whilst firmly gripping the mantelpiece in order to keep her balance. Once the boots were securely zipped she put on her coat and then a scarf which she tucked neatly inside the coat's fur collar. When the coat was buttoned up, she picked up her hand knitted woollen gloves from the sideboard, walked through the kitchen and left Rose Cottage by way of the back door porch.

Outside, from on top of the aluminium coal bunker, Molly carefully picked up a holly wreath made by her grand-daughter, Anne, and securely holding a piece of string to avoid pricking her fingers, she carried it down the garden path and out through the gate into the street.

A cold north wind whipped down the deserted road causing crumpled, wizened, brown leaves to dance in the gutters as Molly stepped onto the pavement and closed the gate. Turning left, she walked as briskly as her aged legs were able; she was after all a woman of eighty two years. Not that a stranger would ever guess, for she wore her years well, kept herself active, valued her independence and swore blind she would never be a burden to her ever growing family.

Outside the church Molly stopped and glanced up at the old turreted tower from which the red leaves of the Virginia creeper had long since withered, faded and dropped onto the grass verges where autumnal winds had blown them into neat heaps beneath the hedgerows and surrounding stone walls. Under Molly's gaze the church clock struck the hour and rang out the time to those within earshot.

Holding the railing with her left hand, Molly climbed up the old granite steps and walked beneath the lichgate where she stopped to read the new notices pinned on the wooden board. It was her turn to do the flowers on December the twenty first along with school teacher, Meg Reynolds; a special Sunday too, the last in Advent, the Sunday in which the Service of Nine Lessons and Carols always took place. Molly smiled with satisfaction; she enjoyed arranging the flowers, especially near to Christmas, when she could put a few silver branches into her offering along with sprigs of holly. She therefore looked upon the task more as a privilege than a chore.

On the other side of the lichgate Molly stepped onto the gravel path and followed it through the churchyard, past the old lichen covered gravestones of the long forgotten dead and into the new part where flowers, mostly chrysanthemums, nodded in the breeze beneath clean headstones which glistened in the watery sunshine. Beside a grave in the last row she stopped, knelt and laid her wreath beside the fresh flowers she had left just two days before. She then stood and told her late husband, Major Benjamin Smith, of the family's plans for Christmas, how she had kept herself occupied for the last two days, how much she missed him and for the hundredth time she thanked him for the thirty four glorious years of married life they had shared.

In no hurry to return to her empty cottage, Molly sat on the bench bought ten years earlier by Bertha Fillingham in memory of her late husband, George. Molly thought it a lovely tribute to a lost partner and wondered if she might do something similar. For the occupancy of the graveyard was continually growing and she knew that she was not alone in enjoying the peace and solitude offered in Trengillion's final resting place.

From her coat pocket Molly pulled a packet of cigarettes. She took one from the box and popped it between her lips. As she lit it she felt a pang of guilt. Ten years earlier she had given up smoking and thus for ten years had been free of the habit. But in the days following the major's death she had started again. She knew he would not have approved but it made her feel better, at least she felt better mentally, but if she were honest she knew it was doing nothing to enhance her general health.

Molly glanced along the mounds of grass beneath which lay the major's neighbours. Two weeks before his passing, the village had lost Bertha Fillingham, and in the summer of the previous year, Molly's neighbour and friend, Doris Hughes, had peacefully passed away. Both ladies lay on the major's right hand side, while to his left lay Cyril Penrose, a Trengillion farmer who had worked hard all his life on Long Acre Farm.

As Molly sat reflecting on the changes, she noticed Gertie Collins, daughter of the late Cyril approaching with a holly wreath not dissimilar to the one she had brought for the major.

"Snap," Molly heard Gertie say as she waved the wreath in the air. "I see our Anne's been busy."

Molly put out the stub of her cigarette and smiled broadly. Gertie seemed to have that effect; the ability to brighten the day of those in her company and often without needing to open her mouth.

Stooping, Gertie lay the wreath on her father's grave and then sat down on the bench beside Molly. "I think Anne must have stripped the holly bush at the Old Vicarage bare. She's made them for all our family."

Molly nodded. "She made two for me as well; one for the major and one for my front door."

Gertie rubbed her gloveless hands together to warm them. "She's a clever old stick and I love the way she dots sprays of pretty dried flowers amongst the holly leaves."

Molly agreed and glanced towards Cyril's grave. "How's your mother keeping?" she whispered. "I saw her the other day and thought how pale she looked, but then I know what she's going through and believe me, time does help although it's especially tough this time of the year; you know, Christmas and all that. So many memories come flooding back and the major always liked Christmas." Molly blinked away the tears welling in her eyes. "The carol service was a favourite of his; he liked to go carol singing too, even though he didn't have much of a voice. It'll be strange this year: like your mother, it'll be my first Christmas as a widow."

Gertie sighed. "Oh dear, but you mustn't be glum, the major had a good and long life and so did Dad, and Mum's alright except for a rotten cold which I suppose was probably why she looked a bit pale when you saw her. Having said that, I saw Jean this morning and she said Mum's feeling a lot better and they were going to do some festive baking."

"That's nice, she's very lucky having a caring family. Our Stella and the grandchildren have been very good to me as well, and Rose too, she pops in every day, bless her."

"And Ned as well no doubt."

Molly laughed. "Oh yes, he's a frequent visitor and as big a fusspot as ever."

Gertie pushed away a strand of hair which had blown into her eye. "I'm really glad Mum has Tony and Jean living with her and running the farm because it's nice for her to see Dad's hard work is continuing in their capable hands. Not that he did much up there in the end but he did like to potter about and pretend he was still the gaffer."

Molly smiled. "It's not easy, Gert, for us elderly to accept we're no longer able to do things which at one time we'd not have given a second thought to."

Gertie sighed. "I suppose not."

"Do your mother and Jean get along well?"

"Oh yes, in fact Jean looks after Mum as if she was her own gran. Tony couldn't have found himself a better wife."

Molly nodded. "Good. I like her too; she has a lovely temperament. Mind you; your other son did alright marrying our Anne. What a perfect team they are. What with your John's wonderful building skills and Anne's artistic flair they've turned the Old Vicarage into one of Trengillion's finest properties."

Gertie giggled. "Yes, and on top of that they've still managed to have two children along the way. I don't think Tony and Jean will have children though, not for a while yet anyway, they're both so tied up with the farm they'd never have the time and to be honest I don't think Jean's the maternal sort." Noticing Molly was shivering, Gertie took her arm. "Come on, I think it's time we made a move, it's too cold to sit around and we don't want you laid up for Christmas."

"Oh dear, what a dreadful thought," said Molly, fondly patting Gertie's hand. "Spending Christmas in bed, I mean, although I did do it once before many years ago when I was a child and I had the flu. I remember feeling so bad that I didn't even care that I was missing

Christmas. Mind you, I was pretty fed up when I got better. I felt I'd been well and truly cheated."

She rose to her feet, blew the major a kiss and then left the churchyard, arms linked with Gertie who chatted all the way back to Rose Cottage.

John Collins and his work partner, Steve Penhaligon, who was also his brother-in-law, drove along the rugged track to a barn at Long Acre Farm where they kept their building supplies and tools. As they emerged from the barn, having parked their truck inside, John's twin brother, Tony, came out from the farmhouse to greet them.

"Come inside and join us if you can spare the time. Jean and Gran have been baking mince pies for your return and I've a damn good batch of home brew ready if you want something stronger than tea to wash them down."

John rubbed his chilled hands together. "Brilliant, but I mustn't have more than one pint because I've got to choose a Christmas tree before I go home. Not that Anne knows, she thinks I'm going to get one tomorrow, but I thought I'd do it today for a surprise."

Tony looked up at the sky. "But it's nearly dark so how will you be able to choose a nice one if you can't see properly?"

Steve nodded. "That's just what I said, Tone. Leave it 'til tomorrow John; that's when I'm getting mine and Sue and the kids are coming up as well, to help choose it."

John shrugged his shoulders. "Okay, I'll do that."

Tony led the two men into the farmhouse. "We've already got our tree," he said, waving his hand as they turned the corner in the hallway, "so make sure you pay the women a few compliments. Gran still seemed a bit low because of the cold she's had and so Jean insisted we got in a tree to try and cheer her up. I think it's worked judging by the laughter I've heard today."

In a field where once sheep had grazed, Jean Collins grew Christmas trees. The idea had first come to her shortly after her marriage to Tony in 1978, for she already had twenty small trees growing in pots which she had raised from seed a year or two before, hence she was thrilled when her new grandfather-in-law, Cyril

Penrose, encouraged her to start her own small nursery and he relished in its success as much as Jean. For as the trees flourished she sowed more seeds and eventually Long Acre Farm became the place to go for Christmas trees. Every year since they had graced the living rooms, lounges, sitting rooms and hallways of Trengillion homes and beyond.

Nettie Penrose sat in her beloved rocking chair beside the farm's original and newly fettled Cornish Range. She waved as her grandsons walked into the warm kitchen with their brother-in-law, Steve. In turn they each kissed her cheek and asked after her health.

She chuckled from behind the half-empty pint glass in her hand. "You know, lads, I've been a farmer's wife for fifty years or more, and except for taking a rest following the birth of our Gertie, I've never so much as had a day off." She took a sip of beer. "I may have been a bit peaky lately but you can put that down to the loss of your dear grandfather, God rest his soul. But right now, I'm feeling as fit as a fiddle and I reckon I'm good for a few more years yet." Her eyes twinkled. "I hope so anyway, because Tony's got this home brewing malarkey off to a fine art, and he's made a batch of stout for Christmas which he says will be ready in a few days."

John grinned as he pulled up a chair beside his grandmother and Tony handed him a full glass. "Thanks, Tony. Cheers."

Steve sat down at the large pine table as Jean began to serve warm mince pies.

"Now," said John, patting his grandmother's hand. "Are you all coming to us for Christmas dinner or not? Anne keeps badgering me to persuade you but I know you've a mind of your own and are often reluctant to leave your bloomin' rocking chair. But please do come, we'll all be there then and the children would love to see you. Why, only the other day Ollie asked why Granny Net was misrul."

Nettie tutted. "Bloomin' rocking chair indeed, you cheeky so and so. May I remind you there were times in the past when I didn't sit down between dawn and dusk, and for that reason I think I'm entitled to take my ease a little now."

"That's more like it, Gran, it's good to see you've not lost your fighting spirit. So can I take it you'll join us for Christmas then?"

"Well actually I was going to tell you before you insulted me that we've chewed things over, Tony, Jean and myself, and we'd like to accept your invitation. I reckon it'll do our Jean good to have a rest and be waited on, not that your Anne doesn't need a rest too, she works hard does that girl and she's a credit to you and your little 'uns."

John looked relieved. "That's brilliant, Anne will be pleased. She's been making preparations for weeks."

"Hmm, preparation is half the fun of Christmas, I used to love it when your mum was little. Will Molly be there? I hope she will; she and I have a lot in common, having both become widows this year. Funny old thing, time! I remember when she first arrived here back in fifties, all dressed in bright colours, feathers, and so forth she was. We thought she was really weird back then with her fortune telling and skulduggery, but she's one of us now and I feel privileged to know her."

John bit into a mince pie. "Yeah, she'll be there; in fact if you three come there'll be twenty in all, so you might even need to bring your bloomin' rocking chair."

"Twenty," laughed Nettie, "you'll never get a turkey big enough and if you do it won't fit in the oven."

"We've an eighteen pound turkey in the freezer and it does fit in the oven because we tried it and we have the Rayburn as well as the electric cooker so there'll be room for the spuds and trimmings. Anne's going to roast a joint of pork too because some folks aren't too keen on turkey. So that should be enough, especially as six of the twenty are children anyway, and they never have much of an appetite on Christmas Day, even though we try and stop them eating too many sweets."

"Talking of sweets, I saw your mum buying a bar of chocolate in the post office earlier when I went in for a bag of flour," said Jean, offering round more mince pies, "and she told me Diane's chosen the date for her wedding at last. She and her fiancé, I can't remember his name, settled it over a romantic dinner last night and apparently and she's over the moon. Susan popped in to tell your mum after Diane rang her this morning to pass on the news."

"Diane's chap is Mike, Mike Westward," said Steve, taking his third mince pie.

Jean nodded. "Ah, yes, of course, I remember, nice bloke and he plays rugby, doesn't he?"

Steve nodded.

"So when is the wedding then." John asked.

"June," said Jean, "June the thirteenth."

"Thirteenth!" Nettie exclaimed. "I hope to goodness that's not a Friday."

Jean shook her head. "No, it's definitely a Saturday because I've already jotted it down in next year's diary."

"Well, so that's nearly everyone in the Pact hitched now then," said Tony, sitting on a stool with a full pint glass. "Only Jane, Graham and Matthew left and I reckon Graham will be settling down soon because Ginny's there every weekend, although I'm not too sure how serious Jane is about Giles and vice versa."

"And don't forget Lily," John added, waving his finger, "she's still unattached. Anne had a letter from her the other day and it seems there's no man in her life or if there is she's keeping quiet about him."

"Whatever do you mean by the Pact?" asked Nettie Penrose, peeking over the rim of her glasses. "It sounds quite sinister to me."

During the long hot summer of 1976, the young twenty somethings of Trengillion, dreading they might one day all lose touch with each other, made a pact stating they would never leave their native Cornwall. Furthermore, should any Pact members still be unmarried in the year 1990 then he or she should marry whosoever in the Pact was also unmarried in order that no-one be left to live a life of solitude; for they had all known each other for as long as they could remember and looked upon the possibility of losing touch with dread and sorrow.

Five Pact members married within the first three years. Anne Stanley, who back in the carefree days of that halcyon summer, worked on the reception desk at Trengillion's prestigious Penwynton Hotel, wed fellow Pact member, builder John Collins in the summer of 1977, and one and a half years later, twins, Oliver Grenville Collins and Jessica Amber Collins, known by all as Ollie and Jess, were born. Their birth caused great amusement, for Ollie was born first, five minutes before Big Ben struck the midnight hour on New Year's Eve and Jess was born seventeen minutes later on New

Year's Day, hence the twins were born not only on different days and months, but in different years also.

Elizabeth Stanley, Anne's older sister, formerly a primary school teacher, married Gregory Castor-Hunt, also in the summer of 1977. Elizabeth, and Greg a solicitor who worked in Helston, bought and lived in their first home, Cove Cottage, which for many years had been a holiday home for a family who were frequent visitors to Trengillion. Elizabeth and Greg also had two children, Willoughby Edward Castor-Hunt and Talwyn Jennifer Castor-Hunt, known to all as Wills and Tally.

Susan Collins, the only daughter of Gertie and Percy Collins and sister of twins, Tony and John, married builder Steve Penhaligon, partner and work colleague of her brother, John, in 1978. They lived at number four Coronation Terrace; a row of four 1950s houses belonging to the local authorities. Since their marriage Steve had been keen to purchase a plot of land and build a house of their own, but Susan liked Coronation Terrace; her parents were near neighbours which was ideal when a babysitter was required for their two children, Denzil, named after Steve's late father, and daughter, Demelza.

Matthew Williams insisted he was a confirmed bachelor and was perfectly happy living at home with his parents, Betty and Peter Williams at Fuchsia Cottage. Since leaving school his sole occupation, like his father, had been fishing. In his early days he worked as crew with Ron Trevelyan from Polquillick and dated Ron's daughter, but in 1982 he had his own boat built, the *Betty Jane* and began fishing from Trengillion.

Matthew's older sister, Jane Williams, had her own small business, a beach café in the fishermen's loft jointly owned by her father, Peter, and his partner, Percy Collins. She cautiously began the business shortly before her relationship with a chef from the Penwynton Hotel ended, and to her delight, business flourished with each ensuing year. She was still unmarried, but had a steady boyfriend, Giles Wilson, a farmer, relatively new to Trengillion, who along with his brother, Brendan, jointly owned Higher Green Farm overlooking the village in the vicinity of the Witches Broomstick.

Diane Reynolds was the only female member of the Pact still living at home with her parents. Her mother, Meg, taught at the village school and had done so since she first qualified as a teacher in 1950. Her father, Sid, several years older than his wife, had retired from his reporting job with a local newspaper and the family also lived in Coronation Terrace. After leaving school, Diane worked for the Bristol and West Building Society, but had since moved on to a secretarial job where her boss, Mike Westward, was also her fiancé.

Diane's younger brother, Graham, an enthusiastic estate agent working in Helston, finally achieved his dream of becoming a property owner in 1981, when he bought a two bedroomed terraced house in Penwynton Crescent, Trengillion. He had a regular girlfriend, Ginny, who lived and worked in Truro, but she always spent the weekends with Graham and the couple appeared to be deeply devoted to one another.

Lillian Castor-Hunt remained a mystery and was the only member of the Pact who lived outside the county. Currently she was working up-country in her chosen career as a nurse, and had recently been promoted to ward sister, but none of her friends knew anything of her love life, not even her older brother, Greg.

The only two members of the Pact no longer in touch with the aforementioned, were Roger and Colin Withers, sons of Trengillion's erstwhile publicans, Raymond and Gloria, who ran The Badger, formerly The Sherriff's Badge for seventeen years. The Withers family left Trengillion in 1983 after sixteen years of service, or disservice as some might claim, to the community. They remained in the licensed trade, however, and took on another pub in the Falmouth area. Roger and Colin, meanwhile, had both married and gone their separate ways.

CHAPTER TWO

On the outskirts of the village situated at the end of a winding driveway lay Penwynton Hotel, a three storey building constructed in the sixteenth century and formerly the home of the Penwynton family who achieved great wealth and good fortune during the prosperous days of tin mining. Much of Trengillion owed its existence to the Penwyntons, for apart from land occupied by their residential family home, they owned farmland and farms, and many of the cottages in the village were initially built to house their workers. The Hotel's current owners were Mary and Dick Cottingham and Mary's sister and brother-in-law, Heather and Bob Jarrams, who took on the old house and turned it into a Hotel in the 1970s.

From the Hotel's basement, as darkness fell on Friday evening, Dick Cottingham and Bob Jarrams fetched two step-ladders in preparation to hang Christmas decorations ready for the festive season and the influx of visitors due the following weekend. Many of the expected guests were regulars who returned every year to meet old friends and enjoy the friendly family atmosphere.

Mary Cottingham and Heather Jarrams, had decided well before Christmas to have the dining room, function room and reception area, decorated on a purple and yellow colour scheme interspersed with lashings of gold tinsel and gold baubles, hence an abundance of purple and yellow spray paint had been used to colour dried leaves, seed heads, branches, twigs, thistles and the large heads of faded hydrangeas.

While the men hung garlands of the foliage entwined with tinsel and ribbons from the ceiling in the reception area, the ladies filled vases and urns with yellow chrysanthemums and placed bowls of purple hyacinths on surfaces where their strong scent would be most effective.

"I think I'm getting a bit long in the tooth for climbing ladders," said Dick, wiping his brow, "I actually feel quite queasy up here."

"Then come down," commanded Mary, beckoning him to return to ground level, "and we'll get our Linda to do it. Heights don't bother her or she'd never be able to go hang-gliding."

"Did someone mention my name?" a female voice called. Four heads turned to see Linda closing the front door with Annette, the oldest of her three young daughters, by her side.

"Right on cue," grinned Dick, descending the ladder, "that's my girl."

"Your dad's suffering with a touch of vertigo, Linda; be a treasure and help Uncle Bob hang that garland."

"Of course, that's why I'm here and Annette insisted on coming with me. Samantha and Debbie were too sleepy so Jamie's putting them to bed early. They played rounders in the school playground today, you see, and I think it's tired them out."

Linda took off her coat and hung it on the bottom of the banister. "The flowers are looking really good, especially the hydrangeas. To be honest I thought the yellow ones might look a bit over-the-top but they're actually quite magnificent."

Heather nodded. "We thought so too. It was your mother's idea and when she first suggested it I said they'd be colourful enough if we just let them dry naturally in pink, white and blue, but the purple and yellow are stunning and much more eye catching."

"We put our decorations up today," said Annette, removing her gloves and tucking them into her coat pocket, "and I've got a little Christmas tree in my bedroom, but it's not real, it's silver and white."

"How lovely," said Mary, bending to kiss her granddaughter's rosy cheek, "and I went shopping yesterday and bought you something to put with your decorations; I'll just go and get it."

As Mary left the vestibule, Annette took off her coat and sat on the bottom step of the staircase beside Dick. "Grandpa, do you think it will snow for Christmas? Dad said it won't cos it never does in Cornwall, but there's always a chance it will, isn't there? And it'd be really exciting if it did."

"Oh dear, I think your dad will most likely be right. I remember wanting a white Christmas when I was eight like you, but I don't actually remember having one and that was up-country where it gets much colder. We usually had plenty of snow afterwards though."

"I'm not eight, I'm nine and a half," corrected Annette, indignantly, as her grandmother re-appeared.

Mary handed Annette a plastic carrier bag. "Here you are, sweetheart. It's for you and your sisters to put with your other decorations. I hope you like it."

Annette eagerly opened the bag and from it took a red box. To her delight, inside was a twelve inch tall Father Christmas, complete with sack and a bell on the end of his hat.

"Look on his back," said Mary, "under his jacket there's a key. Turn it and wind him up."

Annette did as instructed and stood the figure on the floor. To her delight the jolly figure sang Jingle Bells and rocked to and fro. "He's lovely, Grandma, thank you ever so much. I can't wait to show the others."

While Annette wound and rewound Father Christmas, her mother climbed the ladder and helped her uncle hang the garlands. And when the reception area was finished they gathered the remaining decorations and moved on into the function room.

"Oh, my goodness," Linda cried when she saw the Christmas tree, "I didn't realise you were going to spray that too."

"Well, do you like it?" Her mother asked.

Linda tilted her head to one side. "Hmm, yes, I think so. At least I think I will when it's decorated, but it looks a bit stark and overwhelming at present."

The eight feet tall artificial tree which had graced the function room for the past five years, in Mary's eyes looked shabby and tired. And so to give it a new lease of life she had sprayed it yellow to match the rest of the decorations.

"I agree with you," said Dick, shaking his head, "I think the yellow's far too bright and summery."

"But that's why I like it," Mary said in self-defence. "It looks cheerful and happy and I'm sure it'll get lots of compliments over the coming weeks."

"What are you going to put on it?" Linda asked, picking up the end of a garland and stepping onto the ladder.

"Purple baubles, purple dried flowers, gold ribbons and tinsel."

13

Before Linda had a chance to respond the telephone rang.

"I'll get it," said Dick, raising his hand, "seeing as I'm not being much use."

He left the dining room for the reception area and returned ten minutes later with a huge grin on his face.

"Well, you'll never guess what. But that phone call was your boy, Danny. He said he'll ring you tomorrow for a proper chat, but he just wanted to know now if we'd have room for him to stay because he wants to come down for Christmas apparently and ..."

"...what," interrupted Heather, her face a picture of delight, "is he back in England then?"

"It appears so," grinned Dick, "and back for good I'd say from what I could make of it. As I said, he's going to ring you in the morning for a natter, so you'll find out more then. He said he couldn't stop now because he's off out somewhere or other."

"You naturally told him we'd have room for him," said Bob, eagerly.

"Of course, we're not going to be full and even if we were there's always accommodation in the Mews."

"Is he coming on his own?" Heather asked, apprehensively.

"I guess so, he said me not we."

"Looks like he's ditched the lovely Jasmina then," laughed Linda, obviously pleased by the prospect. "Or perhaps she's ditched him. Either way I always said it wouldn't last."

"Well it's lasted for eight years," said Heather, wringing her hands with delight, "and I can't wait to see him again. I hope he's not put on too much weight though. Americans are inclined to eat far too many burgers and suchlike and he wasn't as lean as he used to be when we last saw him."

"When was that?" Mary asked, "It must be a couple of years since you went out there."

"It was two years ago last month. Oh, I do hope Jasmina's history; I know I shouldn't criticise his choice of partner but I really didn't like her and she didn't like me either for that matter."

"Well, thank goodness he didn't marry the woman, that's all I can say," added Bob.

"I think this is going to be a really good Christmas," said Linda, "I've not seen Danny since 1976 when he was down just after our

14

wedding and he's not met any of his nieces yet. Do you hear v
we're saying, Annette? Your Uncle Danny is back from America a
he's coming down to Cornwall for Christmas. Isn't that brilliau
news?"

Annette tilted her head to one side. "Is he the uncle you've told us
about? The one who used to be a pop star?"

"That's right; he was the bass guitarist with a group called
Gooseberry Pie back in the sixties, but the group split up a long time
ago before you were born, back in 1974."

Annette frowned. "So why did he go to America?"

"Hmm, to live with a very rich middle-aged woman," smiled
Linda, "and supposedly pursue his career in photography."

"Photography being a euphemism for nothing," laughed Bob.

"Do they have white Christmases in America?" Annette asked,
dreamily, ignoring the vacuous answers to her previous question.

Linda nodded. "Yes, I believe they do, some parts anyway. Why
do you ask?"

"Cos perhaps Uncle Danny will bring us luck and we'll have a
white Christmas after all, just like in all the songs."

Early on Saturday morning, Jane Williams tooted outside Fuchsia
Cottage, the home of her parents. From inside her mother, Betty
appeared with a half-eaten slice of toast in her hand and rushed to the
waiting car to join her daughter.

"It's no good," she said, scrambling into the passenger seat, "I've
been trying hard to get out of your father some idea of what he'd like
for Christmas, that's why I wasn't quite ready, but it's as hard to get
any help from him today as when we first got married. Shopping for
men is a nightmare, I really don't know what to get."

"Hmm, I agree," sighed Jane, releasing the hand brake. "I don't
think Giles has any interests other than the farm and throwing pints
down his neck in the pub, or if he has I don't know what they are. I'll
probably end up getting him a pair of wellies. Anyway, where shall
we go, Helston, Falmouth or Penzance?"

"I don't mind, you decide, I like all three."

"Then we'll go to Penzance, I've been to Falmouth and Helston
quite a bit lately so Penzance will make a nice change."

"That suits me fine and I must admit I do like walking up the Causeway Head. Have you much to get, other than possible wellies for Giles, that is?"

"No," said Jane, waving to Graham and Ginny as the car passed the turning into Penwynton Crescent, "I've already bought most of my gifts and wrapped them too, which is brilliant as I'll have time to get a new pair of party shoes. You know, something sparkly and impractical. Do you need much?"

"No, just something for your dad and our Matthew and I fancy pampering myself too, so I might even buy a new dress as my old favourite is looking very dated now and I rather like the padded shoulders that are fashionable at present."

"Sounds good to me. Are you in a hurry to get back?"

"No, I've kept today free of appointments so that I can have the whole day off. Most people want their hair done as near to Christmas as possible anyway. How about you, have you anything to rush back for?"

"No, I'm footloose and fancy free 'til this evening when Giles is taking me to the Hotel for dinner."

"What, the Penwynton? The farm must be doing alright then."

Jane laughed. "I don't know about that. Giles won a voucher in the pub's Harvest raffle for a meal for two at the Hotel and it's only valid 'til the end of the year, so we thought we'd better use it before the Christmas rush."

They arrived in Penzance just after nine, parked in a back street and walked up the main road past the railway station into town.

"Fancy a coffee?" Jane asked, as they passed by the Wimpy Bar.

"Yes, but I doubt there will be anywhere open yet and we really ought to buy something before we take our ease."

"Yes, you're right, no refreshments until the men's gifts are purchased."

By mid-morning the town was busy with shoppers and in Woolworths, where they waited to pay for a pack of blank audio cassette tapes, the queues stretched back several yards down the store.

Jane found a pair of flimsy silver sandals she liked in the first shoe shop they entered and whilst they were there she also bought Giles a pair of strong Wellington boots.

As they passed a jewellers, Betty paused and looked in the window. "How about a watch for your dad? The one he has now is getting a bit unreliable and I think he might like one of these new digital ones that you don't have to wind up."

"Sounds like a good idea; Giles has a Casio which he's very pleased with."

"Come on, let's go and take a look inside."

Betty bought a watch for Peter and she also bought a pair of earrings for her closest friend, Gertie. "I've actually already got a present for Gert," she said, as they left the shop, "but I couldn't resist these. Gert bought a new dress the other day and the red stones in these earrings will go with it really nice."

"They'll suit her too, she seems to like dangly earrings. Fancy lunch now or would you rather wait a while?"

"Oh, let's take a break now, I could do with a nice sit down."

They stopped outside Poppins café and looked in through the large glass fronted window; to their dismay all the tables were taken. But as they prepared to walk on and try the Buttery, they saw a couple rise and put on their coats. Jane and Betty lingered in the doorway and as soon as the couple left they quickly nipped inside and seized their vacated seats.

Betty kicked off her shoes as soon as her bottom touched the chair. "Oh, that's better, and now my sense of smell is being tantalised by the whiff of food I realise just how hungry I am. In fact I think I could eat a horse."

"I'll settle for fish 'n chips," smiled Jane, passing her mother the menu. "I shouldn't but I don't care. Anyway, I reckon we've burned up loads of calories traipsing around this morning."

"I think I might do likewise," said Betty, casting her eyes over the menu, "but first I must have a cup of tea and a fag."

After the waitress had taken their order, they looked through their purchases. "Well, I've finished except for a new frock," said Betty, with a satisfied grin. "How about you?"

"All done, thank God. So we can take our time looking for your new dress."

It was raining when they left Poppins and by the time Betty had found a dress the Christmas lights were on. But in spite of the damp and their heavy, cumbersome bags, both still had enthusiasm for the sight of the colourful lights reflecting on the wet roads and the buzz of excitement in the air.

"Have you put your decorations up yet?" Betty asked, as they stopped to admire a particularly festive shop window.

"Yes, I got the tree from Jean yesterday. It's only three feet high but it's really bushy and looks ever so nice. How about you?"

"Our tree's potted up and standing outside by the shed and I shall decorate it tonight if your dad goes to the pub, which I expect he will."

CHAPTER THREE

Bordering the village field known as the Rec and nestled in a leafy valley, stood the Old Vicarage. Built of granite in the mid seventeen hundreds, it had for many years belonged to The Church. But following the retirement of Trengillion's last vicar, the Reverend David Ridge, the property had stood empty and neglected for several years awaiting its fate. For the church's new incumbent was housed in another location due to the amalgamation of local villages and the sharing of one vicar for the whole parish.

Anne and John Collins bought the house shortly before their marriage in 1977, as they were able to put down a substantial deposit due to a sum of money Anne had inherited from her paternal grandfather, Michael Stanley, which enabled John to get a mortgage on the strength he was a qualified, self-employed builder who would be able to do the vast amount of work needed to bring the house into the twentieth century. Thus after the work was finished the result was a fine impressive house, boasting four good sized bedrooms, two bathrooms, a huge kitchen with flagstone floor, a scullery-cum-utility room, a dining room, three reception rooms, the largest of which had a huge inglenook fireplace, a large cellar and an attic which ran the entire length of the house.

Outside, secluded gardens achieved their privacy by means of a nine foot high granite wall which ran along three sides of the boundary. The wall-less side was bordered by trees and a variety of wild and cultivated shrubs.

Behind the house, lawns ran into the valley, where a pond, built by John, was surrounded by flower beds and dense shrubbery. Leading from the lawn, through a small white, wooden gate and picket fence, lay an orchard, housing apple, pear, plum and cherry trees, all prospering in their sheltered location where their beautiful scented blossom in springtime was protected from the south westerly winds by the trees in the valley. And on the south facing garden wall, within an old lean-to greenhouse with original brick base and refurbished framework, Anne's tender plants lay snuggly tucked for the winter.

At the end of the driveway, beside the house, a small, single storey building, formerly a stable and coach house, had been converted into a double garage.

On Saturday morning, twelve days before Christmas, John drove the work's truck along the driveway of the Old Vicarage, with Anne, Ollie and Jess by his side and a six foot tall Christmas tree, chosen from Long Acre Farm, joggling around in the back. At the end of the tarmac drive, John parked outside the garage and the children, impatient to begin the task of decorating, leapt and jumped around the truck giggling and squealing with excitement.

While John planted the tree into a large pot and firmed it with stones and garden soil, Anne took the children indoors, where, after removing their coats, they sat beside the fire and eagerly rummaged through the boxes of decorations which John had earlier retrieved from the attic.

The tree, once ready, was dragged by John and Anne into the largest of the reception rooms known by the family as the big room, and to prevent the loss of too many needles, it was placed as far away from the inglenook fireplace as possible, in a corner between the window and the door. Before decorating commenced, John carefully twisted two sets of fairy lights around the tree as evenly as possible. It was then the turn of the children to participate which they did with exuberance, eagerly hanging as many baubles, bells, chocolate Father Christmases and robins as far up the tree as their short arms could reach, while Anne decorated the upper section of the tree with a little more artistry. Once finished, strands of tinsel were carefully woven through the branches to hide the green electric wires and lametta was draped across the branch tips where it shimmered in the heat from the fairy lights.

"It's beautiful," Jess whispered, her chubby hands pressed together as though in prayer. "It's the bestest tree in the whole wide world."

"Better than the one at school?" asked John, knowing his young daughter's fondness of the school tree.

"Yes," she giggled, impishly, "but don't tell Grandpa. I think our tree's nicer cos it's more sparkly."

"And it's got chocolate on it," added Ollie, "and lights."

The Grandpa referred to was Anne's father, Ned Stanley, who was also the village school's headmaster, a position held since January 1954. He and his wife of thirty three years, Stella, lived at the Old School House and the couple looked forward, though with a little trepidation, to Ned's retirement, which unless ill health dictated otherwise, should occur in the summer of 1991.

The Old School House, once owned by the authorities, now belonged to Ned and Stella, for they made the final payment to the building society when Ned reached his sixtieth birthday the previous August.

Two days before the village school broke up for the Christmas holiday, the children were due to put on their annual production of a Nativity play in the church. They had been practising for weeks so that the evening would pass without a hitch and several of the children, Jess Collins included, knew all the words to the script irrespective of the parts they had been allocated.

Jess, a natural for the performing arts, had desperately wanted the part of Mary, but because her grandfather was the headmaster and did not want to be accused of nepotism, the part went to Eleanor Grey, best friend of her cousin, Tally. Jess thought the decision grossly unfair. How would she ever be able to show off her talents if she was never given the chance? For the part of a non-speaking angel lacked a challenge to even the most non-theatrical child.

"I feel dreadful over Jess's disappointment," said Ned, one evening when Anne dropped in with a poinsettia she had bought in town for her mother. "Little Eleanor does a good job but she doesn't put her heart into it like I know Jess would."

Anne laughed. "I know how she feels. It was the same when Liz and I were at school. The other kids used to say we were really lucky having our dad as headmaster, but we weren't. We had to be model pupils and we dipped out on the treats, like Jess. But don't worry,

Dad, she'll get over it: we did, and at least I know she and Ollie are in good hands with you and Mrs Reynolds."

"Hmm, but it's not much of a consolation, is it?" said Stella, removing the cellophane wrapping from her plant and placing it in a ceramic pot. "Perhaps we ought to pay for her to have drama lessons, or dancing lessons even, something that might bring out her talents."

"No, you don't need to do that, Mum, she'll be alright once it's over and done with, and Christmas will soon be here; that'll take her mind off it."

On the morning of the great day, Jess and Ollie went to school with their costumes made by Anne. In spite of the dissatisfaction with her part, Jess liked her outfit because it was pretty, her tinsel halo in particular. Ollie on the other hand had no thoughts regarding his costume and was quite happy with the part of a non-speaking shepherd, for it meant he had no words to learn, unlike his poor friend Darren, who had been saddled with the part of Joseph.

When the children were seated in their classroom for registration, Mrs Reynolds, her face flushed with anguish, announced that regrettably Eleanor Grey had been up all night coughing and therefore would not be at school nor would she be able to play the part of Mary. It was even suggested the play might not be able to take place, but cancellation would be the last resort. Jess felt her heart begin to race.

"Please, Mrs Reynolds," she said, waving her arm frantically in the air.

"Yes, Jess, what is it?"

"I know all Eleanor's words and I know her songs too. I can play Mary, please let me, I'd love to do it."

Mrs Reynolds smiled. "Yes, Jess, I'm sure you're more than capable. We're all going to the church to have a run through the whole play after assembly, so we'll give you a try and anyone else who thinks they could play the part and we'll see how you all get on."

Jess was happy beyond belief and threw herself into her new found role with unbridled dedication and enthusiasm, for as no-one else felt confident enough to claim the limelight, the part was hers.

"She's a natural," said Meg to Ned, as they escorted the children back to school.

22

Ned grinned. "The Lord moves in mysterious ways, so they say."

The church was full that evening for the play and Jess was as good as her word. She played the part as though she had attended every rehearsal and spent many hours learning her role.

For Anne the evening was very emotional, the sight of her daughter's slight figure dressed in the pale blue outfit made for Eleanor, brought tears to her eyes, and as the children sweetly sang, Away in a Manger, the years slipped away and she herself was back in her primary school days.

The following morning, Anne walked round to the post office to buy stamps and post the last of her Christmas cards. As she walked back through the village she met Linda delivering local cards by hand.

"Brilliant: seeing you saves me walking down to the Vicarage," laughed Linda, flicking through her bundle of white envelopes and handing one to Anne. "Not that I mind walking to the Vicarage, it's a very pleasant walk, it's just that I want to get the house spick and span before the children break up from school tomorrow."

"Thank you," said Anne, "I know what you mean; it's so much easier without children under your feet. Will you be having Christmas dinner at the Hotel?"

"Oh yes, we'll be eating after the guests have been fed, as usual. This year should be great fun though because Danny's back in England and he's coming down on the twenty third."

Anne felt the colour drain from her face. There was a time when she had been besotted with Danny Jarrams, and the last time she had seen him he had told her they would never be anything more than friends. She had been mortally wounded at the time, and even though, deep down, she knew he was right, his words had hurt her deeply. Time, however, had healed the wounds, her marriage to John was a success and she would not have wished her life to have followed a different path. The prospect of seeing Danny, however, made her feel light-headed.

"How long will he be here for?" Anne asked, feeling she ought to say something.

"Goodness knows," laughed Linda, "you know Danny. But apparently his big love affair with Jasmina and America is well and truly over and he's staying with Guy in London at present."

"Guy?" Anne queried.

"Yes, you must remember him; he was Gooseberry Pie's drummer, the blond bloke with the big ears."

Anne laughed. "Of course, yes, I remember him, but we didn't know he had big ears 'til years later when he went solo and had his hair cut short. So what's Danny going to do now he's back over here? I thought he'd gone to the States for keeps."

"Don't know really, but no doubt we'll find out when he gets here. You'll most likely see him anyway, because we're bound to go out with him for a drink at the inn and when we do I'll let you know, so you and John can join us."

Anne smiled, weakly. "Lovely, I'll look forward to that."

CHAPTER FOUR

Following his retirement in July 1985, George Clarke, Ned's school teaching friend of many years, and his wife, Rose, moved to Trengillion where they purchased Ivy Cottage in the heart of the village. The sale brought about by the death of Doris Hughes who had lived there all her life.

As young men, Ned and George both taught at the same London school until Christmas 1953, when Ned left to take up the position of Headmaster of Trengillion School. The two friends, however, kept in touch over the ensuing years; therefore it felt right that George and Rose should choose to spend the remainder of their days in the village they had come to regard as their second home.

"It doesn't seem like Christmas with no decorations," sighed Rose, drawing the curtains in the sitting room of Ivy Cottage, "though I suppose I could hang up the cards."

"Hardly seems worth it," George replied, "we'll be gone in a couple of days."

"Yes, I know, but the place just looks so bare compared with everywhere else and I do like to see a bit of tinsel even at my age."

George tossed the weekly newspaper onto the coffee table. "How about popping down to the inn for a bite to eat then, it's nice and Christmassy in there and it'll save you bothering to cook."

"But I've already taken a couple of lamb chops from the freezer for tonight, so we ought to eat them. I abhor waste."

"So do I, but we can have them tomorrow. You look a bit peaky to me; a relaxed evening by the pub's fire and a nice glass of Merlot will do you good."

"All right, I must admit that would be nice. I'm not feeling very wonderful. I hope I've not gone and caught the cold doing the rounds."

"Good heavens, you better not have. We can hardly spend Christmas with your parents if you have, it wouldn't be fair spreading germs and so forth to them at their ages."

Rose smiled. "You don't have to pretend you want to go, George, I know you don't and if the truth be known then I'd rather be here too. But they're my parents and it may be the last Christmas I'll ever be able to spend with them both. Dad's such a poor old thing now and Mum's not much better."

"I know, love," said George, patting her arm, "I just wish we could do both, spend Christmas here and go to Blackpool too."

"Well, we'll definitely stay here next year, whatever happens. And let's hope Christmas dinner is such a success at the Old Vicarage, that Anne and John invite us and everyone else again next year too."

"Absolutely, now while I feed Pumpkin you get yourself ready and then we should be able to get to the inn just after opening and bagsy the best seats."

Over the past twenty years Trengillion had witnessed the name of its inn change four times. Originally it was called The Ringing Bells Inn, but in 1967 the owner at that time, Frank Newton, sold it to Raymond and Gloria Withers, and Raymond, a gun crazy fanatic of the Wild West, unwisely changed the name to the Sheriffs Badge. However, during Raymond's occupancy, a tragedy in Trengillion caused him to relinquish his love of guns thus rendering the name obsolete, and as most of his clientele referred to the inn as the Badge anyway, he changed the name to The Badger.

In 1983 the inn changed hands again and this time it was bought by the present licensees, Gerald and Cassie Godson. Gerald, in his earlier life, had been a successful Member of Parliament, but following a bout of ill health his wife suggested he ought to step down. At first he had refused, he occupied a safe seat and enjoyed his work immensely, but after an agonising deliberation he finally conceded if his health was not one hundred per cent then to continue would be unfair to his constituents, his party, his country and his loyal wife.

The Godsons fell in love with the inn during the summer of 1983, after the General Election in June of that year, during which Gerald had promoted and supported the young man who eventually became

26

his successor. And the Godsons finally moved to Trengillion in the September after selling their home, formerly an old manor house.

Before Christmas, however, they changed the name of the inn to the Fox and Hounds which caused even more upset than when Raymond had named it The Sheriffs Badge. But gradually the locals accepted the new name, if for no other reason than it at least sounded like the name of an inn, and only a few, who were against blood sport, boycotted the place initially. But their self-inflicted exclusion did not last long, for they soon realised their stance was doing little more than making them cut off their noses to spite their faces. For the Godsons were competent publicans, professional and likable and although they kept three horses and were keen followers of the hunt, they were discreet about their passion, aware of the sensitivity caused, and as the hunt never went anywhere near Trengillion there was no reason for anyone to take offence.

Two years before the Godsons bought the inn, Higher Green Farm, up on the cliffs near to the Witches Broomstick, sold for the second time in seven years. For the Denby family, who bought it from Pat and May Dickens' in 1976, did so under the misapprehension that running a farm would be an idyllic and easy lifestyle. They soon realised, however, that farm life and getting up in the very early hours to milk the cows in winter, was anything but idyllic, and eventually the frequency of wading through the mud splattered farmyard during wet spells of weather, crushed their spirits beyond redemption. Hence it was no surprise to anyone when after five years they sold up and returned to London, where Peregrine Denby was reinstated in his previous occupation, banking.

The new and present owners were two brothers, Giles and Brendon Wilson, who successfully ran the farm in an efficient and responsible manner. As well as maintaining the dairy herd, they also had a herd of beef cattle in order to diversify, and grew wheat, potatoes, cauliflowers and cabbage on fields which during the Denby years had reverted to grassy meadows.

On the evening of Monday December the twenty second, dedicated church goers and villagers keen on singing and conviviality, assembled inside the Fox and Hounds in preparation for a walk around the village singing carols. It was a tradition which had begun back in 1918 following the end of the First World War, and the proceeds were always divided equally between the church and the Royal British Legion.

To the delight of Sid Reynolds, who had taken on the role of organising the event since the retirement of his father-in-law, the Reverend David Ridge, the turnout was high in spite of dark threatening rain clouds. And after a quick drink to lubricate their throats, the singers, armed with candles flickering in jam jars, torches and paraffin lanterns, left the inn where they assembled beneath a succession of street lamps to sing nominated carols from their hymn sheets.

Carol singing was always an enjoyable event, whatever the weather, although many changes had occurred during its sixty eight year history, most notable of all being the arrival of the television. For in the early years, before even the advent of the wireless and the gramophone, villagers had stood appreciatively on their doorsteps glad of the entertainment, often joining in with the singing which conjured up warm feelings of friendship and goodwill. Competing with the television, however, meant their present day efforts were not heard until a sharp rap of a door knocker or the shrill ring of a bell brought people to their doorsteps, more often through a sense of obligation than appreciation. And even then, many, keen to return to their soaps, commercials and quiz shows, closed their doors before the last notes had faded from beneath their nearest lamp post.

Once the village round was completed, the singers returned to the inn where their efforts were rewarded with mince pies and glasses of sherry, a tradition begun in the nineteen thirties by the then landlord, Frank Newton.

"I always reckon this is the best bit," said Albert Treloar, downing his sherry and ordering a pint, "'though I must admit I do like a bit a singing and it was smashing hearing Helston Town Band playing carols outside the Guildhall last Saturday. I find carols quite emotional, you see, even though I'm not a bit religious."

"You're a heathen then, are you?" Sid grinned. "I know we don't very often see you in church."

"Well, I wouldn't say I'm a heathen. I mean, I do believe in something but I'm not quite sure what. Anyway, I don't need to go to church very often because our Dorothy's been enough for both of us over the years. Not that I'm criticising her, mind, she's a good woman, my sister, and she was a damn hard worker in her day."

"Yeah, she is and I sort of know what you mean about religion. To tell you the truth, I only started going to church to create a good impression to old Vicar Ridge, seeing as I fancied his daughter. My, that all seems a very long time ago."

"Where is Meg? She usually comes singing, doesn't she?"

"Yes, but she's got a bit of a sore throat, so thought it'd be better if she stayed in the warm, but I think the real reason is our Diane's likely to call and then they'll be wanting to discuss weddings and so forth."

"Hmm, rather you than me, I must admit I've been spared all that with Madge's daughter having two boys. Stephen's still a bachelor of course, but David got wed without any fuss; at least there was no fuss as I was bothered with."

"Mince pie?" Gertie asked, doing the rounds with a stainless steel platter.

"Yes please," said Sid, taking a serviette and mince pie.

"Not for me," said Albert, shaking his head, "they make the beer taste funny. That's the trouble with Christmas, too much sweet stuff."

"Ah, there we differ then, because that's what I like best," said Sid. "Christmas pudding, mince pies, sherry trifle and rich fruit cake, you can't beat 'em."

Danny Jarrams arrived at the Penwynton Hotel on the twenty third as planned and after he had settled in he walked with his father, Bob, to visit his cousin, Linda, and Jamie, her husband at their home in Penwynton Crescent.

Linda was relieved to find that Danny had changed very little; he had not put on weight as she and her aunt had feared nor lost his sense of humour. His voice, however, was different; he spoke with a slight American twang and occasionally used American words and phrases.

"So, what happened to your love affair with the States and Jasmina?" Linda asked, without beating about the bush. "I thought both were the B-all and end-all."

Danny sat down on the settee. "It all went sour and I suppose if the truth be known I started to miss good old Blighty. Min's lifestyle started to get me down too. Brandy for breakfast, drinking throughout the day and parties most evenings, I felt if I stayed much longer I'd end up an alcoholic. It's aged her terribly too, drinking and smoking that is. She's not half as good looking as she was a few years back."

Linda frowned. "That's a bit harsh, dumping her because she's started to look her age. I mean, you knew she was years older than you when you first shacked up with her."

"Yeah, but she was a handsome woman then. Anyway, I don't think my departure has ruined her life, she's still got loads of admirers so she'll not be alone for long. But that's enough about me. How are you guys doing? Your house is looking really cosy, in fact everywhere is looking good, especially your mum's tree at the Hotel; it's brilliant. Some American guests were taking pictures of it when I left."

"Were they?" smiled Linda, "that's sweet. I've not seen it since it's been decorated."

"Well you should." Danny leaned back, clasped his hands behind his head and closed his eyes dreamily. "Gee, I'm so happy. It's good to be back and for the first time in years, I'm actually looking forward to, what I hope will be, a good old fashioned family Christmas."

CHAPTER FIVE

Christmas Day began early at the Old Vicarage when Anne and John slipped from their bed just after six to begin the day's preparations: for Anne the task of preparing the turkey and peeling potatoes, sprouts, carrots and swede, all home grown, and for John the task of lighting fires in the big room and the dining room.

Anne yawned as she stood at the large, wooden kitchen table, laying rashers of streaky bacon over the turkey's breast and legs. It had been well past midnight before she and John had finished wrapping presents for the children the previous night and she knew she had many chores to complete before the day was out. But at least help would be at hand when her mother and sister, Elizabeth, arrived. Her sister-in-law and life-long friend, Susan, had also promised to give a hand.

Warmth from the previous evening still hung in the air as John opened the door of the big room, thus drawing out the sweet scent of pine wood from the Christmas tree and the delicate perfume of dried lavender displayed in a wooden bowl on the hearthside table. As John closed the door to keep in the warmth, dangling twists of colourful foil rustled from the beams, and crinkled lengths of red and green streamers danced with balloons in the brief movement of air.

John switched on the light and pulled back one of the red velvet curtains; it was still dark outside and so he drew it again, conscious as he did so of small feet tiptoeing across the floor in the rooms above. The twins were obviously awake, but he knew they would not be down before invited to do so, for it was a tradition in the Collins household that all family members opened their presents together, after breakfast, around the tree in the big room.

As there was still sufficient heat in the coals on the grate, John did not have to make the fire up from scratch, instead he carefully raked out the excess ash, laid fresh small pieces of coal on the glowing embers and then while he waited for the fire to burn up he went outside to fill both coal scuttle and log basket. Once this task was completed he went into the dining room where the air was chilly, for the room had seen no fire since the previous Christmas, although it did benefit a little natural warmth and airing from the late afternoon sun all year round.

When John was satisfied both fires were burning brightly, he put up fireguards, closed the doors and joined Anne in the kitchen where, with the turkey wrapped in foil and in the oven, the couple drank tea and ate hot buttered toast. When their mugs and plates were empty, Anne made porridge for the children, determined that they should at least begin the day with sensible eating, even if it did not continue.

At eight o'clock the twins were fetched downstairs where their excited chatter filled the kitchen with an air of optimism, as they expressed their hopes, desires and anticipation regarding the gifts Father Christmas might have left in their stockings and beneath the tree in the big room.

Inside Cove Cottage, Elizabeth picked up colourful wrapping paper from the floor dropped by Wills and Tally, while their father, Greg, spoke to his parents, Willoughby and Tabitha Castor-Hunt, up-country for Christmas as guests of his younger sister, Lily. Elizabeth sighed, she was sure neither she nor Anne had ever made the mess Wills and Tally seemed to make with alarming regularity.

"Mum and Dad send their love," said Greg, when he came off the phone, "they'll be back for New Year's Eve though, because Lily's on duty that night and they thought they might as well come back home as be up there not knowing anyone."

"That's good, I know they like being home for New Year's Eve, because your mum told me so last year. Did they say how Lily is?"

"She's fine apparently, 'though Mum reckons she's working too hard because she doesn't seem as cheerful as usual. They're trying to persuade her to come down for a visit in January and Mum's pretty sure she will."

"Nursing must be hard work," said Elizabeth, standing up two cards which had toppled over on the mantelpiece. "Poor Lily, I hope there's nothing wrong. We don't see her half as much as we ought, but then that's the price you pay for leaving your home town. I'm glad we decided never to leave Cornwall."

Greg nodded and looked at his new watch, a present from his wife, "What time did you say we'd be at the Vicarage? It's half past ten already."

"Is it? We really ought to be there by eleven, eleven thirty at the latest, there'll be so much to do what with laying the table and so forth, although I know John will do his fair share and Mum's probably there already."

"Well, just say the word, I'm as good as ready so we can go whenever you like."

"In that case give me ten minutes to change and I'll be ready too, and then while I'm upstairs perhaps you'll give Grandma a ring because we're picking her up on the way."

"Aren't we walking then? I thought we were, after all it's not very far."

"It is when we've lots of presents to carry," smiled Elizabeth, pushing the last piece of paper into a second brim-full carrier bag, "not to mention a sherry trifle, two dozen mince pies and a chocolate log."

"Okay, enough said," grinned Greg, "I'll ring your gran."

After a hot, bubbly bath, Molly Smith dressed in her best bottle green skirt and favourite red blouse, put her new emerald green cardigan over the top, hung a string of pearls around her neck and slipped matching earrings into her earlobes. She then made her bed and went downstairs for breakfast. After washing up, she went into the living room and switched on the radio to hear a church service for company.

Since she would be out for the day, she did not light the fire, so she dusted the room, glad of a chore to keep her on the move thus preventing her from getting cold. As she dusted the wooden case of the clock, the telephone rang; it was Greg. Molly was pleased with the call, for although she did not normally mind being alone, there was something unpleasant about solitude on Christmas morning. Perhaps it was because it reminded her of the lonely years she had spent following the break-up of her first marriage to Ned's father many years before, or because it made the major's absence more poignant.

33

After the call, with only ten minutes to spare until the arrival of Elizabeth, Greg and the children, Molly went over to the sideboard and took her make-up bag from the middle drawer. She then dabbed on some face powder, applied some lipstick and sprayed honeysuckle perfume onto her wrists and behind her ears.

From beside the settee she lifted two carrier bags crammed with presents for the family. Molly generally enjoyed Christmas shopping, but she found with each ensuing year it was becoming more of a chore than a pleasure and for that reason she had selected many of her gifts from Candy Bingham's catalogue to negate the necessity of tramping around the shops.

Inside the kitchen of Higher Green Farm, Nettie Penrose wept after opening a large present from Tony and Jean. It was a painting of her late husband, Cyril, copied from an old photograph of him on his favourite tractor.

"It's beautiful," said Nettie, wiping her eyes. "It must hang here in the kitchen so that I can see it every day. Wherever did you find someone to paint with such skill, the likeness is astounding?"

"We didn't have to go far," said Tony, proudly, "John recommended, Anne, but Anne insisted her mum should do it because she said she's much better at portraits. We're glad you like it, we're pretty impressed too."

"So Stella Stanley did it. Well I never. I'd no idea the girl was so gifted. I shall tell her so later; it's the best present I've ever had. Thank you so much, both of you."

"Close your eyes," giggled Gertie, as she peeped around the sitting room door of number two, Coronation Terrace, where her husband, Percy, was sipping from a can of lager. "I've got my new frock on and I want you to tell me what you think."

Percy quietly groaned. He hated commenting on women's fashions, it was so easy to say the wrong thing, although during thirty four years of marriage he had learned a little of what not to say. As he sat up straight the door was flung open and Gertie danced into the room with a twirl. "What do you think?"

Percy was relieved and surprised by how much the dress suited his wife and so was not lost for appropriate words. "It's smashing, Gert. Really smart and the colour's very festive."

"It is, isn't it?" Gertie laughed, twirling for a second time. "I've always liked red because it suits me, but it's a colour to be wary of because it often makes people look fat. I don't look fat, do I, Percy?"

"No, sweetheart, you don't, in fact that particular style makes you look slimmer."

"Oh, thank you, the high heels are partly responsible for that, they make my legs look thinner. Are you nearly ready? We mustn't be late because we might be needed to give Anne a hand and I can't wait to see everyone and give them their presents."

Steve Penhaligon left his wife, Susan, and two children, Denzil and Demelza showing each other their Christmas presents at the family home in Coronation Terrace and slipped out of the back door for his annual trip to the churchyard. It was something he had done every Christmas for as long as he could remember, although in the early days the pilgrimage had been with his mother and siblings.

In the churchyard Steve walked through the long grass to a remote shaded corner where his father, Denzil, rested beneath the arched branches of an ancient yew tree. It always grieved Steve that he had no memory of his father, a fisherman, who had died just before Christmas in 1950 when he had drowned after going to sea in spite of a bad weather forecast.

By the grave Steve knelt, tore away a stem of ivy creeping towards his father's tombstone, laid a holly wreath amidst the long, dry grass and weeds and berated himself for his negligence. For every year on Christmas Day he vowed to visit the grave throughout the year and save it from neglect and lack of care, but every year it slipped from his mind and the grave fell more and more into disrepair.

As he stood he heard the crunching of footsteps on the gravel path and the chatter of happy voices. Intrigued by the presence of so many he peered around a large holly tree where he observed a procession of gaily dressed parishioners walking down the path, leaving church after the Christmas Day service. Steve watched as they walked beneath the lichgate and out onto the street. Some climbed into cars parked along the

35

roadside, others made their way home and a few went round the corner and into the inn. Steve glanced at his watch: it was five minutes past eleven. He knew Susan wanted to leave for the Vicarage around eleven thirty and so concluded that gave him just enough time for a very quick pint.

To his surprise, there was already a considerable number of people in the bar, bearing in mind the inn had only just opened up. Most were men, getting out of the way while the women cooked the dinner, but there were a few females too enjoying the special magical atmosphere that only a Christmas morning can bring.

"I thought you'd be with the rest of the family at the Old Vicarage this lunch time," said Peter Williams, standing at the bar when Steve ordered his pint.

"I shall be soon, but I've just been to the churchyard to put a holly wreath on Dad's grave. It's something I do every Christmas Day and I reckoned I'd time for a crafty pint before Sue would think I'd been gone too long."

Peter laughed. "I've been told I mustn't have more than one, but I reckon I'll squeeze in at least three. There's nothing much for us blokes to do at home anyway, especially with no little 'uns to entertain, so I'm sure I'll not be missed."

"Just the family this year?"

"Yes, plus the Wilson brothers, but I bet they'll be in here before they go to Fuchsia Cottage."

"Talk of the devil," laughed Steve, as farmers Brendon and Giles Wilson appeared through the inn door.

"Glad you're here, Pete," grinned Giles, joining his girlfriend's father and Steve at the bar, "we were going straight to your house, but the buzz of jovial voices enticed us in as we were walking by."

"I reckon there could be a few irate women before the inn closes its doors," said Brendon, noting the speed with which many men were downing their pints. "This place is packed and mostly with blokes. Could be a few dinners ruined.

"Oh, no," said Cassie, handing Steve his pint from behind the bar, "we'll be closing at one o'clock prompt. I know what it's like to have the day spoiled when men are late coming home."

She cast an accusing glance in the direction of her husband, Gerald, which he received with a cheeky, broad grin.

36

CHAPTER SIX

After Christmas dinner at the Old Vicarage was eaten and when all the washing up was done, the family gathered in the big room and distributed gifts bought for each other. This created much joy, laughter and squealing especially from the six children.

"How are your parents, Stella?" Nettie asked, as Anne handed her presents from beneath the tree. "I haven't seen them for a while, but then that's because I've not been to the Over Sixties Club lately."

"They're fine, thank you," said Stella, loosening the belt of her skirt. "They've gone up to Wiltshire for Christmas and New Year to stay with my big sister."

"Very nice too. I've only ever been out of Cornwall once and that was to Plymouth just after the War, but then there was never any need to go gallivanting about with the family all being here abouts."

"Did you never want to travel, Nettie?" Molly asked, as she fought a parcel with a particularly stubborn piece of Sellotape.

"No, I've always said there's no place like home. And of course with the farm to run there's always been such a lot to do and you can't just go off and leave it. Besides, Cyril wouldn't have wanted to go away, not even for a weekend, and I was much the same myself."

"I've never wanted to travel either," Molly agreed, "The major was the same. He said he saw enough of foreign places during the War and with there being so many beautiful places in this country there never seemed much point in going abroad."

"Talking of foreign places," said Stella, removing her shoes to replace them with the sheepskin slippers she had just unwrapped. "I saw that pop star chap yesterday, you know, what's his name, the one you girls were dotty about years ago. His parents run the Penwynton Hotel."

"Oh, Danny Jarrams," said Anne, feeling colour rise in her face, "Linda said he was coming down for Christmas. Apparently he's home from the States for good and is living with the band's old drummer, Guy, in London."

Susan raised her eyebrows. "Is he still as gorgeous as ever?"

"Wouldn't like to say as he was never my cup of tea, a bit too young," smiled Stella, lifting her right foot in the air. "Gosh these slippers are smashing, thanks, Liz and Greg, I'm going to keep them on."

"I saw him the other day too," said Tony, "and I thought he looked much the same. I recognised him straight away but then that was probably because he was walking through the village with his dad."

"Whose are these?" John asked, holding up two Woolworth's carrier bags full of gifts which he had found tucked behind the settee.

"Oh dear, they're mine," tut-tutted Molly. "I meant to put my offerings under the tree with the rest but forgot. It only takes one glass of wine these days and I forget my name. Pass them here please, John. Silly me. It's too late now to put them under the tree and I spent ages wrapping them too."

With the bags hanging from her arm, Molly distributed her gifts to all present. The final two were a brace of small identical parcels which she handed to Anne and Elizabeth. The sisters eagerly unwrapped their gifts and in unison squealed cries of delight. For Anne, in a white oblong box lay a beautiful necklace of white daisies each entwined like a daisy chain and with matching earrings, and for Elizabeth, a row of dainty blue forget-me-nots, also with matching earrings.

"I didn't know who to give which to," said Molly, as she removed the lid from a bottle of perfume she had received and took a sniff. "Oh that smells really nice. And so I wrapped them in the same paper and then wrote your names on after, so even I didn't know who had which."

"Well, you did the right thing," said Anne, bending to kiss her grandmother's cheek. "Daisies are my favourite flowers, especially white ones. Thank you, I shall treasure it always."

"And I love forget-me-nots," said Elizabeth, draping the delicate necklace across her fingers. "They have such a romantic name. Thank you, Gran."

"My mother loved forget-me nots," said Molly, touched by the delight of her two granddaughters. "In fact if you look at the bottom of the box, Liz, you'll find a piece of card on which is a little verse she was always reciting when I was a girl."

Elizabeth pulled the card from the box and read:

Forget-me-nots, sweet conveyers of love
Tended by cherubs in Eden above,
Sprinkled by angels from heavenly skies
Reminders to mankind that love never dies

So, when I am gone, I beg, please do not mourn,
I'll watch o'er you each day from sunrise at dawn,
'til stars fill the skies and daylight has gone,
for I shall not be dead, but just passed on.

With wings I shall flutter and dance with the breeze,
I shall shout in a storm and rustle the trees,
I shall run with the wind and roar with the sea,
My pain shall be gone and my spirit be free.

Forget-me-nots, sweet conveyers of love
Tended by cherubs in Eden above,
Sprinkled by angels from heavenly skies
Reminders to mankind that love never dies.

"It's beautiful," said Elizabeth, placing the card back in the box. "Do you know who wrote it?"

"No idea, probably even Mum," laughed Molly, "she was always quoting bits of this and bits of that and scribbling verses down on paper. I think of her every time I recall it."

"I've never heard it before," said Stella, thoughtfully, "not that I'm the oracle of all knowledge. The only poem I recall referring to forget-me-nots is by Henry Wordsworth Longfellow. You know the one:

Silently, one by one,
in the infinite meadows of heaven,
blossom the lovely stars,
the forget-me-nots of the angels."

"Hmm, yes, but I think the rose takes a bit of beating," said Nettie Penrose, hastily, before anyone else felt compelled to quote more

39

poetry. "It's always been a favourite of mine, although goodness only knows why they have to have those ghastly thorns. The times I've cut myself on them is nobody's business."

"I'm inclined to agree," Molly grinned. "They are beautiful, especially the scented varieties."

"Rose," Stella shouted, banging her head with the palm of her hand, "I knew there was something I meant to do before we came out. I was going to phone Ivy Cottage to see how Rose is and I completely forgot, how remiss of me and on Christmas Day too."

"She's feeling a lot better," said Molly, dropping the new bottle of perfume into her handbag. "I saw George this morning when he got back from taking Pumpkin for a walk. He said she was going to get up today and she was even feeling a bit hungry."

"Oh, thank goodness," said Stella, "I hated the thought of poor George cooking the Christmas dinner and then eating it all alone."

"I didn't know Rose wasn't well," said Susan, tut-tutting at Steve who had over-run his allotted time at the inn earlier and was now fast asleep in the corner. "I assumed they weren't here because they'd gone to Blackpool."

Stella nodded. "That was there intention but Rose came down with the flu the day before they were due to go. Shall I draw the curtains, Anne? It's looking quite dark outside now."

"I'll do it," said John, standing. "Roll on summer, I do hate these short days and long, dark nights."

"Do you?" Molly asked. "I love them. I find long summer days far too long now, but then that's probably because I don't have the energy to make use of them like I did back along."

"I can never make my mind up," mused Stella. "I saw a cartoon once depicting a man lying on the beach with the sun beaming above, and in a thought bubble he was sitting in an armchair beside a blazing fire. And then in the next picture the same man was sitting beside the fire with the beach scene in the thought bubble. I find myself like that, never sure which I like best."

"Well, it's summer every time for me," John laughed. "I'm a real sun worshipper."

"Would anyone like a cup of anything?" Anne asked, "I'm gasping for a cup of tea."

"The ladies all asked for tea but the men opted for something stronger.

"I've just been thinking," said Gertie, her brow wrinkled in perplexity, "about forget-me-nots, that is, and I wonder how they got their name. I mean to say, it must be something romantic."

Molly laughed. "Oh, it is romantic. That's if it's true. You see, it's claimed that once upon a time, a knight was walking with his bride along a river bank and he stopped from time to time to gather the little blue flowers growing in the grass. However, when he handed them to his sweetheart, he slipped, lost his footing and fell into the deep and treacherous water where he panicked and began to sink. The weight of his armour, you see, pulled him down. But before he disappeared beneath the water he tossed the flowers onto the river bank to his bride and cried, 'Forget me not!' Those were his dying words and ever since, the little blue flower has been known as the forget-me-not."

"What a plonker," hissed Tony, from behind his glass of beer. "Silly bugger should have looked where he was going."

"Tony, behave," said Jean, suppressing a laugh, "there are children present."

Molly smiled. "I shouldn't worry, Jean, I think they're all too engrossed in Ollie's Scalextric to hear what we're saying. And I'm inclined to agree with you, Tony, if it's true he was very foolish and careless."

"Do you know the folklore for every flower, tree and shrub, Grandma?" Elizabeth smiled, recalling Molly's tales of the elder.

"Most," she laughed, "I might sound like a bit of a crackpot but I've always been fascinated by such things."

As Molly spoke, she watched Ned from the corner of her eye as he opened his presents and when he picked up the last one, which was from her, she watched with interest as he slid ribbon from the soft parcel and tore the paper in two. When he saw something bright green and knitted his face dropped."

"Pick it up," ordered Molly, eagerly.

Watched by all present, Ned picked up the object. As the folds dropped open the shape of a large, sloppy, green jumper emerged.

"Show everyone the front," said Molly, clapping her hands with glee.

Without uttering one word, Ned turned the jumper around. On the front was a large ugly reindeer wearing a Christmas hat and with a nose redder than Ned's face.

"Try it on," said Molly, rising to lift up one of the sleeves. "I should like to see you in it after all it took me ages to knit."

"No-one spoke as Ned removed his jacket and slipped the jumper over his head.

"Stand up," commanded Molly, excitedly, "so that we can all see it properly." Ned stood. "Well, sweetheart, what do you think?"

"It's, umm," poor Ned muttered, "it's, umm ..."

"... hideous," said Molly, "is that the word you're after?"

"But ..."

Molly threw back her head and roared with laughter. "I'm sorry Ned, I bought it at a jumble sale back in the summer and it was my intention to unpick it and make a cardy for myself. But then after I'd washed it George saw it hanging on the line and he suggested saving it and giving it to you as a joke. I must say you kept a lot calmer than I thought you would."

"Thank God for that," groaned Ned, flopping down in the chair, "for one awful moment I thought you were serious. Oh, but you wait 'til I see George"

Inside Ivy Cottage, Rose Clarke, with a blanket around her shoulders, sat beside a blazing fire toasting her toes, sipping from a glass of sherry, while in the kitchen her husband George read the heating instructions on the wrapper of the Mrs Peek's Christmas pudding he had bought from the post office the previous day. Once satisfied it could safely be micro-waved, he took the small turkey from the oven and proceeded to dish up the Christmas dinner.

Rose smiled when he entered the front room pushing the hostess trolley laden with two plated up dinners, a dish of cranberry sauce and two crackers.

"Oh George, it's really sweet of you to make a fuss of me like this, but I'm sure I'd be alright to sit at the table."

"No, no, you're to stay in here where it's warm; it's too chilly in the dining room but then that's because I've not bothered to light a fire."

"Oh well, it's a first I must admit. Having Christmas dinner on my lap, that is."

After pulling both crackers and placing the flimsy hats on their heads, George lay a tray on Rose's lap and passed her the cranberry sauce. He then sat down on the opposite side of the fireplace with his own dinner likewise on a tray.

"What do you get when you cross a snowman with a vampire?" Rose asked with a smile as she read the joke from her Christmas cracker.

"Hmm, err...don't know," said George.

"Frostbite," giggled Rose, "isn't that dreadful?"

George grimaced and then picked up the slip of paper on his tray. "What's the most popular Christmas whine?" he asked.

"Umm, I don't know...umm, Liebfraumilch," suggested Rose.

"No," George laughed, "it's I don't like Brussel sprouts."

CHAPTER SEVEN

The weather between Christmas and the New Year was mild and damp but that did not deter villagers from attempting to wear off the results of excessive eating by taking walks over the cliff tops and along the lanes before returning to their homes for consumption of yet more turkey, boiled ham, chocolates, oranges, chestnuts, alcohol, pickles, and bubble and squeak. On one such walk, Rose, feeling much better after the flu which had kept George and herself at home for Christmas, walked along the back lane leading down from Higher Green Farm to the cove. In spite of the damp, the fresh air and gentle breeze helped clear her head, and her skin which had cracked and dried due to the constant heat in the house, tingled with a healthy glow.

From the top of the hill Rose looked down across the valley and onto the village. When she had left Trengillion back in 1953 to marry George and live in London, she had supposed Trengillion would never be her home again; she had been delighted therefore when George suggested retiring to Cornwall, and at times it seemed as though she had never been away.

Rose looked at the trees nestled in the valley, dark and lifeless against the grey sky. She liked winter, especially in the countryside near to the coast, where it was possible to walk and think with only the birds and the rumbling of the sea to distract one's thoughts.

As she rounded a corner, she caught a glimpse of the Castor-Hunt's black car disappearing across the field leading to the back of Chy-an-Gwyns. Rose watched as it approached their garden and a flock of starlings preparing to roost, flew up and away from the apple tree, disturbed by the sudden intrusion.

"Summer seems such a long way off at this time of the year, doesn't it?" Tabitha Castor-Hunt sighed to her husband, Willoughby, as they stepped from their car. "Everything looks so dead and lifeless, even the sea looks dull and dreary."

"Cheer up, old girl. Look, there are some daffodils poking up through the earth under the kitchen window and I daresay the snowdrops are nearly ready to flower by the front gate."

Tabitha smiled. "Forever the optimist, eh Willoughby?"

She left the back garden and followed the curved path around to the front, while her husband took their luggage into the house. "You're right of course," she called, as he returned outside to lock the car. "The snowdrops will be in flower very soon and the camellias are smothered in nice fat buds too."

Willoughby walked to her side, took her hand and led her through the front garden gate and onto the cliff path. "Look properly at the sea, Tabbs. It may be dull but it's never dreary, each wave is different, the smell is bliss, and the melodramatic sound is pure music to my ears."

Tabitha laughed. "I should know better than to criticise anything in the vicinity of Chy-an-Gwyns: you really do love this house, don't you?"

"I love it more each time I leave it and come back. I hope when we're gone either Greg or Lily will live in it. I should hate to think of it leaving the family and falling into the hands of strangers."

"Oh, don't talk of going, Willy, not when I was just beginning to cheer up. There's plenty of life left in you yet."

"I'm nearly eighty, Tabbs, I can't go on forever, 'though I'd very much like to, or would I? I don't know."

"Well unfortunately that's one thing in life over which we have no control. But I shouldn't worry about the future of Chy-an-Gwyns, if I were you. Lily won't ever return to Cornwall, of that I'm sure, but Greg will offer buy her out. Why, I think he loves the house nearly as much as you and I know Elizabeth is very fond of it too, because she told me so many years ago when she was just a girl."

"There are lights on in Chy-an-Gwyns," said Elizabeth, as she drew the living room curtains inside Cove Cottage, "so your mum and dad must be back."

"Oh, good," said Greg, looking up from the bank statement he was checking, "I must ring them later and see how Lily is. Hopefully they'll have persuaded her to come down here and see us soon; we've not seen her since Easter."

"Hmm, and that was only a flying visit. Do you think it's going to rain tomorrow?"

"No idea, why?"

"I need to wash my favourite pink blouse. I got cranberry sauce on it the other day and I want to wear it on New Year's Eve. Oh well, I'll wash it tomorrow anyway and if it rains it'll just have to dry on the radiator."

"Would that be a hint pleading the necessity of a tumble drier by any chance?" Greg asked.

Elizabeth giggled. "Well one would fit perfectly in the little outhouse if I moved things round a bit and it really would be useful because things don't dry too well being so near to the sea."

"Mum always said washing dried well at Chy-an-Gwyns," said Greg, "and that's near the sea."

"Yes, but it's high up and well away from the salt spray and it's much windier up there too."

Greg tucked the bank statement into a cardboard folder. "Alright, we'll trawl the shops in the January Sales next week. I think we can just about afford it."

"If we're going shopping, can I have some new shoes," said Tally, sitting on the floor and carefully slipping the arms of her new Cindy doll into a coat. "Mine are getting too small and I want some like Eleanor's."

Greg peered at his daughter over the top of his reading glasses. "Are they really too tight, Tally, or are you just saying that because you want shoes like your friend?"

"Oh, they're definitely too tight," Tally answered, with a sheepish look of guilt. "I tried Eleanor's on and they fit me much better."

"Well, we'll see," sighed Greg. "Is there anything you need, Wills?"

"Not really, Dad, I had everything I wanted for Christmas."

"That's my boy," grinned Greg. "That's my boy."

The following evening after Tally and Wills had gone to bed, Greg walked up to Chy-an-Gwyns to see his parents, and Elizabeth, appreciative of a little time to herself, sat on the sheepskin hearth rug, with only the glow of the fire and the soft lighting on the Christmas tree to illuminate the room.

Elizabeth leaned back her head on the base of the fireside chair and watched the baubles on the Christmas tree gently twisting in the heat generated from the lights. She was proud of the tree: it was the best they had ever had, symmetrical in shape and decorated, in her eyes, to perfection. For Elizabeth liked to see coloured baubles hanging beside similar coloured lights, red beside red, green beside green, yellow beside yellow and so forth, and over the years the children had learned to copy her ideal, hence the tree, decorated by all, was very pleasing.

Elizabeth turned her head; hanging on the wall beside the tree was a picture of the children taken at school. Elizabeth sighed, it seemed like only yesterday that she and Anne had been at primary school and now they both had children of their own. It made her wistful, she often missed being a school ma'am too, but she had vowed after the birth of her children that she would not seek a teaching position until both were at senior school and she meant to honour by that vow.

Elizabeth laid back her head on the seat of the chair. Above the fireplace hung her silver branch. She recalled the day she had walked over the cliffs by the old mine and down the lanes looking for the ideal branch and had eventually found it by the bridge where the stream flowed out from Bluebell Woods. She got the idea of painting a branch silver from Blue Peter when she was in her teens and had painstakingly painted every crease and crevice with a tiny brush. The result was stunning, and every Christmas since, the branch had taken pride of place over the fire, originally at the Old School House when she had lived with her parents, and now in her married home, Cove Cottage.

Feeling relaxed and content, Elizabeth stood and went to the kitchen where from the fridge she took a half full bottle of Liebfraumilch and from the cupboard a glass engraved with her name. She put both on the table and then removed the cellophane covering the Christmas cake and cut a large wedge. Briefly she pondered whether or not the slice was too big, but her conscience assured her it was permissible, for it was after all, still Christmas.

With, bottle, glass and cake on a plate in her hands, she returned to the sitting room and took up her place on the hearth rug.

The reflection of the fire flickered on the side of Elizabeth's full glass of wine as she stood it on the hearth slate and made herself comfortable. All was silent save the distant rumble of the sea at high tide and the wind whistling down the chimney. Elizabeth loved to hear the wind, especially at night. Since childhood, she had imagined it to be the voices of angels chanting songs of sorrow and joy, the voices of those gone to another world.

Elizabeth laughed; her weird and wonderful thoughts were very much like the protestations frequently made by her grandmother, though not in the presence of her father. For Ned had instructed Molly when the children were very young that their heads must not be filled with notions of mystery, magic, enchantment and soothsayers.

Sipping wine, her mind wandered back to days gone by, playing with friends, the struggle of adolescence and the joy of falling in love. As she recalled Greg's return to Trengillion and their first kiss, her daydreams were interrupted by the ringing of the phone. Elizabeth put down her glass and crawled across the floor to where the phone sat on an occasional table. To her amusement it was Greg, saying he would be home later than he had originally said, because he was taking his father to the inn for a pint.

The Fox and Hounds was a popular venue over the Christmas holiday with many people having not to return to work until the New Year, and as Cassie and Gerald Godson always made patrons, old and new, very welcome, business was brisk.

"The best thing about Christmas is I can have a drink every night for twelve days on the trot without anyone commenting on it," said Albert Treloar, nodding with satisfaction, "but as soon as all the twinkly lights and sparkly things get taken down people start saying I drink too much, not that I care."

"Well you should care," said Madge, his wife, as they sat with locals in the snug bar, "and you do drink too much. I'm always telling you so. I dread to think what the state of your poor liver must be."

"Oh, don't be too hard on him, Madge," laughed Brendon Wilson. "It's hard work running a farm, a chap has to have a bit of fun, eh Albert?"

"Humph," grunted Madge, taking a handful of peanuts from the bowl on the table, "fun indeed! You're nearly as bad young man, but at least you do still work. Albert hasn't done a stroke for years now, not on the farm nor in the house and he drinks more than ever and look at the size of his beer belly."

Albert pulled down his jumper in an attempt to cover his round stomach. "I don't need to work now because David and Judith are more than competent enough and I don't want them to think I'm horning in. In fact I must admit it amazes me how good they are considering they've got no farming blood in their veins."

"But David must have," said Brendon, puzzled. "He's your grandson."

"No, not strictly speaking," said Madge, struggling to communicate with a mouthful of peanuts. "He's Albert's step-grandson, and so is his brother Stephen, of course."

"You mean young Stephen who works at the post office."

"That's right, he's learning the ropes from his parents because they want him to take it over one day when they're ready to retire. And hopefully in the meantime he'll find himself a nice little wife because it's too much for anyone to do on their own."

"Hmm, perhaps I've had too much beer, but I still don't see how David, and Stephen too for that matter, aren't Albert's grandsons, if Milly's your daughter," said Brendon, puzzled.

"But it's simple, I already had Milly, their mother, when I married Albert," said Madge, "and I must admit he's been very good and always treated the boys and Milly like his own."

"Oh, I see, how stupid of me. And what about David's wife, Judith, then? You say she has no farming background, so is she a local girl?"

"Local inasmuch as she comes from Mullion, said Madge. "Her father was a mechanic and her mother ran a guest house, so she knows all about hard work."

Over the years it had become a custom to celebrate the coming of each New Year with a party at the Old Vicarage. It started in 1979 when

49

Anne and John's twins were babies and they invited Elizabeth and Greg, and Susan and Steve to join them with their tiny offspring to celebrate the twins first birthday and to stay for the night. That way their children could be put to bed upstairs with their cousins and no-one would have to worry about baby-sitters. The evenings soon became a huge success, and so Anne and John let it be known theirs was an open house and all were welcome with or without offspring. And since the Vicarage was in close proximity of the inn, by way of the village field which ran twixt the two, many people were able to enjoy the hospitality of Anne and John at the Vicarage for party games and conversation, and a good laugh at the inn where the evening swung with a fancy dress party.

New Year's Eve of 1986 followed the same pattern as previous years; Jess and Ollie had their friends round for a birthday party in the afternoon and then in the evening, after their friends had gone, the six cousins were joined by the three daughters of Linda and Jamie Stevens, and Larry and Candy Bingham's two boys, Charlie and Sam. Hence in the dining room the youngsters had their own party - the second in the day for some - and were allowed to stay up for as long as they could keep awake. The children relished their bit of independence and their parents, crammed into the big room, knew they could rely on their offspring to behave. The presence of Ned guaranteed this, for not only was he grandfather to six, but headmaster to all. By half past ten, however, most children were ready for bed and by eleven o'clock all were safely tucked up in their makeshift beds and fast asleep.

In the big room the assembled guests sat in candlelight and chatted over mulled wine, spirits, liqueurs, and Tony's homemade beer, the quieter option to the party at the inn and the perfect antidote for anyone who could take only so much noise. For the party at the Fox and Hounds precluded all conversation due to the particularly loud local band playing the latest hits.

For the striking of the midnight hour, villagers were torn between the two options, hence it was mostly just family who toasted the New Year at the Vicarage, the exceptions being, Linda and Jamie Stevens, Candy and Larry Bingham, Rose and George Clarke, and Meg and Sid Reynolds. And as the words of Auld Lang Syne rose from the inn, the Old Vicarage and homes throughout Trengillion; high in the tower of the ancient church, the bells rang out to welcome in the New Year.

CHAPTER EIGHT

"I read Dickens' A Christmas Carol on Christmas Eve this year," said Ned, whilst John poured him a brandy, as he and the remaining guests sat around the fire in the big room shortly after midnight. "I'd forgotten just what a damn good story it is, I don't think there's anything else as can touch it, not with a moral message anyway."

"Hmm, I often say I must read that at Christmas," Larry Bingham said, "but somehow I never seem to get round to it. There's always so much to do in the weeks leading up to the big day, not that I do a great deal as the look on Candy's face will no doubt tell you."

Candy giggled, her face flushed by wine and the heat of the fire, as she nodded to endorse the words of her husband.

"Well, it's a classic, there's no doubt about that, but I still think there's nothing like a true ghost story," said Rose, attempting to crack a Brazil nut. "Especially if it's local."

Sid Reynolds threw back his head and laughed. "But surely the statement 'true ghost story' is an oxymoron. I mean, you'd have to believe in ghosts for such a story to be true and that's ridiculous."

"No, I don't think you could claim 'true ghost story' to be an oxymoron," said Meg, emphatically. "Lots of people believe in ghosts and there's no way of proving them wrong."

"Poppycock, science says it's not possible, Meg. You only have to look at the facts, and as regards 'true ghost story' being an oxymoron it's no different to saying 'fictitious fact' or 'true fiction'. Ghost stories are good for entertainment but that's as far as it goes."

Meg shrugged her shoulders. "You're a beastly killjoy, Sid Reynolds. I believe in ghosts, always have and always shall."

"Hear, hear," said Stella, raising her empty advocaat glass smeared inside by her finger in order to get out every last drop. "Long live ghosts."

"Now that probably is an oxymoron," laughed Anne, passing the advocaat bottle to her mother.

"You're an educated man, Willoughby, what do you make of all this ghost nonsense?" asked Sid."

"Well, it's not a subject I've given much thought to during my life, I must admit, but a friend of Tabbs experienced a rather peculiar happening, didn't she, love?"

"Hmm, I assume you mean, Sadie?" sighed Tabitha.

Willoughby nodded.

"Oh, please do tell us about it," begged Stella, her glass brim-full again. "It's the perfect night for hearing spooky stories."

Tabitha smiled feebly. "Alright, just let me get my train of thoughts sorted." She leaned forward in her chair, her face distorted with concentration. "Gosh, it was quite a while back, longer than I care to remember because I've been retired for ages, but then I suppose the actual year doesn't really matter anyway." She leaned back. "Okay, well, here goes. Sadie was a work colleague of mine and also a friend and at that time we'd both have been in our thirties because it was just after Willoughby asked me to marry him. Sadie lived with her widowed father, her mother having died five years earlier, and she had a boyfriend called Terry whom she'd been dating for several years. Terry was thirty nine and for his fortieth birthday she wanted to do something special because he was adamant he didn't want a party, so she booked a week's holiday in a hotel so they could go away together. Terry was really sweet, I liked him a lot; he was a true gent in every aspect. Anyway, the night before they were due to leave, Sadie dreamed of her mother who begged her not to go. The following morning, Sadie recalled the dream but dismissed it as an unfortunate coincidence and so she and Terry went away as planned. The hotel they stayed in had originally been a stately home and they had a beautiful room in the west wing. I think it may have been in Scotland, but I'm not sure, it may have been the Lake District. It was somewhere up North anyway. On the very first night, she dreamed of her mother again and this time she begged her to return home. Disturbed by the dream, Sadie couldn't sleep and so she dressed and slipped out of the building where she sat in the hotel gardens by a lake in the moonlight to think over her mother's warning. I recall her saying it was a humid, balmy night with a warm westerly wind blowing across the lawns. The peace, however, didn't last. For as she sat ruminating she heard a terrific bang from behind. There was a gas explosion deep in the heart of the building in the kitchen. The hotel was ablaze in minutes and much of it was burned to the ground. There were no survivors in the west wing. All perished including Sadie's boyfriend, Terry."

"Good heavens!" Elizabeth muttered, as Tabitha's words sank in. "Sadie must have been terrified when the reality hit her."

"She was," gulped Tabitha, wiping a tear from her eyes, "and she felt awfully guilty too, because had she heeded her mother's warning in the first place then she and Terry would both have been spared. She never lived it down, it plagued her for many years after and she never married. Poor, poor Sadie."

"Ah, but to dream of the dead is not the same as claiming to see the dead, is it?" Sid reasoned, noting several pairs of eyes awaiting his explanation. "I mean to say; Sadie's mother wasn't a ghost, was she? She was a...um...a ..."

"A what?" asked Tabitha, amused by his predicament, "after all she must have entered Sadie's dream from the spirit world and she was aware of her daughter's danger. Don't you find that a little unnerving?"

"Well, yes, maybe," grinned Sid. "What do you think, Molly?" Sid asked, eager to turn the spotlight onto someone else. "I believe this kind of talk is right up your street."

Molly smiled as she sat with feet tucked in the armchair as she had done since a girl, listening to the banter. "You're right, it is a subject very dear to my heart," she whispered, "and of course I believe in ghosts and spirits, the same as I believe in life after death and especially so since my dear husband has gone. Furthermore, I've no doubt whatsoever that Sadie's mother spoke to her from beyond the grave. "

"I wonder if there's any truth in the legend of the seamen who died during the Great Blizzard," mused Susan, nervously biting her nails. "You know, the ones who perished off this shore and whose boat is supposed to appear whenever Trengillion suffers a blizzard."

"I've not heard that before," said Candy, moving from the floor to the settee. "Please tell us more."

Susan shook her head. "I don't really know much more than that. Can anyone help me out?"

"I can, the blizzard was in March 1891," said Percy, with a hint of pride. "Granddad often spoke about it to me when we were kids. He remembered it, you see, and I wrote a piece about it back in my school days."

"Really?" said Gertie, impressed. "Tell us more then."

"Well, it all started when severe east, nor' east gales blew across the whole of southern Britain along with continuous snow. Heavy snow it was, dry and powdery because the temperature was well below freezing. Anyway, as that weather front moved away, along came another which brought even more snow and gales. The poor old South West was crippled for a whole week, and Devon and Cornwall were virtually cut off from the rest of the country by whopping great snow drifts. The damage was terrible, and at one time ten bleedin' trains were snowed up, including one over at Hayle, which was stuck in an enormous drift, fifteen feet high and a quarter of a mile long. Imagine that! I drew a picture of it from my imagination but it wasn't very good. Anyway, two hundred people died and six thousand animals too. The gales brought down trees everywhere and fifty ships were wrecked in the channel, including the one you spoke of, Susan; the ghost ship. It got smashed to bits, you see, near to the Witches Broomstick and in broad daylight too. No-one survived and the poor buggers on board were all buried in our churchyard in a mass grave. There's a memorial stone for them but you've probably never noticed, it's on the left hand side of the church not far from the wall. I often looked at it as a boy because it saddened me, but it never deterred me from going to sea."

"Good heavens! I've never heard anything about that before," said Candy, "and I thought snow down here was rare."

"It doesn't happen very often, though we've had our fair share this last year or so," said Nettie, moved by her son-in-law's story, "but the last really severe year I recall was 1963. That was pretty bad and before then it was the long bitter spell in 1947. We thought that would never end." She tutted. "It was a miserable time for farmers, especially up-country."

"Was it during the Great Blizzard of 1891 that Elijah Triggs went missing?" Tony asked. "I've often wondered how long ago it was but never really bothered to find out."

Nettie shook her head. "No, he disappeared ten years earlier than that in 1881; that was a bad winter too but not as bad as 1891. Not that I remember either, of course, because both were well before I was born."

"Would it be a silly question to ask who on earth Elijah Triggs was?" said Candy. "I thought I was quite well informed of local folklore but he's not a name I've ever come across before."

"No, I suppose you'd not hear tales of him these days as he's long forgotten," said Nettie, with a laugh, "but we were all very much aware of his story when we were kids. Elijah Triggs was a farm hand, you see, and son-in-law to old Henry Richards, who was a wealthy farmer. Henry, so I've always believed, wasn't a very nice man, because he made poor Elijah Triggs marry his daughter, Polly, when she ended up in the family way. According to my mother, Elijah always denied the child was his. Well, at least he did to his friends and family, but he knew better than to say so to Henry. He was a giant of a man was Henry, so I believe, so Elijah married Polly and kept his mouth shut."

"What! Poor sod," spluttered Matthew, with an air of disgust, "I'd like someone to try and push me around like that; I'd soon tell him where to get off."

"Yes, but he no doubt wanted to hang on to his job," said Ned. "I can see the dilemma the poor chap would've been in. Which farm was it incidentally, Nettie. Was it yours?"

"No, no it was Higher Green Farm and at that time it'd been in the Richards' family for God knows how many years. But when old Henry retired he sold it to Pat Dickens' granddad. He had no sons to leave it to, you see, and that would have been around the turn of the century I should think."

Candy screeched with delight. "Oh, wow, so it's where I work. Brilliant, I take it Polly's child was a girl then and she was an only child at that."

"Hmm, she was, and I suppose Polly didn't marry again when Elijah went missing in case he turned up. It must have been very peculiar at the time."

"So what exactly happened to this Elijah bloke?" Gertie asked. "Did he do a runner?"

Nettie laughed. "Well, that we'll never know, but I'll tell you the story and you can make up your own minds." She cleared her throat, took a sip Baileys and then licked her lips. "Well, it was way back in

January 1881 that as snow fell from the heavens an easterly gale developed and turned it into a real nasty blizzard which caused havoc all over the southern half of the country. Drifting snow blocked rail tracks further up the line, like the year Percy told us about. They had snow drifts ten feet high up-country, but it wasn't so bad here, though it were bad enough and it still caused a lot of disruption. Anyway, it was Elijah's job to take the milk churns to the milk churn stand at the crossroads by the old Ebenezer chapel which of course was in use back then. He did it every day so knew the route like the back of his hand. On the first day of the snow he set off as usual with his cargo. He must have reached the churn stand because he dropped off the milk and picked up the empty churns, but he never returned home and he was never seen again, not him, nor the horse, nor the cart, nor the empty milk churns neither. Though it's been claimed over the years, that at certain times, it's possible to hear the clatter of horse's hooves and the rattling of the churns on the back of the cart. But I've never heard it and I've never met anyone with two penneth of common sense to have heard it either."

"Oh, my goodness, that's sent shivers down my spine," said Anne, "because I've never heard that story before."

"Me neither," said Elizabeth, selecting a chocolate from a box offered by John. "How come you've never told us that one, Gran?"

"Because like you I've never heard it either," said Molly, "but I'm absolutely enthralled. What a wonderful tale. If only I was a few years younger I'd do a bit of investigating. So has no-one any idea what might have happened to him, Nettie?"

"Well, there were all sorts of daft ideas, like he may have lost sight of the road, bearing in mind it were only a dirt track then, and he might have ended up on the moorland beyond the old chapel and even have gone into the small pond there that's supposed to be quite deep. It's even supposed he may have veered off towards one of the old disused mines and fallen in. There were after all plenty of them back then and safety standards weren't as tight as now, and if he couldn't see where he was going then God only knows what happened to the poor blighter. And of course it was impossible to follow his cart tracks because the snow was heavy and his tracks would soon have been covered."

Larry Bingham roared with laughter. "So let me get this right. We not only have a ghost ship that sails off these shores during blizzards and heavy snow, but we've a ghostly horse with cart and milk churns driven by a missing farm hand as well. That's brilliant, let's hope we have lots and lots of snow ere long."

"A loud rapping on the window startled the cosy gathering in the big room and caused some of the females to scream. Realising it was not made by any unearthly presence, John went to the front door to see who had knocked. Outside he found Giles and Brendon Wilson, arms linked and teetering on the doorstep.

"Come in," laughed John, not a little relieved that the callers were down to earth farmers. "No Jane, I see, Giles?"

"No, we just dropped her off home. I think she's had one glass of Martini too many. Silly moo could hardly stand."

"I see: well, we were telling each other ghost stories, one of which is about a one-time worker at your own farm."

"Ah, you mean Elijah Triggs," chuckled Giles, as the two men crossed the threshold and John closed the front door. "Pat Dickens told us about him after we'd bought the place. Has anyone seen his ghost then? It'd be brilliant if they had."

"Put the value of our farm up too," grinned Brendon.

The two brothers joined the other guests in the big room and stood briefly in front of the fire to warm their hands, while John poured them each a glass of homebrew from Tony's five gallon, plastic pressure barrel.

"Cheers," said Giles, raising his glass. "Hey, Linda, where's your pop star cousin gone? I thought he'd be in the pub tonight, he told me he would be when I got chatting to him the other day."

Linda attempted to stifle a yawn. "I know, but his old friend, Guy rang him yesterday and begged him to go to some party or other. He didn't really want to go but he needs to keep on the right side of Guy because he has digs with him. He intends to come back in a day or two though."

"Good night at the inn was it?" Tony asked, throwing a couple of logs on the fire.

"Hmm, so, so," said Giles. "I had a chat with Harry Richardson, when the band took a break. Gosh he's looking old, poor sod. Anyway, he told me the people who've bought the Old Police House move in in the New Year. Their name is Ainsworth and they've got four kids, so that'll boost your pupil numbers a bit, Ned."

"Yes, I did know about the four children. Mr Ainsworth phoned up the school a few weeks back. Did Harry say when they were due to arrive, not that it really matters?"

"No, but he got seventy four grand for the house. This beer's bloody 'ansome, Tony. Well done."

"Thanks, there's plenty more where that came from, so drink up."

"Seventy four thousand pounds," Molly exclaimed. "The major was right, he said it was a damn good investment back in 1976."

"What did Harry pay for it then?" asked Giles.

"I believe it was ten thousand," said Molly. "Can anyone confirm that?"

Sid nodded. "Yes, you're spot on. I remember our Graham telling us and we thought he'd done alright too."

"Right, let's hear some of your ghost stories then," said Brendon, sitting on the floor beside the settee with legs crossed. "Let's see if you can scare Giles and me."

A log suddenly hissed in the fire sending a cloud of smoke up the chimney.

"Hmm, damp wood," said John, puzzled, "it must have fallen from the back of the pile onto the dry stuff when in the log shed."

"Thank Goodness for that," giggled Susan, "for a minute I thought it was going to turn into an apparition."

"Ooooo, from ghoulies and ghosties and long-leggedy beasties and things that go bump in the night, good Lord deliver us," laughed Sid.

CHAPTER NINE

The New Year got off to a miserable, mild, wet start, but after a couple of days the rain ceased, the sun came out and the weather turned cold and frosty, just in time for those who had been on holiday for a fortnight to return to work.

On Sunday the fourth, as day dawned, Rose and George, two weeks later than originally planned, finally left Ivy Cottage and Trengillion for Blackpool to visit Rose's elderly parents. And the following day, the twelfth day of Christmas, a family, new to Trengillion, moved into the Old Police House. It was Gertie who first came across the new arrivals, for after the removal van had departed she found a doll lying in the path outside the Old Police House, thus giving her reason to knock on the door on assumption it had been dropped by the removal men. After handing over the doll to Mr Ainsworth, she was asked into the house to meet the family.

"He seems really nice," said Gertie, as she sat in the kitchen of the Old School House that afternoon telling of her first encounter to Ned and Stella. "Although I'm sure he was looking at my crooked teeth all the time I talked. He's a dentist, you see, and has gone into partnership with Ken Bradshaw. I wasn't too keen on his wife though, I couldn't get much out of her; she seemed a bit of a busy body, a bit snooty too and it ended up with her asking all the questions which stopped me finding much out about them. Still, there's plenty of time to find out more, I suppose."

"Well, it seems to me you did quite well to establish the fact he's a dentist," laughed Stella. "I'm sure I'd not have had the shrewdness to have established that."

Gertie giggled. "Oh, it didn't take much to get that out of him. He was very forthcoming, but then being new he's probably touting for business. You'll no doubt see the kids soon, Ned; they're all primary school age and there are hundreds of them. Mrs Ainsworth wanted to know all about you, so I put in a good word and I sang Meg's praises too."

Ned laughed. "Thank you, Gert. Actually there are only four children and as they're here now I suppose they'll start school when we go back tomorrow, but the number is all I did know until your visit."

"What are their names?" Stella asked.

"Ian and Janet Ainsworth," said Gertie. "They're the parent's names anyway, I don't know about the kids. Oh, and they have a dog too, a white poodly thing with a daft hairdo."

"A poodly thing," laughed Stella, glancing up at the clock. "Oh, my goodness, look at the time." She leapt from her chair. "I must dash, I have to pick up Mum and Dad from Redruth station in forty five minutes."

"So, what are they like?" Ned asked, as Stella, quickly put on her shoes and brushed her hair. "The Ainsworths, that is."

"Well, at a guess I'd say they're both in their early forties. He's about six feet tall, got black hair going grey round the ears, hazel eyes and a little moustache. He's rather handsome, I must admit, and she's a mousy blonde with a big nose and funny shaped bow legs."

Stella threw back her head and laughed out loud, as she put on her coat. It was quite obvious Gertie, and Janet Ainsworth, were hardly likely ever to be the best of friends.

That same Monday afternoon, Elizabeth and Greg took the children into Helston shopping to buy a tumble drier and new school shoes for Tally. The purchase of a tumble drier was straight forward; Elizabeth found just what she wanted in ETS. The search for shoes, however, proved more difficult, for Tally had set her heart on a pair like her school friend, Eleanor, bought from John Farmers in September past; but the said shop had only one pair left in the required design and they were the wrong size. Tally was distraught. The shop assistant offered to order a pair especially for her, but they would not be in until the end of the week and so too late for the beginning of the new term the following day. Tally sulked.

"Why can't you have something different," said Elizabeth, exasperated by her daughter's stubbornness.

"Because I don't like any of the others," said Tally, unreasonably. "But we've not even looked at any others," said Greg. "Come on Talls, at least try some on."

With grudging reluctance Tally tried on several pairs of shoes, most of which she claimed hurt her feet, but then the assistant brought out an attractive black matt leather shoe with a T bar and scalloped edge which appealed to her juvenile sense of fashion. Tally tried on both shoes and looked in the mirror; she would never have admitted it but she actually liked them more than Eleanor's.

"These are quite nice and they're comfortable," she said, sitting down beside her mother. "I think I'll make do with them."

"They only came in last Friday," said the assistant, "but we've sold several pairs already."

"We'll have them, please," said Elizabeth, taking her purse from her handbag.

With shoes in box and carrier bag, the Castor-Hunts left the shop and headed for the car park before Tally had time to change her mind.

That evening the News reported Ronald Reagan, President of the USA, had undergone prostate surgery, thus raising speculation regarding his fitness for office. In the United Kingdom, bank robbers had absconded with thirteen million pounds in used notes and the weather forecast predicted further freezing temperatures.

"I'd better order some more coal tomorrow," said Ned, picking up the empty coal scuttle, "we seem to have used up a lot lately."

"You'll be back at school tomorrow," Stella reminded him, "so I'll do it, but I think it's about time we thought about getting central heating installed. It'd be so much easier and cleaner too, if we had oil, that is."

"Hmm, I agree." Ned looked down at the empty scuttle in his hand. "And I must admit, repeatedly filling this thing and cleaning out the fireplace every day does get a bit tedious and I only do it during the school holidays. Having said that, I thought you liked to see a coal fire."

"And so I do, especially at Christmas, but it'd be nice to have the whole house warm and we can still have a fire when we want one, especially when it's bitterly cold."

"Okay, I'll have a word with Larry Bingham when next I see him and see what he advises."

"Does he do heating then as well as plumbing?"

"Hmm yes, he put central heating in for Frank and Dorothy last summer and I know he did a good job because Frank told me so."

That same evening, Frank and Dorothy Newton drove down to the Fox and Hounds to see a few friendly faces; both were glad to get out of the house and away from the television. Because of the drink/driving law, Dorothy drove, as she was happy to sip fruit juice if it gave Frank the opportunity to have a pint and a chat with other men. For the death of Major Smith had left a huge void in Frank's life; he deeply missed the major's company, his wise thoughts and his opinions on current affairs; he also missed the conviviality and having someone with whom he could put the world to rights.

The inn was fairly quiet, just as Frank and Dorothy, as customers, liked it, and so they were able to sit in the snug by the blazing log fire where they were joined by retired farmer, Pat Dickens, and Dorothy's brother, Albert Treloar.

"How's Madge?" Dorothy asked, as Albert placed his pint glass on the table and took a seat beside her. "I hear she's had this wretched flu that's still doing the rounds."

"Yes, she has, poor old gel; she came down with it just before New Year but she's a lot better now." Albert laughed. "It'll take a lot more than flu to kill off my Madge, she's a tough nut, I'll give her that."

"Hmm, she's lucky then," said Pat, unzipping his jacket and removing his mohair scarf. "Some have had it quite bad and when you get to our ages it can often be fatal. Having said that, May had it and was up and about in no time, but then like your Madge she's pretty tough too. It must be all the farm work that made 'em that way, either that or it's the care we've taken of 'em."

"Cheeky," said Dorothy, pouring pineapple juice into her glass. "When it comes to being cared for, you're both on the receiving end.

Neither of you could have had a couple of better women, though I did have my doubts about Madge at first."

"Hey, did you hear about the bank robbery on the News?" Frank asked. "Thirteen million pounds nicked. Whatever would anyone need that sort of money for?"

"I'm sure I could find something to spend it on," said Percy, who had just arrived, "and I daresay Gertie could do even better than me."

"Yes, but thirteen million," laughed Dorothy, "that's an awful lot of money. I'm sure I wouldn't know what to do with it."

"Well, it'll be shared between at least four," said Pat, "cos that's how many robbers they reckon there were. They've got a nerve though, going into a busy bank like that in broad daylight. I wouldn't risk it even if I knew the plan was pretty well near perfect."

"Yeah, but it must be a really good feeling if you can get away with it," said Percy, wistfully. "I mean, look at the *Italian Job*, I'd love to have been involved with that; what a hoot."

Pat laughed. "But it wasn't real though, was it? And what's more we don't know whether they ever got the ruddy bus back on the road. I know what you mean though, but I think there's a lot to be said for keeping the right side of the law, even if it does mean staying poor."

"You're not poor," Albert scoffed. "You got a bloomin' good price when you sold up."

"Yes, but nothing like as much as old Peregrine Denby got when he sold to the Wilson lads. He got double what we did; jammy bugger."

On January the sixth, the beginning of the Epiphany, it was back to school for children and teachers. Not that the children minded, for the holiday lost its magic once Christmas was over and so all were glad to be going back to discuss with their friends the presents they had received.

Inside Cove Cottage Tally put on her new shoes. She liked them and was glad she had them, but there was still a nagging doubt in her mind as to whether or not it might have been better to have waited until the end of the week in order that she had a pair like Eleanor. Eleanor was after all, a leader where the subject of fashion was involved. Hence, when she walked to school with Elizabeth and

Wills she was somewhat downcast. The sombre mood, however, did not last, for when Tally met up with Eleanor in the playground she found her friend was not wearing her old shoes, she too had a new pair and they were exactly the same as Tally's. Tally thought it was wonderful. Providence. A miracle, and so when Mrs Reynolds asked them to write a composition about something that had happened during the school holiday, Tally did not write about Christmas but chose instead to tell the story of her new shoes.

At the Old Vicarage, Anne, after taking down the Christmas decorations, was lured outside by the dry morning where she attempted to do a little gardening in preparation for spring. But after pruning a few roses she found her fingers were numb with cold and her nose was dripping constantly. Accepting there would be plenty of time during the coming weeks to finish the tasks, she abandoned the garden and returned indoors.

With the decorations gone, the house looked bare, especially the big room and the corner where the tree had stood. Anne contemplated how to overcome the bareness but finally conceded it was just something they would have to get used to.

On Thursday it rained during the night and was sunny the following day, so Anne finished pruning the roses and trimmed back the dead chrysanthemum flowers to give more light to the spring bulbs emerging in profusion through the earth. She then cut the dried flower heads and stems from the Sedum Spectabile and hung them in the kitchen to dry thoroughly, her intention being to make an arrangement of dried flowers and evergreen winter foliage to brighten the Christmas tree's vacated corner. As soon as the sun sank that evening, the temperature dropped, but Anne was pleased with her modest contribution to the garden's upkeep, for every job done made spring feel a little nearer.

In the flat above her café, Jane Williams looked through the substantial amount of yellow cotton fabric, decorated with shells, fish and all things nautical in various shades of blue, which she had purchased in the January Sales that morning. With it she intended to make new curtains and cushion covers; it was imperative therefore that she changed the colour of the walls in the café during the winter months, for the current combination of peach and tangerine she concluded would look hideous.

Jane's café was named The Pickled Egg; a name she chose for two reasons. One, she enjoyed pickling eggs in various ways and they were a popular take-away snack for sun-bathers, and two, the name conjured up the image of an egg having had one drink too many. Hence the board above the window displaying the café's name, depicted an egg sitting on the rim of a jar with dishevelled wisps of hair peeping beneath the peak of a cap, clothing awry and with a very merry expression on his jolly face, whilst in his hand was a portion of chips. It was Stella Stanley who had painted the board which was popular with locals and holiday makers alike. So much so that some locals suggested Jane applied for a licence. But that she refused to do, saying she had not the slightest desire to be in competition with the inn; her ambition was quite straightforward: the preparation and presentation of simple, good value, family food.

The Pickled Egg opened every year from Easter until the last full week in October which usually coincided with half term. During the school holidays she employed any willing girls from the village who wanted to earn some pocket money, and during term time, Gertie helped out, along with Jane's friend, Susan.

In the winter months, Jane lived on the profits made during the summer. Her living accommodation was cheap to run: a modest two bedroomed flat above the café, and her free time gave her ample opportunity to make preserves, plan new dishes and touch up the décor where necessary.

As Jane put the fabric back inside the carrier bag, the telephone rang. On answering it she found it was Giles asking if she would like to go into town for a Chinese meal that evening. Jane accepted the invitation with enthusiasm and after replacing the receiver went to the bathroom to wash her hair. As hot water splashed into the wash basin, Jane sighed with contentment; she was happy with her life; she had a business she loved; family and friends in the village and a boyfriend whom she hoped one day might ask her to be his wife.

CHAPTER TEN

Sunday January the eleventh was another cold day and so while John took Ollie and Jess to the recreation ground, Anne covered over her tender plants in the greenhouse with sheets of polythene and newspaper and put up-turned buckets over the half-hardy plants in the garden.

After dark the weather turned colder still, and inside the Old Vicarage, Anne sat with the twins cosily on the settee by the fire in the big room, glad that her plants had protection, listening to the children read in turn from their school reading books. When Jess had finished she went upstairs to return her book to her school bag, but within minutes of her departure, Anne and Ollie heard a scream followed by the thudding of small feet rapidly running down the stairs. Anne leapt to her feet as Jess flew into the room, her face glowing with excitement, her arms waving towards the window. "It's snowing," she panted, "quickly, come and see; it's snowing real snow, great big flakes, you can see it from the landing window."

Ollie leapt from the settee sending his reading book onto the floor. "Can I go and see, Mum, please?"

"Of course," said Anne, picking up the fallen book, "and I'm coming too."

The falling snow was clearly visible from the landing window, daintily swirling in a glowing patch of light emanating from the outside lamp overhanging the front door. Anne and the children watched, huddled together on the cushioned window-seat, enthralled, as the delicate flakes gently fluttered downwards and settled on the lawn and surrounding trees and shrubs.

"Will Daddy be able to get home alright?" Ollie asked, much concerned. "The drive's getting awful white and you can't see the edges very well."

Smiling, Anne put her arm around the shoulders of her son. "Oh yes, I should think so, it's not far to the farm and the Land Rover is specially made to tackle bad weather as well as muddy fields."

"What, like really big snowdrifts?" asked Ollie, with awe.

"Yes, and slippery roads too. Anyway, Daddy should be home soon: he said he'd be back by eight, so the snow won't be much deeper by then and it might even have stopped."

Jess looked aghast. "Please don't say that, Mummy, I want it to snow all night so we can play in it tomorrow."

"You have school in the morning," Anne reminded them, "and for that reason I think it's time you two got ready for bed, and then when Daddy gets back he'll come up and read you both a story."

"I'm going to look at The Snowman book 'til he gets back," said Ollie, jumping down from the window-seat and crossing the landing towards the bedroom, "cos I'm going to build a snowman tomorrow when we come home from school."

"And I'll ask Daddy if he'll read The Snow Queen," said Jess, skipping across the landing.

"Oh, I'm sure he will," smiled Anne, following the children into their room. "It would be an excellent choice on a night such as this. Now get into your pyjamas quickly; your beds should be lovely and warm because I put your hot water bottles in them over an hour ago."

Ollie and Jess each had their own bedroom but neither could sleep without the other; they claimed it was too scary and spooky to be alone once darkness fell and so Anne and John agreed to leave them together until they decided for themselves that they wanted their own space. For John, himself a twin, knew only too well how attached twins could be to each other, although it must be said that both he and his twin, Tony, were equally fond of their younger sister, Susan.

The following morning, Cornwall's inhabitants awoke to a glistening white world where their once familiar landscape lay hidden beneath a sparkling blanket of snow. The tranquil scene resembled a Christmas card sprinkled with silver glitter; its smooth, even surface disturbed only by the tiny footprints of birds and small creatures who had ventured out in search of food.

At the Old Vicarage, before breakfast, John switched on Radio Cornwall to hear the latest news regarding the weather. He was surprised to find the broadcasters made very little of it, although they did warn it was freezing hard and some roads were very dangerous in places.

Steve Penhaligon phoned while John was eating his toast and they both agreed to work as usual for they were keen to get their present job finished in order to begin another the following week. Ned, however, concerned about the safety of his pupils living in remote areas around Trengillion, decided the village school would not open, hence there was much rejoicing amongst the youngest generation.

Later in the morning, Anne, keen for adult company with whom she could discuss the weather, walked with the children through the village and down to Cove Cottage to visit her sister, Elizabeth. Conditions out were bad and far worse than she had anticipated. Snow was falling heavily, the wind had strengthened and visibility was deteriorating rapidly. Anne shivered, as the cold wind and snow blew onto her face and stuck to her eyelashes. Desperate to reach the warmth of her sister's house, she attempted to walk quickly, but Ollie and Jess, oblivious of the cold, wanted to make snowballs and throw them at any moving target. Anne chivvied the children up; the sky was thick with snow and her toes were rapidly becoming numb. The children, alarmed by their mother's red nose, watery eyes and shaky voice, did as she asked.

On arrival at Cove Cottage Anne was astonished to find it was Greg who opened the front door, with Tally and Wills chattering excitedly beside him.

"Just got back," he grinned, in answer to the surprised look on his sister-in-law's face. "Conditions in Helston are dreadful and so we all agreed to abandon the office. Just as well really, because as we left we witnessed an avalanche of snow cascade off the roof of Abbott's dress shop and it missed a couple staggering down the road by a matter of inches." He stepped aside to let them in. "You should see it; the traffic's virtually come to a standstill and there are stranded cars everywhere. I've not seen it as bad as this since 1963. Remember that, Anne?"

"Of course," she replied, removing her boots, standing them in the small front porch and indicating to Ollie and Jess to do likewise, "although I was only seven at the time and Mum wouldn't let us go out for long. Not that I really minded because I hate being cold."

"Like big sister then," said Greg, shutting the front door and leading them along the passage. "Come in here and we'll put the kettle on. Liz is on the phone."

They took off their coats and hung them in the kitchen to dry. The children complained saying they wanted to go back out but Anne and Greg both agreed the weather was too severe to play outdoors.

Elizabeth, sitting on the floor in the living room, frowned as she put down the telephone receiver; she then went to the kitchen to see to whom Greg was talking. "Anne, I didn't realise it was you. Is your phone working? Ours isn't, it's completely dead."

Anne shook her head. "I don't know but then no-one has used it since Steve rang this morning. Perhaps the wind has brought down some of the lines?"

"Either that or there's ice on the lines," said Greg, placing a carton of orange juice and the biscuit tin on the table for the children. "That's a nuisance because I was going to phone Mum and Dad to see if our Lily has arrived safely."

Elizabeth sighed. "I was trying to ring Grandma to make sure she's alright, but I expect Dad will have been round to see her. She'll be really fed up though if she can't get out."

"Lily is here," said Anne, warming her hands on the radiator, "she rang me last night to say she's longing for a chat and I guess that would have been about ten o' clock."

"Oh, she did, did she?" Greg tutted, taking three mugs from the cupboard. "She didn't ring us. I shall have to have a sharp word with my little sister."

Elizabeth, seeing Tally was struggling to open the carton, poured orange juice for the children. "Do you still want me to baby-sit tonight? I mean, I take it the snow won't put you off going out."

"Yes please, if you don't mind, although it'll be a nightmare getting up to the farm if this snow continues for much longer."

"You'll have to get Tony to pick you up on the tractor," laughed Greg. "Or should I say the trailer."

"Hmm, I think I'd rather walk than ride in a dirty old trailer, but I'm pretty sure the Land Rover will be alright anyway. John's mum and dad are playing safe though and walking up at teatime before it gets dark."

"How old is John's gran this year?" Elizabeth asked.

"Eighty two, she's just that bit younger than Grandma. I hope Jean has cooked something hot and filling, not that it's ever cold in

69

the farmhouse kitchen, but I expect we'll eat in the dining room since it's a special occasion."

The snow continued to fall steadily until after dark and nowhere in the country did the temperature rise above freezing. Even the Scilly Isles rapidly disappeared beneath a blanket of snow: a very rare occurrence indeed.

John and Anne, after much deliberation, decided to walk up to Long Acre Farm, and as they prepared to leave the Old Vicarage, Elizabeth arrived, clad in heavy coat, hat, scarf, gloves, thick socks and Wellington boots.

"God, it's evil out there," she shivered, stepping onto newspapers Anne had laid in the hallway to prevent wet boots spoiling the carpet. "But then at the same time it's really lovely too. It's still snowing and it's ever so slippery in places, so do be careful."

"Mum and Dad popped in just before teatime," said John, "on their way up to the farm. The pipes in their outside loo are frozen solid and so are everyone else's in their terrace. Just shows how cold it is."

"I'm glad we've got everything well and truly lagged," said Elizabeth, hanging her coat on the pegs. "Greg's a real fusspot about things like that. Anyway, don't worry about getting back if you decide to stay the night. I'll be alright here because I doubt there'll be any school tomorrow or work for Greg either."

John nodded. "That might be a good idea but with the phone lines down we'll not be able to let you know."

"No, well it doesn't matter. If you're not back by midnight I shall make myself comfortable on the settee. I quite like the idea in fact, and I did warn Greg I might not be back tonight."

"Thanks, Liz, you're a real treasure," said Anne kissing her sister's cheek. "You'll find plenty of blankets in the ottoman in the spare bedroom. Please make yourself at home; there's a nice bottle of red wine on the table in the kitchen and plenty to eat in the fridge if you're peckish."

"Why can't Liz sleep in the spare bedroom?" John asked, zipping his thick padded jacket up and over his chin. "It seems the obvious place to me."

"Because it's grotty and smells fusty through lack of use and I'm sure she doesn't want to sleep in that grotesque old fashioned bed either. I know I wouldn't."

"And I'd be much happier down here in the warm anyway," Elizabeth said, "because I can watch the telly until I doze off."

"Right, if you're okay, then we'll be off then," said Anne, pulling her hat tightly over her ears."

"Err, what about the children?"

Anne laughed. "Oh no, I'd forgotten about them. They're in their room, tucked up in bed looking at books, but I'm sure they'd love it if you read them a story."

"Okay, will do. Now off you go, have a good time and please convey my best birthday wishes to Nettie."

After the departure of Anne and John, Elizabeth went upstairs where she found Ollie and Jess not in bed but kneeling on the cushioned window seat on the landing watching their parents walk away from the house and onto the driveway. When they were no longer visible, Jess jumped down and took her aunt's hand.

"We're glad you're here, Auntie Lizzie, cos the snow's very pretty but it's scary too. What will we do if it never stops and the house gets buried?"

"But it will stop," smiled Elizabeth, as she was escorted towards the window seat by her niece. "It always does, so enjoy it while it's here and then tomorrow you can build a snowman."

"Why wouldn't you and Uncle Greg and Mummy let us build one at your house today?" Ollie asked.

"Because it was horrible out; much too cold, too windy and with the snow falling heavily any snowman built would have been buried before it was finished anyway."

"Suppose so. We're going to build one down there," said Ollie, pointing to a part of the garden where usually grass lay bordered by shrubs. "A whopper and then we'll be able to see him from up here just like the little boy in the book."

"Talking of books, Mummy said you might like me to read to you both. Would you?"

"Yes please," squealed Jess, jumping down from the window seat and running into the bedroom towards the bookcase. Elizabeth followed.

71

"Please read this one, Auntie Lizzie; it's my favourite because it's about Father Christmas."

"But Christmas has gone," laughed Elizabeth, stooping beside the bookcase where Jess sat with her chosen book. "Are you sure this is what you want?"

"Yes, cos it feels like Christmas again now, even though real Christmases are usually wet or foggy. I'm going to pretend it's Christmas and imagine all the decorations are still up and Father Christmas is going to come tonight with his reindeers and sleigh."

Elizabeth read the chosen story and two others beside, she then tucked Jess and Ollie in their respective beds and kissed them goodnight.

Downstairs, she pondered over whether to open the bottle of red wine or stay alert and drink coffee; the lure of the wine won when she realised it was her favourite, Cabinet Sauvignon. With opened bottle and small stemmed glass in hand, she left the kitchen and walked along the hallway to the big room. Inside she found the fire burning brightly and Anne's sheepskin slippers laying on the hearth rug. Elizabeth sat on the floor and warmed her feet by the fire, she then tucked them snugly into her sister's slippers; for since removing her Wellington boots on arrival, she only had socks to protect her feet from the cold.

With feet warmed, she crossed to the window and peeped behind the thick curtain. The drifting snow glistened in the glow from the room's light, highlighting the delicate flakes still falling and softly settling on the white ground. And in the borders, lifeless garden plants, rigid and dusted with frozen snow, cast eerie shadows across the crisp, white blanket.

Elizabeth shivered, let the curtain fall back across the window and returned to the warmth of the fire. She contemplated watching television, but there seemed to be magic in the air which she felt would be destroyed by the intrusion of collective voices. She sat down on the settee took a sip of wine and picked up a book lying on the occasional table beneath a brass lamp; it was R F Delderfield's, A Horseman Riding By. Elizabeth turned to the first page; she had enjoyed the television series made by the BBC the previous decade and so began to read. At the end of the second chapter she lay down the book and wandered into the kitchen, her dinner had long since settled and she felt hungry. In the fridge she found a dish containing half a cheese and onion quiche; she cut out a large piece, laid it on a plate along with six pickled shallots and returned with it to the big room. When her supper was eaten she washed it down with a sixth glass of wine which emptied the bottle.

By the end of the third chapter Elizabeth felt her concentration lapsing, the print was small and her eyes were beginning to ache. Before she was half way down the first page of the fourth chapter, the book slid from her lap and she was fast asleep.

Elizabeth shivered when she awoke, the fire was burning low and her mouth felt dry. She picked up the book from the floor and laid it back on the table. The clock on the wall told her the time was eleven thirty five. She stood, crossed the room and went to the kitchen where she made a mug of tea, and then sitting at the huge pine table, she drank it and ate three chocolate digestive biscuits. Feeling refreshed, she tipped more coke into the Rayburn and then went upstairs to get blankets from the spare bedroom, checking en route to make sure that Ollie and Jess were both fast asleep. They were.

The spare bedroom struck cold when she opened the door; the light bulb was dim and the large, old fashioned, black, iron-framed, single bed which dominating the room, cast a dark shadow across the bare floorboards. The bed had been left in the house by Vicar Ridge when he retired and vacated the Vicarage. His daughter, Meg, said it had been in that particular room since before the Ridges had first moved in when she was very young and for some strange reason, because they didn't need to use that bedroom, the Ridge family felt it should stay where perhaps it belonged. Elizabeth knew Anne disliked the bed and would have preferred a new modern divan, but there was something about the old iron frame that compelled her also to let it remain in situ.

From the ottoman in the corner Elizabeth took two large pink blankets. As she closed the lid she thought she heard the voice of a child whispering. She laid the blankets down on the ottoman and stood perfectly still listening; when she heard the voice again she left the room, assuming either Ollie or Jess had woken, but to her surprise both were still asleep and lying as she had seen them just minutes before. Puzzled, Elizabeth returned to the spare room and picked up the blankets, but as she reached for the door's latch to leave, she heard the voice again and realised it was there, with her, in the spare room. Slowly, she quietly tiptoed across the bare floorboards, listening carefully, trying to locate the exact spot from where the voice appeared to emerge; to her surprise the source was the chimney. Elizabeth dropped the blankets onto the bed, stooped down low and shuffled herself inside the fireplace. From high above her head, the notes of a tuneful song mingled with the wind whistling across the chimney pot. Elizabeth strained her ears to learn more; the song was just recognisable; a child was softly singing *I had a Little Nut Tree*. As the nursery rhyme finished and the notes faded, the wind dropped, and the chimney fell silent.

Confused, and feeling claustrophobic, Elizabeth was eager to get back into the room but as she turned to leave the fireplace her foot slipped on loose soot in the hearth. In panic she reached out to avoid banging her head and her fingers pushed against a granite stone which moved. Not wanting the loose stone to fall noisily and disturb Jess and Ollie, she pushed it back; as it fell into place she heard a distinct clonk. Realising the sound was not of granite knocking against granite, for it sounded hollow, Elizabeth pulled out the stone and then pushed her hand into the vacated gap where her fingers touched a cold, smooth, curved surface. Intrigued, she placed her other hand into the void and gently pulled out the object. It was an ornate ginger jar complete with lid.

With hands trembling, Elizabeth shuffled herself from the fireplace and gently stood the jar on the wooden floorboards. Carefully, she lifted the lid. She gasped; inside was a child's, folded, Victorian, black leather boot, neatly fastened with a row of dainty buttons; the size of its worn sole was a little less than the length her out-stretched hand.

Elizabeth shivered. She was too tired to try and fathom out what significance the shoe might have and so gently dropped it back in the jar and replaced the lid. And after pushing back the loose stone into its gap in the chimney, she quietly crept from the room, clutching jar and blankets.

Once back downstairs, she made up her bed on the settee. She looked at the clock; it was past midnight and so she knew it was unlikely that Anne and John would return before morning.

In the early hours Elizabeth woke abruptly, momentarily not remembering where she was. She sat up and rubbed her eyes. The dim glow from the remains of the fire jolted her memory as to her whereabouts. Feeling unsettled by the darkness she reached out for the lamp on the table. Comforted by the light, she glanced around looking for the reason for her abrupt waking. The clock denoted the time was a quarter past three, so she knew the disturbance could not have been the return home of Anne and John.

Elizabeth rose from the settee and crossed unsteadily to the door and out into the hallway. Her head was muzzy and aching, her eyes still misted with sleep. As she passed the open dining room door, instinct compelled her to take a peep inside. The room, lit only by the reflection of the snow through the large mullioned window, struck cold and silhouettes of the furnishings and ornaments loomed sinister in the shadows. Elizabeth shivered and turned, keen to get back to the warmth of the big room. Crossing the hallway she stopped and her heart began to race. Numbed by fear she looked up at the ceiling. A rustling noise indicated something was shuffling across the bare boards. She stifled a scream. The room above was the spare bedroom and the only room on the upper floor not carpeted.

Feeling sick through fear and consumption of too much wine, Elizabeth crept along the hallway and quietly climbed the winding staircase. At the top she tiptoed along the landing towards the spare room. Outside the door she listened with her ear close to the oak panels. To her horror the rustling sound was clearly audible. Elizabeth held her breath, undecided whether to run or enter the room. She chose the latter. But to her surprise, when she opened the door and switched on the light, she found the room quite empty, both of presence and sound.

With a deep sigh of relief she quietly closed the door and then checked that all was well with Ollie and Jess. Both were still sleeping soundly. Feeling dizzy and faint, she fled down the stairs to the comfort of the settee. Once settled she pulled the blankets snugly around her body but she did not switch off the light and for the remainder of the night slept with one eye open.

At half past seven Elizabeth was woken by Ollie and Jess, both dressed, pulling at her arm asking if they could go out and build a snowman, for the snow, they informed her, had stopped falling, the sun was shining and they were very much afraid it might melt.

Elizabeth sat up and groaned. "You must have breakfast first and then we'll see. Your mum and dad will be home by then perhaps."

"Alright, but will you make us breakfast then please?" Ollie asked. "But we don't need to have porridge cos it takes too long."

"Do you normally have porridge then?" Elizabeth yawned, putting on Anne's slippers.

"We do when it's cold," said Jess, "but the sun's shining today so it doesn't matter cos it's probably quite warm outside."

Elizabeth stood, crossed to the window and pulled back the curtains; the glare caused her to squint. "Oh, the snow looks so beautiful in the sunshine," she whispered to herself. "I really must take some pictures when I get home."

The kitchen struck warm, but Elizabeth still opened the door of the Rayburn to let out more heat, she then looked outside the kitchen door at the thermometer hanging on the wall.

"Well, I don't think this snow will be going anywhere yet," she shivered, dashing back inside and closing the door, "the temperature is way below freezing and so you've plenty of time for porridge."

Ollie groaned but did not argue; Jess clasped her hands together and tilted her head to one side. "If it's freezing out, we can go ice skating, can't we, Auntie Liz."

Elizabeth spooned porridge oats into a saucepan and covered them up with milk. "Well, yes, umm, probably, but where?"

"The sea," said Ollie. "The sea will be frozen cos it's water and water freezes."

Elizabeth smiled. "I'm afraid the sea won't have frozen, Ollie. It would have to be a lot colder than this for that to happen."

Jess frowned. "It will have to be a pond then. There must be one somewhere."

Ollie pointed to the kitchen window. "There's one in the garden."

"Don't be silly," said Jess, indignantly, "it's much too tiny." She turned to face Elizabeth. "Do you know any ponds, Auntie?"

Elizabeth placed the saucepan on top of the Rayburn and gently stirred its content. "Umm, well, the only one I can think of is on the scrubland behind the old Ebenezer Chapel." She paused and slapped her forehead. "What am I saying? You must never go skating on a frozen pond, lake, pool or whatever. It would very, very dangerous because if the ice was too thin then it would crack and break and you'd fall into the water." She shuddered at the thought.

Jess giggled. "We can't go anyway cos we don't have any ice skates."

As Elizabeth and the children were eating their porridge Anne and John returned home.

"God, it's freezing out there," said Anne, removing her gloves and warming her cold hands on the Rayburn, "and for once it really is. It's slippery too and the snow's quite deep in places. You must tread very carefully when you go home, Liz. I nearly came a cropper on a couple of occasions."

"Yes, of course I will; it was pretty slippery when I came round last night. Anyway, did you have a good time?"

"Yes thanks, it was really, really nice. John's mum and dad stayed overnight at the farm too, so we were rather late to bed. Was everything alright here?"

"Err, yes," said Elizabeth, hesitantly, recalling the evening through a hazy blur, "everything was fine, although I had a bit too much wine which along with quiche and pickled onions set my imagination into overdrive. Having said that, I might have been dreaming."

"Might have been," laughed John, hanging his coat on the back of the door, "surely you can differentiate between a dream and reality."

"Normally, yes, but I was half asleep and it was to do with weird and spooky goings-on in your spare bedroom."

Anne frowned and sharply nodded in the direction of the children who had both pricked up their ears.

"Oh yes, I understand, of course it was a dream, definitely a dream, and a very silly one at that." She smiled at the children.

Ollie scowled. "What did you dream, Auntie Lizzy?"

Jess looked afraid. "Is our spare bedroom really spooky?"

Elizabeth laughed nervously. "Err no of course not and the dream was nothing, nothing at all." She turned to Anne and hurriedly asked, "So, what did you have for your dinner last night?"

"Roast lamb," said Anne, puzzled by her sister's sudden strange behaviour, "and very nice it was too."

"Can we go outside now?" Ollie asked, tugging at Anne's sleeve. "Please, Mummy, we've been ever so good and eaten all our porridge."

"Alright, but you must wrap up well as it's very, very cold outside, even in the sun."

"Come with me kids," said John, "and I'll help you out while Mummy talks to Auntie Liz."

As John closed the kitchen door Anne looked at her sister with eyebrows raised.

Elizabeth sighed and nodded towards the door. "Come with me."

In the big room Elizabeth reached down behind the settee and pulled out the ginger jar. "I found this hidden in the chimney in your spare bedroom. Look inside."

Anne did as instructed. "An old shoe. But I don't understand. Why would anyone put a shoe in a ginger pot and hide it inside a chimney? It doesn't make sense."

"I agree and if you've no objection I'd like to show it to Grandma to see if she can shed any light on it."

"Of course, please do. I'm as intrigued as you to know what, if anything, it might mean."

As Anne returned the shoe to the jar and replaced the lid a puzzled look crossed her brow. "But what on earth were you doing in the spare bedroom chimney?"

Elizabeth groaned. "Oh dear, there was a reason and if I tell you you'll no doubt think me really daft."

Anne handed Elizabeth the jar, her eyebrows raised in anticipation. "The umm, dream would it be, by any chance?"

Elizabeth nodded. She then went on to tell of her experience the previous evening.

Before she set off for home, Elizabeth went upstairs to return the blankets. The spare room struck bitterly cold but she attributed that to the lack of heating. She crossed to the corner and dropped the blankets inside the ottoman and then walked to the chimney and listened for any sound. All was quiet, save the wind whistling over the chimney stack. Elizabeth laughed; the room felt neither eerie nor unfriendly. "Anne's right," she said, "the child's voice was a combination of the wind and my imagination and the rustling was probably a mouse." Comforted by her conclusion, she left the room.

CHAPTER ELEVEN

Inside the kitchen of Rose Cottage, Molly stood at the sink washing her breakfast dishes. As she placed the last item on the draining board, Ned emerged through the back door, snug and warm in his rarely worn sheepskin coat.

"Is it as cold out as it looks?" Molly asked, as he quickly closed the door and removed his knitted hat. "I guess it must be because there were beautiful patterns all over my bedroom windows this morning. I wish you'd have seen them as they were quite spectacular, but sadly they've gone now the sun's shining."

"Humph, that's not good, is it? We must think about getting this house double glazed this summer," said Ned, removing his leather gloves and laying them alongside his hat. "We can't have you freezing in your bed."

Molly dried her hands. "Oh, but it's only cold upstairs; my living room is lovely and cosy. Go in and see and I'll make you a coffee."

After coffee, Ned filled Molly's coal scuttle, brought in enough logs to see her through the rest of the day, made sure she had plenty of food in the fridge and then shovelled the snow off the path leading from the back door of the porch to the gate by the road.

"Now, you're not to leave the house," Ned ordered, reaching for his coat when the chores were all done. "It's very, very slippery out, bitterly cold too, and freezing hard."

Molly sighed. "I can assure you Ned I've not the slightest desire to go out as beautiful as everywhere looks. I'm much too fond of warmth."

"Good," said Ned, pulling his woollen hat down over his ears. "Now, what do you propose to eat today?"

"Oh, sweetheart, please don't treat me like a child," Molly spluttered, indignantly. "I may be eighty two but I still have my wits about me. But if you must know I had porridge for breakfast, I intend to have bangers and mash for lunch and a tin of tomato soup for tea, or maybe oxtail or even vegetable, I'll see how the mood takes me.

On the other hand, I might even have a cheese sandwich or perhaps ham or even scrambled eggs on toast."

"Ned smiled; his mother's response quashed any doubts in his mind as to her well-being.

"Good, but if you need anything, please don't hesitate to ring. I'm only a stone's throw away and I can be here in a jiffy." He tutted. "I wish George and Rose weren't away, but at least they should be back any day now. I don't like the idea of you being on your own, I wish you'd come and stay with us for a while."

"Ned, we had all this out when the major passed away, so please don't let's go through the same old thing again. I bet Stella doesn't fuss over her parents like you do me."

"No, she doesn't, but then that's because there are two of them to watch out for each other, whereas you're on your own. I don't like it."

Molly smiled. "Ned, please believe me, I'm alright. I don't mind being on my own. I have a good book to read, the television if I want to see a friendly face, and family and friends at the end of a phone line if I want a chat."

"Ah, but the phones aren't working," said Ned, shaking his finger. "I've just remembered that. Apparently the lines have been dead since yesterday afternoon, so really you're very isolated and that's not ..."

"Ned, I'm alright, so off you go, and then I can do a bit of knitting while the light's still good. Thank you for calling and I'll see you tomorrow."

"Oh, alright, if you're really sure you have everything you need, but don't ..."

"Ned, go," commanded Molly, attempting to smother a smile, "you're starting to fuss like your father, Michael. God rest his soul."

By lunchtime the problem with the phone lines was solved and Trengillion's inhabitants were able to communicate once more, as Ned and Stella found out when they had a phone call from Rose in the early afternoon to say she and George were stranded in Helston because the road to Trengillion was completely blocked by snow.

"Oh no, poor you," Stella sympathised, "but I'm not surprised: it's quite horrendous here. Having said that, it's not as hostile today as it was yesterday when the snow fell heavily all day long and the wind howled non-stop. In fact I didn't leave the house at all but then I've not been out today either, nor do I wish to."

"I know what you mean, because we witnessed some of yesterday's weather. It's silly really, because conditions weren't too bad 'til we got to West Cornwall, although the roads were bad enough and it was freezing hard all the way back. We never dreamt we'd get stuck for the last bit of the journey though; it's a real turn up for the book."

"Which hotel are you in?" Stella asked.

"The Angel. You should see the town, Stell, stranded cars everywhere. It seems really weird, not at all like Helston. Everyone's going around on foot too, it's the only way. Were it not for the stranded cars it would look a bit like the olden days."

"Hmm, Anne popped in this morning and said Greg was home when she went to see Liz yesterday. He told her how bad it was in Helston, so much so they had to leave work early and of course we've had more snow since then."

"I take it Greg's not working today either if the road's blocked."

"Absolutely not and Ned's closed the school too so the children have a spontaneous holiday and they love it. I think there's a snowman in every garden. Mind you, they weren't all built by kids; even Ned went out to give the grandchildren a hand this morning after he'd seen his mum."

Rose laughed. "I'm not surprised. Poor George, his big gripe at the moment is he wants to build a snowman but he can't do that until we get back home, that's if we ever do."

"I take it you'll have to stay in Helston for another night then."

"Yes, and possibly even longer if we have more snow. Still, never mind, we've got this far and being stranded in Helston's not half as bad as being stuck further up the line. I'll ring you tomorrow to let you know how things stand."

Inside the spare bedroom of the Old Vicarage, following instructions from Anne, John placed a small piece of cheese on each of two mousetraps and pushed them away underneath the bed so that the twins would not see them. He then crossed to the fireplace, bent himself double and crawled beneath the granite lintel to look inside the chimney in order to locate the loose stone Elizabeth had found dislodged as told to him by Anne. He found it with ease and decided when he was next doing a building job at home he must cement the stone firmly in place to make it secure.

Once out of the fireplace John glanced around the room. It was the smallest of the four bedrooms and apart from the walls and ceiling having been given a coat of white paint it was still much the same as when he and Anne had moved into the Old Vicarage in 1978. John thought it a shame; the room had a deep alcove to one side of the fireplace, ideal space for a built-in wardrobe, but because the room wasn't needed it was unlikely they'd get round to modernising it in the near future.

John liked the room very much but Anne didn't, although he felt sure the real reason for her apathy was more to do with the bed, which she claimed was grotesque and unwelcoming, than the room itself. John sighed. Like the Ridges who had previously lived in the house, he and Anne had agreed the old iron framed bed belonged and was part of its history.

John crossed to the curtainless window and looked outside. The room had a very pleasant view over the orchard and the valley beyond, even more so since its thick coating of snow. With ideas whirling through his mind, he sat down on the window sill and glanced at the bare floorboards, heavily varnished in places and worn in others. He decided that if the floor had a carpet and they hung curtains at the window then perhaps Anne might like the room a little more and the twins could even use it as a playroom. Happy with his plans, he returned downstairs to tell the family of his decision and suggested a carpet and curtain shopping trip at the weekend if the snow had melted.

After Molly had eaten her sausages and mash for lunch and washed the dishes, she made herself a cup of tea and took it to the living room where she sat in an armchair by the window, with feet resting on a cushioned stool.

She watched as a robin flitted between the branches of a cotoneaster bush, sending little cascades of snow to the ground with each movement. Molly smiled, she enjoyed watching the birds and the robin was a particular favourite of hers. Suddenly, she sat bolt upright, remembering Ned's comments regarding the temperature outside; it was freezing hard. Molly drained her mug and stood up. If it was freezing outdoors then the birds would have no water to drink and birds must have water.

From the kitchen cupboard she took out a shallow bowl and filled it with warm water from the kettle, she then went into the pantry and pulled her cake tin from the shelf. Inside the tin were the remains of a fruit cake she had made the previous week. Molly looked at the cake; it would no doubt go to waste for she had eaten very little cake since the major's passing, yet still she kept making it out of habit.

"The birds shall have it," said Molly, decisively, "their need is far greater than mine." She crumbled the cake inside the tin, picked up the dish of water and carried both into the front hallway.

The front door was stiff to open as it was seldom used, but Molly eventually managed with a surge of elbow grease and the threat of replacement with a nice new double glazed door.

A blast of bitterly cold air caused Molly to shiver as she stood on the doorstep and looked to where the front path lay hidden. Ned had not cleared the snow around the front of her house as the path was used only by the postman and there would be no mail delivery if the main road was closed.

Molly frowned, the snow looked deep and had drifted in places. She contemplated changing from her slippers into her boots, but they were in the kitchen and she considered that by the time she had fetched them and put them on she could already have put out her goodies for the birds. Without giving her boots another thought she stepped onto the path; the snow was crisp and crunched noisily. Clutching the cake tin and the dish, she trod carefully so as not to spill the precious water.

Once over the path she stepped onto the lawn; both feet sinking ankle deep with each step she took. In the middle of the lawn she stopped, placed the dish on the snow and scattered the cake crumbs from the tin around it. With a shiver, she turned, eager to get back indoors where she could watch the birds enjoy their feast, but before she reached the front step her attention was taken by a noise in the distance, a rumbling sound like the whirring of an approaching helicopter. She looked up to the sky and through the glinting sun's rays, spotted two dark flecks with blades spinning flying low towards her. After they'd passed overhead she turned and watched as they flew over the village, slowly, as though looking for something. Intrigued Molly walked back across the lawn towards the road, her feet sinking deeper into the snow, covering her slippers and wetting her tights. With eyes fixated she watched the diminishing specks as they hovered in the clear blue sky. Keen to achieve a clearer view and ascertain in which direction they might go next, she hurriedly clambered beneath the cherry tree and onto the rockery. But in her haste, near to the top, her right foot tripped against a hidden stone and the empty cake tin flew through the air. Stumbling, she attempted to grab the branch of the cherry tree, but she missed and toppled headlong onto the garden twisting her ankle as she fell and knocking herself unconscious against the trunk of the tree.

CHAPTER TWELVE

Elizabeth Castor-Hunt felt uneasy as she knelt in front of the hearth making up the fire in the living room of Cove Cottage. Absently-mindedly she poked the low-burning coals forcing ash to fall through the grid, her thoughts elsewhere, recalling the voice of a child singing *I had a Little Nut Tree* in the chimney of the Old Vicarage the previous evening.

Sitting back on her legs, she lay down the poker and watched fresh flames flicker from burnt out coal revitalised by the disturbance. With a sigh her thoughts drifted to the mysterious shoe inside the ginger jar which she had in her position in order to show to her grandmother. She looked at her watch. There was no time like the present; she must go now. Leaning forward she quickly shovelled fresh lumps of coal into the flames, jumped up and safely placed the fireguard on the hearth slate.

In the kitchen she washed her hands and then went to find Greg. He was in the dining room sitting at the table, attempting to do a one thousand piece jigsaw puzzle with Tally and Wills. "Will you three be alright if I pop round to see Grandma? I won't be long."

Greg looked up. "Of course. We're fine here, aren't we kids? You see, Liz, we've decided we must have the edge pieces done before any of us can have anything else to drink or eat today."

At the table, Tally and Wills were rummaging through the large box looking for edge pieces which they then placed in a heap for Greg to piece together.

Elizabeth smiled. "Hmm, I think it might be quite a while then before you're ready for lunch and so I don't need to rush back."

"No, it'll all come together soon, you see. In fact I predict we'll have the edge pieces all joined up long before you get home."

"Really! We'll see," smiled Elizabeth, amused by his optimism.

She left the room and took her thick winter coat from its peg in the hallway. She then pulled on her Wellington boots, hat and mittens and picked up the carrier bag containing the ginger jar.

Outside she walked carefully along the garden path attempting not to slip on compact snow which had escaped Greg's shovel earlier that morning. Once on the pavement she trod on fresh snow which gave her a better grip. Leaving the beach behind, she walked to the top of the incline, past the inn and along the main road. Several people were out, cheeks glowing, clad in vast layers of warm clothing; walking dogs; taking pictures of the spectacular scenery; chatting excitedly and visiting the post office for supplies. She nodded and waved to those she knew.

By the gate of Rose Cottage, Elizabeth paused to remove her thick sheepskin mittens in order to lift the latch on the gate; she then proceeded up the path which Ned had cleared earlier. When the house came into view she was puzzled as to why the seldom used front door was wide open. She walked towards it calling her grandmother's name. By the doorstep deep footprints stretched out across the lawn. Her eyes followed them towards the cherry tree. She squealed when she saw her grandmother lying in the snow.

In panic, Elizabeth dropped the carrier bag containing the ginger jar and hurried across the lawn. At first she feared the worse but as she looked into her grandmother's eyes, they flickered. Elizabeth breathed a sigh of relief but she knew she must act fast for Molly's face was blue and she was beginning to shiver.

Elizabeth knelt down in the snow and assured Molly everything would be alright; she then ran into the house and up the stairs where she grabbed blankets from the airing cupboard. Back outside she quickly wrapped them around the old lady's body, carefully tucking them as far beneath as she was able to reach. Once done, she ran next door to Ivy Cottage, hoping for the help of Rose and George, unaware they were snowed up in Helston and not home. Upon receiving no response to her fierce knockings, she ran back into the cottage and in desperation rang her parents.

Ned, Stella and Elizabeth carefully carried Molly into the house and laid her down on the floor beside the fire. They knew it was unwise to move someone following an injury but all agreed under the circumstances to leave her out for a minute longer than necessary was even more foolhardy.

While Elizabeth and Stella attempted to warm Molly with hot water bottles and massage, Ned reached for the phone to ring the doctor but realised instantly even if he got through to the surgery, the doctor would not be able to call and neither would an ambulance, for the road was blocked.

"Lily," said Elizabeth, suddenly, rising to her feet, "she's home for a while and she's a nurse. Take over from me, Dad, and I'll ring her."

To the relief of everyone, Molly's condition did not appear to be life threatening. She recalled falling, recalled coming round and clearly remembered hearing Elizabeth's welcome voice and lifesaving actions. She did, however, have a small lump on the back of her head, and a badly sprained ankle which Lily appropriately dressed, and only when she had been changed into dry warm clothing and was sitting on the settee drinking tea with her foot resting on a stool did Ned barrage her with questions and reprobation.

"I know you told me not to go out, Ned, but the birds need feeding when the weather's bad and they need water too, and anyway I wouldn't have fallen at all if it hadn't been for those stupid helicopters."

"Is that when you fell then?" Stella asked. "When the helicopters flew over?"

"Yes," tut-tutted Molly, waving her arm towards the window. "They were flying very low, you see, and I got the impression they were looking for something. Naturally I was intrigued to know what it was likely to be. Serves me right I suppose, for being nosey, I mean."

Ned looked relieved. "In that case you'd not been outside for very long at all because Stella and I went out to watch them too and it was only about ten minutes after we'd gone back indoors that we got the call from Liz."

"And thank goodness Liz happened to be calling at that moment," said Lily. "Had you lay there much longer, Mrs Smith, things would have turned out much differently."

Elizabeth suddenly remembered the ginger jar which she had dropped onto the snow when first she had spotted her grandmother. She stood up. "Excuse me, I'll be back in a minute. I have something intriguing to show you." With haste she dashed into the kitchen and out through the back door.

Ned watched her go and then turned back to Molly. "Are you warm now, Mum? I must say, you're a better colour than you were a while back."

"I'm fine, thanks, Ned, and I'm really glad you weren't able to get the doctor or an ambulance. It's so much nicer to be treated at home than having to go all the way to hospital. What's more I'd have felt a right charlatan since there's nothing much wrong with me."

Lily looked concerned. "That might well be the case, but I really don't think you should be here on your own tonight, not after what you've been through. You need to rest and to be waited on."

Molly sneezed three times in succession. "Nonsense dear," she sniffed, fishing a handkerchief from her pocket, "I'll be fine here and I'm as warm as toast now. Look, I've logs and coal to make up the fire with and I can easily hobble into the kitchen to get something to eat."

"There, I knew it, you've gone and caught the flu," said Ned, shaking his head in annoyance, as he watched his mother tuck her handkerchief back inside her pocket, "and I agree with Lily, you really aren't safe to be left alone and you certainly aren't capable of climbing the stairs to go to bed. Either you come to us or I'll have to stay here with you."

"If you must know, my cold is not a result of the fall as I already had a slight sore throat when I woke up this morning, but I didn't say so because I knew you'd fuss. And of course I know I'll not be able to climb the stairs for a day or two. But that's not a problem because I've already decided to sleep on the settee. It'll be really cosy in here and I can have the telly on for company. Please don't worry Ned, I really will be alright."

"But Mum, be practical, your bathroom's upstairs so what will you do when you want the loo?"

"Go outside, there's a perfectly pleasant lav out there which I always use during daytime anyway. It's not a problem, especially since the major had the big porch built so we don't have to go right outside to get to it."

"What do you think, Lily?" Ned asked, as though his mother was not present. "Do you think she'd be alright?"

Lily sighed. "Yes, I suppose so. It's often best not to force people to do something against their will and it's certainly an excellent idea to sleep downstairs, especially with the weather being so cold. But I really think someone should come in to prepare your food otherwise you'll have to put weight on your ankle and even five minutes spent making a sandwich is five minutes too much."

Ned nodded. "I agree, so we'll take it in turns to make sure she's fed."

"Good and I'll call in the morning to have a look at the ankle and the lump on the head."

Molly chuckled. "Thank you for letting me stay, Lily dear, you obviously have a charming and understanding bedside manner."

All turned towards the kitchen door as Elizabeth returned with the carrier bag.

Molly intrigued, gleefully rubbed her hands together. "Now what do you have there, young lady? Something tells me it's quite exciting."

Elizabeth wrinkled her nose. "Well, it's not really. Having said that it might be. Open it, Gran, and tell me what you think."

She handed the bag to Molly who pulled out the ginger jar.

"Oh, it's very pretty, Liz."

Stella nodded. "I'd say it's very early Victorian. Great Granny Hargreaves had one very similar to that and I believe it was a wedding present."

"Hmm," said Ned, "very nice but hardly intriguing."

Elizabeth giggled. "No, not on the outside. Look inside, Gran."

Molly removed the lid and pulled out the shoe.

Elizabeth sat down on the arm of the settee. "It was hidden behind a stone in the chimney of Anne and John's spare bedroom at the Vicarage. I found it quite by accident last night while baby-sitting."

Ned frowned. "How on earth can you find something hidden up a chimney by accident? Unless of course you were playing hide 'n seek with the twins."

Elizabeth bit her bottom lip. She didn't want to mention the child's voice singing and cause a possible disagreement and so she brushed over the subject lightly. "I went to the spare room to collect blankets so that I could sleep on the settee and while in there I could hear the wind whistling over the chimney top…"

"...I didn't think it was particularly windy last night," interrupted Ned. "Daytime, yes, but I'm sure by evening the wind had gone."

"Shush, Ned. It doesn't matter, let Liz finish," said Stella, crossly.

Elizabeth continued. "Anyway, I stooped down and shuffled myself into the chimney to hear better and then when I stepped back out my foot slipped on soot that I'd probably disturbed. To stop myself toppling over I reached out and dislodged a stone. Behind it was the ginger jar."

Molly shook her head. "How fascinating. I've heard of folks concealing shoes and suchlike in chimneys and so forth but I've never actually seen any evidence." She stroked the shoe gently. "It obviously belonged to a little girl, most likely from the Victorian era as they wore button boots such as this." She looked up to see four pairs of eyebrows all raised in a questioning manner. She smiled. "It's all to do with superstition, you see, and dates back many, many years. Surely you've heard of apotropaic, Ned? You too, Stella?"

Ned shook his head. "I've certainly heard of it but for the life of me I can't recall was it is."

Stella smiled. "It's a late 19th century word from the Greek apotropaios and means averting evil."

"Good girl, ten out of ten."

Ned poked his wife in the ribs. "Humph, trust old clever clogs to know the answer."

Elizabeth was nonplussed. "I don't understand. What does a shoe have to do with averting evil?"

Ned groaned. "Oh no, I remember now; more fantasy."

Molly ignored Ned's remark and laid the shoe on her lap. "You see, Liz, backalong folks believed that evil spirits were attracted by the human scent of a shoe, hence they hid them in places where they believed a spirit might gain access, and then once the spirit had slipped inside the shoe it would be trapped and unable to turnaround and escape. They hid them in all sorts of places, in attics, under floorboards, above lintels and as you've discovered, in chimneys."

Elizabeth was intrigued. "Tell me more."

"Well okay. In most cases, as in this case, there is nearly always only one shoe which will have had a lot of wear and more often than not it will have belonged to a child. No-one knows when or why the custom began but I believe in this country the practice dates back as far as the 1500s. The shoe would usually be put into its hiding place when a house was built or later when renovation work was being done."

Lily frowned. "But why a shoe?"

"I believe it's because a shoe is the only item of clothing which takes on the shape of the person who has worn it."

Stella picked up the little boot and turned it over in her hand. "I can understand simple folk wanting to ward off evil spirits and suchlike but it seems a little odd to me that a man of the cloth would go down that road. I mean, surely his belief in God would be sufficient. After all, the Vicarage has always been a vicarage so no other people would ever have lived there."

Ned nodded. "I was just thinking exactly the very same thing, Stell. It doesn't seem feasible, Mum."

"You're both right to a point," said Molly, "but actually a few shoes have been found in religious buildings as well as cottages and houses; in fact I believe one was even discovered in a cathedral."

When Lily left Rose Cottage, Elizabeth left too.

"Are you going to come back with me and see your big brother?" she asked. "He's longing to see you and is a bit grumpy because you rang Anne the other night but didn't even ring him to say you were home."

"Actually I did try to ring him but the line was engaged, so I rang Anne instead and then because it was quite late I thought I'd leave calling him 'til the following morning, but of course yesterday the phone was dead and the weather was far too beastly to risk venturing out. I was going to pop down to see you all today though, honest. But as I'm in the village, then there's no time like the present."

"Brilliant. He was doing a jigsaw puzzle with the children when I left. It has a thousand pieces would you believe? And so no doubt he'll be glad of a reason to abandon it."

Lily laughed. "To be fair, Greg was quite good at jigsaws when we were kids. Unlike me, I never had the patience."

"You won't be offering to help then."

"No fear."

"Actually, you won't get a chance to anyway because when Tally and Wills see you they'll most likely want you to build a snowman. They built one first thing this morning, you see, of which they're very proud but now they challenge everyone who calls to see if they can do better. We've quite a collection in the garden already. I built mine while they were doing theirs and it's the smallest. I don't think the children were very impressed, but it was far too cold for me to be outside for long."

Lily smiled. "I've not built a snowman for years, so I shall enjoy the challenge."

As they approached the Pickled Egg, Jane emerged from the back of the building, both arms outstretched in order to keep her balance.

Lily," she exclaimed, waving her gloved hand, "how lovely to see you again. Are you here for long?"

"A week or so," she replied, "I've a fortnight off work and as I drove down it's up to me when I go back."

"Come to Cove Cottage with us," said Elizabeth, beginning to shiver, "then we can all have a chat like old times. It's too cold to stand out here talking."

"I'd love to, but I'm on my way to see Mum as she wants me to help her do her hair. I always cut it for her, you see, because she showed me how when I was a kid. I must admit I'm a bit nervous though because she wants it layered and in a different style, and then we're going to dye it."

Elizabeth pulled a face. "Rather you than me. If I were in your shoes I'd be terrified it'd go wrong."

"I am," sighed Jane, cautiously treading across the steep incline, "still, I suppose if I botch it, it will eventually grow out, but it won't be a very good advert for Mum's business."

At Fuchsia Cottage, Jane found her mother, Betty, had everything ready and in place inside her salon situated at the back of the house.

Betty greeted her daughter warmly and offered to take her coat. "I've decided to have my hair a nice rich hazelnut brown; after all I've been blonde ever since I was a girl." She laughed. "Even though for the last fifteen years it's been with the aid of colorants. What do you think, Jane?"

"Blimey, that might be a bit drastic, a new style and a new colour. Still, good for you, let's hope it turns out alright."

Betty tied a cape around her neck and then took a seat in front of the mirror. "I'm sure it will, but I won't hold it against you if it doesn't.

Jane took in a deep breath, picked up a comb and clipped up the back of her mother's hair. "Right, here goes," she sighed, taking the scissors from the stand. "Wish me luck."

To Jane's relief the result was near perfection and Betty was delighted.

"Well done, love, I couldn't have done it better myself. If the colour turns out half as good as the style then I'll be very happy indeed.

Once the dying process was complete, Jane set her mother's hair in jumbo rollers and then while Betty was under the dryer she made them both tea.

Gertie called in shortly after as Jane was removing the rollers; when she saw her lifelong friend sitting in one of her own chairs, she was temporarily speechless and sat mesmerised while Jane carefully combed out her mother's hair into its new style.

"This is crazy, Bet," giggled Gertie, shaking her head with disbelief, "but if I'd seen you in town I'd probably have walked straight by you. You look completely different. I wonder what Pete will say."

They soon found out, for Peter, who along with Percy, had been clearing snow from the pathways of Trengillion's elderly residents, returned as Jane sprayed lacquer onto her mother's rich brown curls.

"Bloody hell," he gasped, hands raised to cheeks. "Christ, Bet, what have you gone and done?"

Betty's face dropped. "Oh, please don't say you don't like it, Pete. I love it and I think our Jane's done a wonderful job."

"Well, I'm not saying, I don't like it or that it isn't well done, it's just that you look so, so different." He sat down. "Give me an hour or two and then I'll tell what I think when I've had a chance to get used to it,"

"You donkey," laughed Gertie, patting Betty's brown waves. "Believe me, it looks fabulous, Pete. And I tell you what, Bet, it's made you look fifteen years younger too."

CHAPTER THIRTEEN

That evening, the local television news headlines, reported an air search had taken place during the day for a missing police car containing two officers lost in and around Trengillion in Cornwall. It did not say where the police car was going to or coming from, but apparently radio contact was last made with the car when it was in the region of the old Ebenezer chapel by the crossroads. A helicopter search had been inconclusive and as the main road was blocked by large snow drifts, a land search was not possible until the road was cleared. The report concluded there was deep concern for the safety of two police officers and said the search would resume at first light the following day.

Trengillion's inhabitants were dumbfounded. Many had witnessed the helicopters flying low over the village and although all had been curious as to why, once the aircraft had gone from their vision they thought nothing more of it until they switched on their television sets. The news report, however, left them with more questions than answers, hence many people decided to brave the harsh weather and pop along to the Fox and Hounds for a pint where they hoped someone might have knowledge as to what was going on. But to the great disappointment of all who had gathered, their journeys were fruitless, for no-one had a clue as to the whys and wherefores thereof, so all could only surmise.

"This is really frustrating," said Pat Dickens, banging his half empty glass of beer on the round oak table. "Were this to have happened a few years back then we would have had Fred to interrogate, but now we're kept in the dark and know nowt. It's not really good enough, you know, especially if there are some dishonest or possibly even dangerous folk in our midst. I mean, the coppers must have a good reason to be out here, mustn't they? Cos let's face it, we don't see them very often."

"Maybe Fred's daughter knows something," said Harry Richardson, lighting his pipe and discarding the dead match in the ashtray. "You know, young Sally; she's with Devon and Cornwall Police, isn't she?"

"Yes, she might know something," Pat agreed, a hint of sarcasm in his voice, "but she's in Plymouth now and that isn't the same as being here in this pub, more's the shame."

"Who are Sally and Fred?" Larry Bingham asked, "I don't think I've come across them yet."

"Yes, you have," laughed Frank Newton, "you'll have met Fred anyway. He and his wife Annie live at the Old Lodge House just inside the gates of the Penwynton Hotel. He used to be the village bobby here 'til he retired and a damn fine job he did as well. Sally's his daughter and she's a copper too."

"Oh, I see, yes of course I know who you mean. I didn't know Fred used to be in the Force though. I've always assumed he was associated with the Hotel in some way or another, and whenever we've spoken it's always been about fishing, him being a keen angler and all that."

"He doesn't do much now though, does he?" Pat chuckled. "Getting a bit past it now like the rest of us. Who's for another pint?"

Harry nodded and pushed his empty glass forwards. "He is connected to the Hotel in a way though, Larry, because his son, Jamie, is married to Linda and her family own and run the Hotel. You know Jamie and Linda, don't you? They live near you."

"Of course, yes, I see," said Larry draining his glass and proffering it to Pat for a refill. "Nice couple; he works for the Midland Bank and they have three young girls."

Frank rose and reached for his coat. "I mustn't stay for another as much as I'd like to. Dorothy will be worried if I'm out too long, she knows I'm not too good on my legs now and it's damn slippery out there, that's why I wouldn't let her come and risk bringing the car. I want to call in on Molly on my way home as well and make sure she's alright. You've no doubt heard about her fall?"

Pat tut-tutted. "Yes, your Dorothy rang to tell us. Rum do that, you can't go falling around at our age, especially in the snow. Give her our kind regards and tell her May's going to call in and see her tomorrow."

"I will," said Frank, buttoning up his coat. He then pulled a woolly hat over his head, wrapped a scarf round his neck and part way round his face and pushed his hands into his sheepskin gloves.

"I feel like I'm off to the Arctic rather than home," he grumbled, "I do hate being muffled up like this, but with damn colds doing the rounds and perishing flu as well, I suppose it pays to be cautious."

"There's chicken pox about too," grinned Pat, picking up the empty glasses. "May's sister's grandchildren at the Lizard have both come down with it. Not that I think it's a threat to old timers like us, although I know you can have it more than once."

Frank found Ned with Molly when he arrived at Rose Cottage, both watching the Nine o'clock News to see if there was any mention of the missing policemen; to their disappointment there was not.

"I suppose with all this snow causing havoc they've more than enough stories to fill up the programme with anyway," said Molly, a little down hearted. "But if they don't turn up soon I'm sure it'll get a mention. Local news usually finds its way to national level before long if it's of any importance."

"Have the pub regulars come up with any possible theories?" Ned asked, as Frank removed his coat and took a seat on the settee beside Molly. "I expect it was a hot topic tonight."

Frank laughed. "It was and no, no-one has a clue as to what it's all about. Poor old Pat Dickens is quite frustrated by it, but I expect we'll know what's what soon enough. Anyway, how are you doing, Molly? You look a lot perkier than I'd expected you to be."

"And so I am; it'd take more than a silly ankle sprain to knock me for six and the bump on my head's gone down already. How's Dorothy? Do get her to pop in as soon as this bloomin' snow goes."

"I will," nodded Frank, patting Molly's hand. "Dot's fine. I'm pleased to say and Pat Dickens said to tell you May will be round tomorrow for a natter."

"Smashing, I do enjoy her company and there's a lot to talk about at present."

"Would you like a coffee, Frank?" Ned asked, rising. "I'm going to have one."

"Oh, yes, please, milk and one sugar."

"Mum?"

"No thanks, love, I've had more than enough today. If I have any more I'll never get to sleep."

Ned went into the kitchen but left the door open so that he could hear if Frank had any interesting news to convey.

"Have you met the new people who've moved into the Old Police House?" Molly asked, adjusting the brightly coloured knitted blanket covering her legs. "I've heard he's alright but Gertie says she's a bit snooty."

"Yes, I've met him; Ian he's called, and he's been to the inn a couple of times. I've not met her though or seen any of the children either. I believe they've got quite a brood."

"Four," called Ned from the kitchen, "and they're all polite and well behaved. Janet Ainsworth seems alright too, not that I've seen much of her as the snow arrived pretty close on their heels."

Frank chuckled. "I've heard she's got a white poodle and it's called Fifi. Damn silly name for a dog, but then a damn silly dog if it's all clipped and suchlike."

"The dog's not called Fifi," laughed Ned, pouring water into two mugs, "it's called Glenda. I've seen her out with Janet and she seems a nice little thing."

Pat scratched his cheek. "Is that right? Well it was Giles Wilson who told me it was called Fifi, but I guess he was pulling my leg. I never know whether he's being serious or not. Brendon now, he's much more sensible as long as he hasn't drunk too much, which I believe he's inclined to do."

"It wasn't like that in your day, was it, Frank?" Molly tutted. "Excessive drinking, I mean. Folks knew when to stop when you were landlord."

"Well, there were one or two who had more than was good for them, and yes, on the whole things were a lot different then. But that can be said for most things and money was a lot harder to come by during and after the War. We had to make do and mend back then, didn't we?"

Molly nodded. "We certainly did. I used to make all my own clothes, but youngsters today wouldn't know where to begin; they can't even stitch a button on or repair a hem. Not that it's their fault; it's just the way things are."

Ned walked into the living room with two mugs of steaming coffee. "And pubs were pubs back then too, now lots of them seem to be losing their identity and think they're restaurants."

"I don't really blame pubs for doing food," said Frank, taking his coffee. "Thanks, Ned. Some of the poor souls have shocking rents to pay. The Godsons are alright though because they own the place, of course."

"And they're doing a good job too," said Molly, emphatically. "The major was very fond of them, but he never really got to like Raymond Withers, although she was alright; Gloria I mean."

They chatted for an hour and then Frank rose to leave. "I must go as much as I'd like to stay, but I don't want Dot to worry and she will if I'm not home soon."

"I'll run you back," said Ned, rising and reaching for his coat from the back of the door. "It's quite a way for you to walk and I've got the car outside because I brought Mum some coal as she was getting low."

"Thanks, Ned, I would appreciate that. The snow's freezing hard and I must admit I do dread falling."

Molly waved her hand. "Right, off you go, then I'll get myself into my nightie and snuggle down on the settee. There's a film starting in ten minutes and I should like to watch it, if I can keep awake long enough to see the end."

CHAPTER FOURTEEN

During the night a little more snow fell and so Ned decided to keep the school closed for the third consecutive day and at eight o'clock he walked around to the school and pinned a notice on the door informing parents this was to be the case. Although many already knew for the phone at the Old School House had rung constantly since the break of day.

When the notice was securely in place, Ned crossed the playground, where only the footprints of hungry birds disturbed the fresh layer of snow. By the back wall he stood and looked across the fields to the valley beyond. The view was spectacular. The trees in Bluebell Woods stood erect and graceful, their long dark branches generously sprinkled with layers of snow which glistened like jewels in the early morning sunshine, and beyond the valley, the white fields and hedgerows stretched up towards the grey and creamy yellow sky. Ned thought it a beautiful sight and worthy of capture on film or better still, as a painting, for snow in Cornwall seldom stayed long. Therefore, when he returned home he sought out his camera from the writing desk in the front room and returned to the school to finish off the film he had started on Christmas Day.

"If my pictures are as good as I hope, Stella; will you copy the best one in water colours? I should love to have a painting over the fireplace of the snow lying in the valley."

"Of course, I'd love to and it'd be a challenge as well, because I don't recall ever having painted a snow scene before. How many snaps did you take?"

"Six or it may have been seven, I'm not quite sure. Are there any eggs? I fancy an omelette."

"Yes, fortunately I bought a dozen before the bad weather. If you're having an omelette then I think I'll have one too. I feel in need of something hot, and toast just doesn't quite fit the bill."

After breakfast Ned cleared the fresh snow from the garden path and then walked down the road to Rose Cottage where he found Anne already there.

"Dad," said Anne, rising to her feet from the hearth rug, "just the person. Do you know anyone with a dog we could borrow for a few hours? It doesn't matter what breed it is, as long as it's fit, healthy and well behaved."

"A dog." Ned frowned as he removed his hat, coat and gloves and warming his hands by the fire. "Why on earth would your grandmother want a dog when she's practically housebound?"

Anne laughed and bouncing down on the settee. "She doesn't, I do, but only for a while; I want one to take for a walk, you see."

"Anne, have you taken leave of your senses? I don't know what on earth you're gibbering about."

Anne and Molly both laughed.

"Anne wants a dog so that she can take it for a walk up by the old Ebenezer Chapel," said Molly. "That way she'll be able to have a poke round for any trace of the missing police car without looking nosey. It was my idea."

"Humph, that doesn't come as a surprise." But then Ned's face broke into a broad grin. "Actually it's a damn good idea, but the only dog I can think of is Copper, the Bingham's cocker spaniel and I expect he gets plenty of exercise with the two energetic boys to play with."

"Yes, that's the only one we could think of," said Anne, "although there must be lots of dogs living at Penwynton Crescent with families we're not familiar with, and I've heard the new Ainsworth people have a dog too. But I can hardly ask them when we've not even spoken yet, and I've heard it's a clipped poodle anyway so I wouldn't be seen dead with one of them, especially one called Fifi. It's really very frustrating."

"Actually, Janet's dog is called Glenda," frowned Ned. "Who told you it was called Fifi?"

"Can't remember, probably someone in the pub or maybe it was John. Come on, Dad, put your thinking cap on, there must be someone you know with a dog."

"Ah, how about George and Rose's dozy mutt, Pumpkin; he's staying with May and Pat Dickens while they're away, but I don't expect they'll want to take him out far with this dicey weather."

"Really, that's brilliant, I'd assumed they'd taken him with them," Anne said, clapping her hands with glee. "I'll call round there when I leave here. He seems a nice dog too and he looks quite friendly."

"They were going to take him with them," said Ned, "but May bumped into Rose in the post office and offered to look after him. Rose thought it a good idea as Pumpkin doesn't travel too well and it's a hell of a long drive to Blackpool from here. Having him for company should help poor May too as she's never really got over the death of poor old Rover. It's a pity the weather's not fit for her to take him out though as she was always fond of walking."

Molly sighed. "Yes, she was, especially with Bertha Fillingham. Poor Bertha. Still, fond memories, eh?"

"Where are Jess and Ollie?" Ned asked. "They can't be here, it's too quiet and I know they're not at school."

"Coronation Terrace with Granny Gert; she rang this morning and said to drop them in and then they can help her make some cakes, so I'm enjoying the peace."

"And seeking adventure," Molly added, with a grin.

As anticipated, May was delighted with Anne's offer to take Pumpkin for a long walk, for since the snow fall he had gone no further than their back garden or down to the Fox and Hounds, the latter of which was on May's insistence as she was conscious he needed to stretch his legs; he'd also be company for Pat.

Fortunately Pumpkin knew Anne, for he had seen her many times whilst in the front garden of Ivy Cottage when she visited her grandmother next door. Nevertheless, Anne soon realised as she clipped on his lead and walked with him down the Dickens' garden path, that she had never actually taken a dog for a walk in her life. Pumpkin, however, knew all about walkies; he had three routes, down the lane between the school and the School House to the bottom of the hill; through Bluebell Woods and back by the main road; down the same lane but then carrying on up the hill and along the bridle path over Long Acre farmland and back to the village by way of the coastal path, or down to the cove and up the lane leading to Higher Green Farm. He was a little miffed therefore, when his new handler chose none of the tried and tested routes, but instead dragged him off into unknown territory and through endless cold white stuff to boot.

Initially Anne enjoyed the walk; the air smelled fresh and clean, the scenery was spectacularly picturesque and there was virtually no traffic on the roads. In fact the only vehicles she encountered, were David Pascoe on his tractor pulling a trailer loaded with bales of hay, and an unidentified, four wheel drive vehicle, heading towards the cove. The morning's early enjoyment, however, began to subside long before Anne was anywhere near the Ebenezer Chapel. Firstly, her toes slowly progressed from cold to numb, in spite of two thick pairs of socks enveloping her feet deeply tucked inside her Wellington boots. Her fingers then, likewise, felt nipped, and finally her cheeks tingled and glowed above the knitted scarf covering her mouth. Nevertheless, she persevered with the walk determined to have a snoop around the old chapel just in case there was something unusual there that others might have missed.

After the initial shock of going in what to Pumpkin was the wrong direction, he soon decided he liked the new route, for there were new things to see, new smells to investigate and new hedgerows to snuffle through, although he was a little annoyed that Anne did not let him off the lead as did his mistress, Rose. But Pumpkin did not mind; the restraint of a lead was infinitely better than being let loose in the Dickens' small back garden and even though he was quite partial to a doze by the fire in the Fox and Hounds, it was no substitute for a good long walk.

When Anne reached the crossroads, she paused and looked towards the three directions of roads other than the one she had just walked along for any indication as to the whereabouts of the missing police car. Not, if she was to be perfectly honest, that she expected to see anything unusual; for it was obvious that if nothing had been evident to a brace of helicopters hovering low, then the car clearly had to be concealed somewhere undetectable from the air and not in an open space such as at the crossroads. Realising her search would be fruitless she continued the few yards to the old chapel which stood on the left hand side of the road past the turning into the lane leading to Polquillick.

There was no sign of life in the curtilage of the chapel's boundaries, but by the gates, on top of a dry stone wall, the name on a local estate agent For Sale board was completely hidden by splattered snowballs having successfully hit their target causing the board to tilt to a precarious level. Meanwhile, on the ground numerous sets of paw prints, alongside human footprints, indicated to Anne, that many, like herself, had been compelled to investigate the graveyard out of curiosity, for she doubted the prints were left by prospective purchasers. The old chapel had been for sale for well over a year and many locals were of the opinion the agents would never find a buyer crazy enough to live in such an isolated location, with only the dead for neighbours.

Anne walked along the path towards the door; there she stopped. Footprints leading to the steps suggested others had tried the handle and so she did likewise. To her surprise, the door opened, for she had assumed the chapel would be kept locked. She peeped around the door; it creaked as she stepped inside. The chapel's interior looked gloomy, desolate and bare; the seating had all been removed, the roof had fallen in on one corner and daylight was visible through large dusty cobwebs dangling from the gaping hole. Anne shuddered, she felt a sense of doom and despair. She closed the door behind her, released Pumpkin from his lead and walked further inside. Pumpkin barked at floating specks of dust glinting in the sunlight streaming through a large stained glass window. His bark echoed through the building, sounding eerie and foreboding. Anne shuddered, the place smelt musty, felt creepy and hostile, and she conceded the chapel was the last place on earth she could ever live, and it seemed difficult to imagine happy laughter, chatter and jovial hymn singing had ever penetrated the cold, bare walls.

The sudden noise and vibration of helicopter blades sent Anne rushing for the door; mesmerised by the activity, she stood on the step and watched as the two helicopters flew over the chapel and then disappeared above Trengillion. Relieved to be back outside, she put Pumpkin on his lead; the cold air smelt fresh and clean. Satisfied there was nothing odd or suspicious in the immediate vicinity of the chapel she closed the door quietly. As she stepped back onto the path she heard footsteps crunching through the snow. She turned her head and saw

Danny Jarrams emerge from around the side of the chapel. Anne felt her heart skip a beat and prayed her reaction did not show on her face.

"Anne," said Danny, rushing forward and taking her gloved hand, "did you hear those choppers? No doubt they're still looking for the missing cops. How are you? It's really good to see you after all this time."

"I'm, I'm fine, thank you. I didn't know you were back. At least I knew you were back from America, but I didn't know you were back from London. Linda said you went up there for a New Year's Eve party."

"Yeah, I did, but I got back here the day before the snow started, so that was a bit of luck."

They began to walk down the path towards the road. "I came up here looking for something the police might have missed," said Anne. "Silly really, I mean, they're sure to have a better idea of what they're looking for than me."

Danny laughed. "I did the same. I see you have a dog, he's pretty cute. What's his name?"

"Pumpkin," muttered Anne, "he's called Pumpkin, but he's not mine, he belongs to Mum and Dad's friends, Rose and George Clarke. They're in Blackpool at present; they've gone to see Rose's parents. They were going to go up for Christmas but didn't because poor Rose had the flu. Actually, that's not quite true, because Mum told me they're nearly home now and currently stranded in Helston because of the snow."

"Hmm, that's unfortunate." He patted Pumpkin's head. "So you're looking after him; that's cool."

"Well, no not exactly, he's being cared for by Pat and May Dickens, but I offered to take him for a walk because of um… of um the bad weather. They're quite elderly now, you understand."

Danny nodded. "I see, so how's life treating you, Anne? Linda tells me you have two kids and live at the Old Vicarage. I must say you're looking brilliant."

"Life's treating me well," said Anne, conscious of his eyes fixed on her face. "I'm very happy with my lot in life. John and I have a good marriage and I love Jess and Ollie more than words can tell. How about you? Are you back for good? Linda said you were."

"Absolutely, I'm not sure where I'll settle yet, whether it'll be in London or down here, but it'll definitely be one or the other because I've not the slightest desire to leave the UK again."

"Down here," squeaked Anne, suddenly standing to a halt. "But you once told me you could never live down here, you said you'd die of boredom or something like that. So what's changed your mind?" She turned her head away, hoping he had not noticed her flushed cheeks or detected the anger in her voice.

He sighed. "I was young and foolish back then and too stupid to see the bleedin' obvious."

"The obvious," Anne muttered, striding slowly forward. "I don't understand."

Danny stopped walking and grasped her arm. "Several weeks' back I was sorting through a load of old photographic stuff and I came across the proofs of Linda's wedding pictures. There was a lovely one of you, Anne, looking ever so pretty in your lemon bridesmaid dress. It brought back lots of happy memories. Remember, Anne, how we used to sit outside the Hotel on the lawns and chat for hours? Anyway, as I looked at your picture I suddenly knew I didn't want to be in the States anymore, I wanted to come home. I wanted to see you."

"But…"

"… I know it's too late, and don't worry I'm not intending to break up your happy family, but I can't help thinking what might have been."

"Don't," shouted Anne, releasing her arm from his grasp and turning to walk away. "Don't talk like that, because it is too late, much too late, and as you once said we must only ever be friends."

"I didn't say we *must* only ever be friends, I said we *can* only ever be friends, there's a big difference and I was wrong. If only we could turn back the clock."

"No," shouted Anne, the pace of her steps rapidly increasing. "No, I wouldn't want to turn back the clock. I don't want to turn the clock back, and given my life all over again I wouldn't want to change anything. I'm happy, Danny, very, very happy, you must understand that."

Danny walked faster to keep up with Anne's angry pace, and as they turned the corner they met Fred Stevens emerging from the driveway of the Penwynton Hotel.

"Hello Fred," Anne, gabbled, "are you walking into the village? I'll walk with you if you are because Danny's going in now, aren't you, Danny?"

Danny nodded sheepishly and turned in through the open gates. He did not look at Anne but proceeded down the driveway angry that he'd foolishly said more than he had intended.

CHAPTER FIFTEEN

The following day the main road was finally cleared and a full and thorough search for the two missing police officers and their car began. Numerous inhabitants of Trengillion observed the large police presence in all corners of the village and so many, desperately eager to establish the latest news, spent their day outdoors, taking pictures, clearing snow, walking dogs or any other activity which came to mind in order to look desultory and hide their inquisitiveness. But it was Brendon and Giles Wilson who finally were able to answer the question on everyone's lips: Why was the police car coming to, or going from, Trengillion in the first place?

Rose and George, having finally reached home with the clearing of the road, were at the Old School House telling Ned and Stella of their traumatic journey and the situation in Helston, when Gertie arrived with the latest news.

"You're never going to believe this," she panted, as Ned offered her a seat at the kitchen table, "but Percy's just been to the inn for some baccy and in there he found Giles and Brendon holding forth; they had a visit from the police today, you see, because apparently the missing coppers were on their way to see *them*."

Puzzled looks crossed the brows of Ned, Stella, Rose and George, all speechless and baffled.

"Crazy, isn't it?" Gertie continued. "But the reason is even more bizarre. You see, it's all to do with the big bank robbery, the one that's currently in the news. It's daft I know, but it appears someone told the police that they'd seen a bloke in Trengillion who looks just like the dopey bank robber who was stupid enough to get his face caught by the closed circuit television camera. Apparently he was seen talking to the Wilson brothers in a field on their farmland. You know the field, it's the one the coastal path crosses through."

"The Dandelion field," said Ned,

"Dandelion field?" Queried George.

"Hmm, Mum named it that because there's always a good crop of dandelions there. She used to make wine, you see, when she was younger, so has pet names for lots of places around here."

"So what on earth did the brothers say?" Asked Rose.

"Well, they seem to be amused by it and they've agreed the picture the police issued of the suspect does look very much like their cousin, Ivan from Falmouth, who was at the farm the other day dropping off a spare part for a tractor which he'd picked up for them. Giles showed the police a photo of Ivan taken last summer by Candy when they were haymaking and they agreed there was a likeness. Anyway, they've taken his name and address to check him out."

"I wonder who reported it to the police," said Ned, folding his arms, puzzled. "It seems a bit underhand to me. I mean, surely whoever it was doesn't think Giles and Brendon are in any way linked to a ghastly business like armed bank robbery."

Gertie shrugged her shoulders. "I dunno who it was but I wouldn't be surprised if it's not that dreadful Ainsworth woman. I saw her in the post office yesterday and I reckon she's a real busy-body. Her eyes are too close together and her face appears to be in a permanent frown, like she's looking for reasons to dislike people. She's always plastered in make-up too. She's as unnatural looking as her silly dog."

"Oh, come on, Gert," Ned reasoned, "that's a bit unfair. At present I seem to be the only one with a good word to say for poor old Janet."

"I've not met any of the family yet, but you can't blame a woman for trying to look her best, Gertie," said Rose, recalling the layers of make-up she had worn in her younger days. "It's all too easy not to bother, especially down here when there's nothing much to get dolled up for."

"Have the police gone from the farm now?" George asked, keen to change the subject from women's make-up to something less trivial.

Gertie nodded. "Yes, but apparently before they went they turned the place over, although the brothers said they weren't really sure why, unless the coppers were looking for the police car, which they probably were, because they poked around in the new barn and tossed aside their entire stack of the hay bales. Giles said he wished he did know something about the bank robberies because the police told him there's a twenty five thousand pound reward for anyone with information which might lead to an arrest."

"Twenty five grand," whistled George, impressed, "blimey, no wonder someone was keen to report a possible sighting then; that amount of money's not to be sneezed at. I wish I'd taken a better look at the picture on the telly the other night because right now I've no idea what the bloke they caught on camera looks like."

"Look in the paper;" said Gertie, waving her hand towards a closed copy of the Daily Telegraph lying on the Stanleys' kitchen table. "His picture was in ours again today so I would imagine it's in most. It'll probably mention the reward money too."

"Help yourself," said Ned, seeing George eye the newspaper.

George found an article and groaned. "Hmm, it's not very good, is it? Much too blurred to make out any of the finer details. This bloke could almost be anyone."

Ned agreed.

Rose looked over her husband's shoulder. "Oh dear, trust us to be away and miss all the excitement and we missed Christmas too because I had the sodding flu. Still, we're back now and don't worry about seeing Molly tonight, Ned, I'll make sure she's alright last thing. I popped in to see her as soon as we got back to use her loo; we've got frozen pipes, you see, which is a bit of a pain."

"Oh no, that must be pretty grim," sympathised Stella. "Would you like a bottle of water to take home with you, so you can at least make tea?"

"Thanks, that'd be great. We haven't lit the fire yet so we'll need something to warm us up although the downstairs storage heaters are on low."

"I think Mum's rather enjoying all the fuss," Ned grinned, as Stella filled an empty orange squash bottle at the sink. "She has a constant flow of visitors in spite of the weather and they've never had so much to talk about."

"Yes, she probably is content, bless her" said Rose, "and she'll be very interested to hear your bit of news, Gertie. She does after all like to be kept up to date with things, especially if they're a bit out of the ordinary."

Janet Ainsworth was not a happy woman. It had been her husband Ian's idea to move to Cornwall because he had received an offer to go into partnership with Ken Bradshaw, whom he had met at a dental convention during the summer and renewed a friendship first struck up at dental collage. Janet had been appalled by the idea when first he had mentioned it; she loved life in suburbia and therefore raised all sorts of objections, but her arguments were fruitless, for once Ian made up his mind to do something then opposition was, in most cases, a lost cause.

The Ainsworth children, however, unlike their mother, were thrilled at the prospect of a move to Cornwall. To them, the opportunity to live near the sea sounded idyllic. And the arrival of deep snow, followed by the prompt closure of their new school, so soon after their move, really was the icing on the cake. But to Janet, rural life held no promise of a better life. In her opinion, Cornwall was the back of beyond; large expanses of boring fields, pointless lanes that led to nowhere, cold wet sea and inhabitants whose idea of dining out was pasty and chips in the pub. Furthermore, she anticipated, an inevitable dearth of quality departmental stores, fashionable shops and nice clean pavements to walk on.

For the first time since the snow began, Janet was alone in the house, for the clearing of the road had finally enabled Ian to return to work, and the children, still off school, were out playing in the rec with new found friends, where they were attempting to slide down the snowy incline on all sorts of make-do sledges.

Janet was wiping condensation from the landing sash window, lamenting the loss of her expensive double glazed ones in their previous home, when she saw the first police car drive by. The sight of it brought a smile to her face. She dropped the damp cloth onto the floor and hurriedly opened the window to see where it was heading. As anticipated she saw it drive down to the cove, it then disappeared from view. Desperate to see its next move, she climbed onto the window sill and knelt on the narrow strip on wood. She squeaked with delight, for it was just possible to see the roof of the car as it drove up the lane towards Higher Green Farm.

Janet climbed down and closed the window beaming with satisfaction. She had taken an instant dislike to the Wilson brothers. For the day following their arrival in Cornwall, after the children had gone to school for the first time and Ian had gone to work, she had taken her beloved pet poodle, Glenda, for a walk along the dirty lane leading to Higher Green Farm, and there encountered the brothers on a tractor, one driving the other standing on the back, clothed in tatters and rags. Glenda, alarmed by the huge mud-splattered monstrosity, had yapped and whined as the noisy chugging vehicle passed them by, thus causing the brothers to laugh helplessly. And then one, the slimmer of the two, shouted 'sorry Fifi'. Annoyed and red with anger, Janet had whisked Glenda from the road and walked haughtily around the corner out of sight, vowing with vehemence, to get revenge.

The following day, the opportunity for revenge emerged from nowhere. For as Janet walked Glenda along the coastal path, she heard voices and recognised the twang of the farmer brother who had laughed at her Glenda. To avoid being seen she hid behind a wall and cautiously peeped out to see to whom he was talking. To her delight and amazement, she saw both brothers were there, and they were talking to a man whom she considered closely to resemble one of the bank robbers caught on closed circuit television during the robbery earlier in the week. After the brief encounter Janet curtailed her walk and returned to the village where she had anonymously phoned the police from the village call box.

Inside the Old Vicarage, Anne, alone in the house, threw herself into housework to banish from her mind the conversation with Danny the previous day. John was working and the children were out with Elizabeth and Greg building a snowman and sledging in the recreational field.

The anger which she had felt when first Danny had spoken had long subsided and if Anne was truthful, she was even a little flattered. Not that the flattery in any way changed her way of thinking; Danny was just a friend, not even a close friend, just an old friend. Anne vacuumed and dusted the big room thoroughly where pine needles from the Christmas tree still kept appearing in spite of the carpet having been thoroughly vacuumed after the tree had been undressed and discarded. When the room was clean she polished the silver and then cleaned the windows even though they were not dirty.

But for all the cleaning, her eyes were constantly drawn towards the cupboard on the left hand side of the sideboard, where at the back of the bottom shelf she kept her old 45 rpm records.

Anne left the big room, she would have a mug of coffee, and then vacuum the stairs, but when the mug was in her hands her mind wandered back to the cupboard.

Anne returned to the big room, stood her mug on top of the sideboard, opened the cupboard door and knelt on the floor. After pushing aside two pairs of old curtains her small pile of records was clearly visible. She pulled the records onto her lap and quickly shuffled through them, half way down she found what she was looking for, her very own copy of Gooseberry Pie's, *Crazy Maisie*.

With girlish glee, she sprang to her feet, pushed the plug into the socket and switched on the record player, she then lifted the lid and dropped the record onto the turntable. As the first notes emerged from the speakers, her thought drifted back to her childhood and the summer days when the record had dominated the top twenty. Sweet memories, memories of the ensuing years, when dreams came true, and she and her friends met their idol, Danny Jarrams. But that was only the beginning, for she and Danny became good friends during the years she had worked for his aunt, uncle and parents, as a receptionist at the Penwynton Hotel.

Anne smiled throughout the song and not until the last notes faded did the reality hit her: Danny Jarrams had as good as told her he loved her, and even though she had no intention of pursuing his comments, it gave her a warm feeling, a confidence boosting feeling, but she knew it was something to be kept secret forever for the sake of all those dear to her.

In her flat, Jane Williams sat on the sofa, both hands firmly clasped round a steaming mug of coffee, watching the heavy salty waves tumble onto the sea shore nearby. It was a sight she never tired of watching, every wave seemed different and the crashing sound was a constant reminder of her happy childhood.

On the table her sewing machine stood uncovered and ready for action alongside the fabric she had recently purchased. Jane felt she ought to be sewing but she was not in the mood, the cold spell had sapped her of energy and the long sunny days of summer seemed a million years away.

Jane jumped and was startled by a loud rap on the door at the foot of the stairs; the disturbance was followed by someone calling her name. Realising it was Giles she sprang to her feet and called down to him to come up and join her.

"Hi, love, I thought I'd better pop in and tell you the latest news," he said, nodding as she pointed to the kettle. "Bren and me had a visit from the Old Bill this morning, you see. It seems the missing coppers were coming out to see us when they disappeared because some nosey bugger told 'em our Ivan looks like a bank robber."

"You're joking," Jane gasped, placing a heaped teaspoon of coffee granules into a mug. "But that's ridiculous. I hope you told them not to be so daft."

"Yeah, I think we convinced them they were on a wild goose chase, but then it seemed they weren't so much concerned as to whether or not Ivan was a bank robber, but more about where the devil their mates had got to. They turned our barn over looking for traces of them."

"Well, that's understandable," said Jane, "it must be a bit unnerving when two of your work colleagues disappear into thin air like that. Haven't they any idea what might have happened to them?"

Giles shrugged his shoulders. "Well, if they have they didn't tell us and as soon as they'd searched the barns and the yard they scarpered and wished us a pleasant day."

"Hmm, would you like me to get you a bite to eat while I'm on my feet, I'm starving again, but then it's the cold, I've not stopped eating since the snow arrived."

"No thanks, love, I had a pasty in the pub. I couldn't resist it, they'd only just had a delivery, you see. Apparently they got them from the Hotel because the bakery that normally supplies them is still snowbound." He licked his lips. "They smelt absolutely delicious and they tasted good too."

"Oh, it's not like you to go boozing at lunch time," said Jane, disapprovingly.

"Well, we wouldn't have gone, but Brendon was itching to tell everyone about the visit from the cops and we agreed the best place to see folks was the pub. You'd be surprised how many there were in there, but then I suppose there's not much else anyone can do 'til the weather changes. If you're hungry, why don't we pop over there and I'll treat you to a pasty if they haven't all gone."

Jane scowled. "I shouldn't really, too many calories, but then, sod it, why not?"

Later that day the temperature finally rose above freezing and throughout Trengillion frozen water pipes gradually began to thaw. Some were lucky and their pipes were not fractured, but others were not so fortunate, hence plumber, Larry Bingham, was in great demand and he worked late into the night.

Rose was astounded by how wonderful it was to have running water again even though she had only had to manage without it for a few hours, "We take things too much for granted these days," she said to George, as she filled the kettle on his return from checking that none of the pipes leaked. "Goodness only knows how they managed in the olden days with only communal wells here and there."

"I think I ought to pop up and see Mum and Dad before it gets dark," said Stella, thoughtfully looking up at the sky from the kitchen window of The School House. "It looks to me as though we might be in for more snow, so I'd rather go today while it's relatively fine."

"Yes, you ought," Ned agreed. "You've only seen them once since you picked them up from the station. Would you like me to go with you?"

"Up to you. It'd be nice to have your company but then I'm equally happy going on my own."

"Hmm, I was thinking more of your safety," said Ned, "I mean, what if you should fall? Your parent's house is in rather a remote area and I should hate to lose you after all these years"

Stella turned away from the window and smiled. "I think you're being a bit over protective, Ned. Your mother's fall had obviously programmed your mind to think everyone is likely to take a tumble. Don't worry, I shall be alright, but if you'd like to come with me

115

then please do. I know Mum and Dad would like to see you anyway."

Stella's parents, Connie and Tom Hargreaves, lived in a cottage on the cliffs not far from Higher Green Farm and had done so since their retirement in 1976. Both were in their early eighties and enjoyed good health, which some might have attributed to their love of gardening.

Stella and Ned found Connie in the garden of Sea Thrift cottage wrestling with sheets which had frozen, stiff as boards, on the line. When she saw her visitors she beckoned them to help.

"Must be freezing again," laughed Ned, amused by the rigidity of the white, cotton, bed linen. "But then the weathermen did predict plummeting temperatures again when the sun went down." He frowned. "How on earth are we going to get those in that small basket?"

"With a bit of brute force," said Stella, "I had the same problem yesterday but with much smaller items."

"And they'll soon come back to life when we get them indoors," said Connie. "I often used to be in this predicament when we lived up-country, but I was a lot younger then to cope with it."

Connie spoke the truth, for once the washing met with the warmth of the kitchen it shrank to its normal size and she was able to hang it neatly on the clothes horse.

"How's your mother, Ned?" Tom asked, standing to let Stella have his chair by the fire. "What a to-do, eh."

"She's getting along fine, thanks, Tom, but it could have been really nasty if she'd lain there much longer."

"Your mother slipped yesterday in the snow," whispered Tom, glancing into the hall way to make sure Connie, in the kitchen, was out of ear-shot, "but don't let on I told you or she'll be cross."

"Is she alright?" Stella asked, concerned. "I mean she seems fine."

"I think so, just a few bruises, but you know your mother, she'll never make a fuss."

"Her daughter's much the same," said Ned, patting Stella on the shoulder. "I think it must be a female thing."

116

"Hmm, I don't know about that, my other daughter's a bit of a wimp, always at the doctors and she pops down the antibiotics like there's no tomorrow."

"Not good," Ned agreed, "I'm sure doing so weakens the immune system."

Connie entered the room carrying a full tray. "I didn't ask if you wanted tea, I just made it anyway as you can't have too many hot drinks while the weather's so cold."

"And it's much appreciated," said Ned.

"Have you heard the latest about this morning's police raid on Higher Green Farm?" Stella asked, clearing a space on the coffee table for the tea tray. "Gertie was in telling us all about it a while back."

"Ah, so that's what it was all about. I heard a fair bit of fuss and commotion while I was hanging out the washing," said Connie. "Police sirens and so forth but I wasn't sure where it was coming from though it sounded quite near."

"Well, it was the farm," said Stella, with a laugh. She then proceeded to relay information received from Gertie.

CHAPTER SIXTEEN

As dawn broke the following day, the inhabitants of Trengillion awoke to find more snow had fallen during the night, covering the already white landscape and the frozen ground, thus hiding footprints, paw prints, tyre tracks and all signs of life and activity from the previous day.

From the branches of trees and shrubs, icicles glistened in the early morning sun and throughout the village, in gardens and fields, the hats and scarves of snowmen, gleamed after the light dusting of snow, each resembled the images of their miniature cousins captured in the ubiquitous snow scenes which appear in the shops every Christmas.

Conditions underfoot were treacherous first thing in areas where the snow had begun to thaw and then frozen again in the freezing night time temperatures. Hence, once again the school remained closed and Trengillion's delighted children eagerly looked forward to yet another day of sledging and snowball fights.

Larry Bingham continued to work as many hours as he was able mending fractured water pipes in Trengillion, as did plumbers all over Cornwall and beyond, and because of the water lost due to burst pipes, concern was expressed by the water board who hinted at the possibility of a water shortage.

Many people, young and old, chose to remain in the village during the spell of bad weather and take advantage of essentials supplied by the village post office, hence in the first twenty four hours, milk, bread and fresh produce had sold out and customers had to make do with dried milk granules, tinned vegetables and fruit and buy ingredients to make their own bread. For although the gritters were out early and the main road into town was clear, supplies for the post office were disrupted and village people were afraid to venture into Helston, in case more snow fell and left them stranded.

However, for Susan Penhaligon a journey into town was necessary, for the following day was husband Steve's birthday and she needed to get to John Menzies' to collect a record she had ordered, notification of which she had received before the arrival of snow to say it was in. Therefore, when Steve went off to work with John, to put the finishing touches to a garage they had built in the village, she dropped Denzil and Demelza off to their grandmother, Gertie, and then drove into town.

Susan was surprised by the disruption in Helston, for although the roads were clear and traffic was moving with caution, deep piles of solid, dirty snow ran alongside the kennels in Coinagehall Street, and the paths where shoppers gingerly trod, were very slippery with compacted frozen snow and ice.

To her relief John Menzies' was open, but many other shops were closed because their staff lived out of town. Susan bought the record, a birthday card and a sheet of wrapping paper; she then walked up to Gateway to get provisions for family and friends not available in Trengillion.

The car park was almost empty as she trod carefully over the crisp snow, watching with each step the activity of children on the far side sliding down the incline on an empty milk crate. Susan smiled; the inventiveness of children seemed not to change with the generations and their makeshift sledge worked almost as well as any factory built contraption.

With the boot of her car filled with goodies, including several packets of salt, Susan left Helston for the nail-biting drive home, thankful for the warmth emanating from the car's heater.

Before reaching Trengillion, as she approached the cross roads by the Ebenezer Chapel, a rabbit dashed across the road causing her to swerve. Concerned that she may have injured the creature she stopped and stepped from the car onto the snowy verge where tiny paw prints indicated the rabbit had safely found its way into the hedgerow. With a sigh of relief, Susan returned to the car and opened the door, but then something caught her eye. She closed the car door and walked towards the narrow lane which led down a hill towards Polquillick. On the road, imprinted in the snow, two shiny dark lines stretched away from the main road. Equidistant lines, like wheel tracks but too narrow to be made by a car and with no tread marks, therefore, not made by rubber tyres.

Intrigued, as to what may have caused the lines, Susan went to investigate and walked alongside the tracks where no footprints other than her own disturbed the fresh snow. And then, to her surprise, the tracks abruptly stopped. Susan frowned. It did not make sense. And then suddenly she realised where they had stopped: it was beside the milk churn stand where dairy farmers in years gone by had left their produce for collection. Susan felt uneasy and glanced briefly over her shoulder. Everything was quiet, the main road was devoid of traffic, the birds seemed to have deserted the trees and the only sound was the gentle whisper of the wind whistling across open land. Nervously Susan crossed over the tracks and peered at the stand. Her mouth dropped open. Two perfectly formed, large, dark circles covered with a thin layer of ice stood amidst the bright white snow, each sparkling in the sunlight. Susan shook her head in disbelief. Surely the circles were imprints of milk churns? Without wanting to see more she ran back to the car and drove all the way into Trengillion at a very dangerous speed.

By nightfall, half of Trengillion's inhabitants had been to the crossroads to investigate the tracks and the icy circles, hence the Fox and Hounds was busy that evening with the curious: each desperate to discover if anyone had come up with a plausible theory as to what the mysterious appearance of tracks and circles might mean.

"It doesn't make sense," said Larry Bingham, exhausted but happy, having just mended the last of the fractured pipes, "and as daft as it might sound the only explanation I can come up with is it must have been old Elijah's cart made the tracks."

Sid Reynolds snorted with derision. "Oh, come on, Larry, surely you don't believe in that nonsense, I thought it was only air-headed females who were gullible enough to fall for that old bull."

"Well, I don't know, but can you think of a more logical explanation then?"

"It's obviously a prank," Sid laughed, tapping the table to emphasise his point. "Someone with a weird sense of humour who wants us to believe Elijah's ghost comes back with the snow. Mind you, even I have to admit it's pretty novel as far as practical jokes go."

"But how do you explain there being no footprints?" Percy asked. "I was one of the first up there after our Sue came back as white as a sheet and hers were definitely the only footprints there."

"And what made the track marks?" Peter added, "They must have been made by a vehicle of some kind, but nothing I can think of has wheels that narrow."

"Someone must have an old cart tucked away somewhere, find that and you've found your culprit," said Sid, smugly. "I expect most farms still have at least one or two."

"Ours hasn't," said Tony, emphatically, "and I've never seen one up there in my entire life. Blimey, it must be sixty years or so since folks went around by horse and cart."

"Maybe, but someone has one somewhere, mark my words."

"Okay, let's assume you're right, Sid, and it was a joke," said Percy, "but a cart would have to have been pulled by something, and as we've already agreed there were no prints of any kind and certainly not ones made a person or a horse. So how do you explain that?"

Grinning, Sid rubbed the back of his neck. "Hmm, you've got me there, but then if it was Elijah's ghost driving the cart then there would have to be hoof marks and he'd have left footprints too when he put down the milk churns or picked them up whichever he's supposed to have done. So can you explain that to me?"

"Well, that's simple," Cassie said, having overheard his comment as she collected empty glasses from a nearby table. "Ghosts don't leave footprints, everybody knows that, and I don't expect horses being of flesh and blood would do so either once they've passed over."

"Ah, but what about the cart?" laughed Sid, smugly. "How could that have left tracks if it was a ghost cart?"

Cassie raised her neatly plucked eyebrows. "My dear, a cart has no soul and so it would not be a ghost but merely a tool for a ghost to use to get from A to B."

Sid's indignant face caused his friends to roar with laughter as Cassie departed with a sweet smile of satisfaction.

"Well, damn it," he muttered, "for once I think I'm speechless."

Much later that same Friday evening, Albert Treloar was returning home from Polquillick where he had been to visit his cousin, a retired farmer like himself, but who was a little under the weather having been afflicted with a nasty dose of flu just before Christmas. Albert, feeling drowsy, drove very carefully along the back lanes leading to Trengillion for three reasons; firstly, he had consumed several glasses of Captain Morgan rum whilst in the company of his cousin and he did not want to attract the attention of the boys in blue should they still be in the vicinity of the Ebenezer Chapel. Secondly, the untreated roads were very icy and even though he drove a Land Rover and had forty years' driving experience under his belt, he still felt vulnerable. And thirdly, he wanted to keep an eye out for any sign of Elijah Triggs' ghost. For although he did not really believe in such things, there was something about the night that made such a sighting seem possible, and the mysterious tracks and icy rings which he had discussed at length with his cousin had fired up his imagination.

At the top of the hill where the lane approached the crossroads, Albert slowed down and glanced at the milk churn stand. To his relief it was just as he had seen it earlier when he had driven down the lane on his way to Polquillick; two dark icy circles shining in the light of a full bright moon.

Albert drove very gingerly along the last few yards towards the crossroads; his frightened eyes darting in all directions, eager, yet apprehensive, to witness any unusual activity; for the raised hairs on the back of his neck teased his senses and suggested he was not alone.

At the crossroads he stopped the Land Rover and switched off the engine. The night was quiet. Albert wound down the window, half expecting to hear the echo of horse's hooves gently clopping along the icy road, but all remained silent. When convinced the sighting of Elijah and his cart was not imminent, he opened the door of his vehicle and timorously stepped onto the frozen snow.

Feeling defenceless, Albert leaned his back against the cold wing of the Land Rover for support, both ears pricked up and alert, listening for any unfamiliar noises; but not a sound penetrated the stillness of the chilly night and nothing unusual crossed his slightly blurred vision. With forced bravery he pulled his coat tightly across his chest, left the protection of the Land Rover and crunched across the hidden grass verge, through the frozen snow and towards the old chapel gates, both wide open, but thankfully their ability to swing and creak was curtailed by small drifts of snow.

With a shiver, for the night was bitterly cold and his body temperature low due to the consumption of alcohol, he entered the chapel yard. All around the shadows of gravestones stretched across the white snow in the strong, bright moonlight; arches, crosses, rectangles, graves encased with dark rusty railings, Cornish crosses, and scrolls; the solid structure of each one enhanced by the silvery grey light.

Albert gazed up at the roof of the old chapel where the silhouette of a large bird sat motionless on the ridge tiles, its beady eyes searching for prey. Glad that he was not a bird on such a night, he lowered his eyes and cast a glance across the windows and down towards the door. A sudden crack from behind, like the snap of a twig breaking underfoot, caused him to jump. From the pocket of his overcoat he quickly pulled a large heavy torch, with intent to use it as a weapon as well as for additional light. With an unsteady hand he flashed the circular beam across the crooked, disarray of old tombstones, hoping to see a small animal scampering through the snow. But no living creature crossed the beam of light, and no other sound met his twitching ears.

Albert stepped forward and walked along the hidden path, flashing his torch in all directions. In the distance, an owl hooted, and he was convinced he heard the neighing of a horse over the sound of his thumping heart and the crunching of his feet in the crisp, white snow.

When Albert reached the chapel door he nervously turned to retrace his steps and the torch light fell onto the area beneath the long twisted, leafless branches of an old tree. He gasped and then he whined; every limb on his quivering body froze with fear; his teeth chattered uncontrollably; the torch shook in his trembled hands creating a flickering, eerie beam of light on the frightful image before his staring eyes.

Without stopping to investigate further, Albert ran down the path and back to the Land Rover, shouting and begging for mercy. He started up the engine and drove back to Home Farm like a bat out of hell.

Madge was in bed and fast asleep when Albert crept into the bungalow where the couple lived on farmland Albert's family had owned and worked for many years. And in the farmhouse, occupied by his step-grandson, David, and David's wife, Judith, the lights were also out.

Still trembling, Albert took off his coat in the kitchen, dropped it onto the floor and locked and bolted the back door; he then crept into the living room where he poured a large brandy from the bottle on the sideboard. Still shaking, he sat by the dying embers of the fire and attempted to regain his composure. When the glass was empty he poured another brandy and then, because he was still in a state of shock, yet another. For Albert was desperate to banish from his mind the image he had seen in the chapel graveyard. The image of two frozen policemen, slumped side by side, amongst the dead and buried. Their white faces, ugly, distorted and expressionless, staring into the cold night from beneath their dark helmets. Albert felt he should inform someone, should dial 999, but he knew his voice would slur and sound incoherent, besides, he could not possibly confess to having driven whilst under the influence of alcohol, and it was too late to do anything to help the two coppers: they were obviously well and truly dead.

Albert stood and staggered towards the sideboard for another drink, but before he could remove the lid from the brandy bottle his head began to spin. Feeling giddy, he stumbled back a few paces and toppled onto the settee. Comforted by the softness of the velour covers, he pulled his legs onto the foam filled seating and nestled his head deep into the feather cushions. Within minutes he was fast asleep and snoring.

When Albert woke the next morning he found a blanket over his body and from the kitchen he could hear muffled female voices. He stood and then sat down again; he felt dreadful, worse than he had ever felt before in his life. Holding on to the arm of the settee he forced himself to stand again and unsteadily left the room.

The hallway was bright with the glare of snow glowing through the glass front door. Albert screwed up his eyes to shut out the torturous light and stumbled down the hallway, towards the voices, touching the walls for support as he went.

In the kitchen he found his wife, Madge, chatting with her daughter, Milly, over mugs of coffee. Madge cast him a look of disapproval as he stumbled towards the kettle, clutching his head with both hands.

"Morning Milly," he croaked, feeling the need to be sociable, "what brings you here so bright and early?"

"It's not early," snapped Madge, before Milly had a chance to answer. "It's past eleven. Look at the state of you, your trouser bottoms are soaking wet and you look dreadful, still serves you right. You know you slept on the settee without bothering to take your boots off. You're a disgrace. You and that cousin of yours no doubt had a skinful last night. You ought to be ashamed of yourselves, Albert Treloar. And you drove home too! One of these days you'll get caught and it'll serve you right."

"I've come for some eggs," said Milly, timorously, feeling a little sorry for her step-father. "We've sold out at the post office, in fact the shelves are rapidly becoming bare, although the baker and the milkman both finally got through this morning, thank goodness."

Albert nodded as he poured boiling water onto a teabag and attempted to stifle a cry of pain, for the movement hurt his badly aching head. Madge, sensing his discomfort, felt a sudden pang of pity. "Come on sit down before you scald yourself and I'll get you a couple of aspirin, then you can hear what our Milly's got to say about the latest happenings in the village."

Albert felt the colour in his grey cheeks rise. Milly no doubt had told Madge about the dead policemen. He sighed: he was in no mood for amateur dramatics but he knew he must act surprised.

Milly started to laugh. Albert was confused. Why on earth would she laugh over such a serious incident?

Madge sat down and Albert watched the aspirin disperse in a glass of water.

"Come on, down it," commanded Madge, "and I'll make you a bacon sandwich when I've finished my coffee."

Albert drank his medicine in one gulp and then banged the empty glass down on the table. "So, what's happened?" he asked, his voice faint and nervous.

"Well, it seems someone's been at it again," giggled Milly, "up at the Ebenezer Chapel, that is. It was the milkman who discovered it on his way into the village early this morning. It was dusk of course, but visibility was good because of the moonlight and he was driving very slowly, because even though the main road was clear there were patches of ice here and there. Anyway, as he passed the chapel he noticed the peaks of two policemen's helmets over the top of the wall beneath the old ash tree. At first he thought it was the police in there looking for their missing colleagues again. But when he reached the gate he stopped: there was no police car, you see and so he got out to take a closer look, because on reflection he realised it was far too early for the police to be there anyway as it was barely light." Madge laughed, as Milly tried to suppress a fit of giggles. "Anyway," she continued, "when he got close enough to see he found they weren't coppers at all, but a couple of snowmen wearing policemen's helmets on their heads and with black dustbin liners over their bodies. He laughed, got back in the float and was about to drive off when it suddenly occurred to him that the helmets might actually belong to the missing men, but on looking closer he saw they were plastic fancy dress children's things, you know, the type you buy in Woolworths and so forth."

Madge and Milly both fell about in fits of laughter. "So it seems to us that someone in the village has a real warped sense of humour," Madge roared. "I'd love to know who it is. They must have some pluck though, because you wouldn't catch me up there building snow-coppers in the dark."

"Are, are you sure the helmets weren't real," Albert whispered, "I mean, there's no way the milkman might have been mistaken."

"Definitely not, he was one hundred percent sure on that fact. He says he has to laugh though, because he said he'd have looked a right idiot if he'd called the police, so he reckons it was a close shave."

A large grin suddenly crept across Albert's face and he threw back his head and laughed until the tears ran down his cheeks. Madge and Milly watched in horror, afraid he had taken leave of his senses. When his laughter subsided, he wiped his eyes and told them the truth about the previous evening. After which he found his headache had completely vanished.

126

CHAPTER SEVENTEEN

That same Saturday morning, the village buzzed with gossip telling of the imminent arrival of a regional television company eager to obtain a follow-up story regarding the missing police car by unearthing previously unbroadcast news from locals worthy of inclusion on their Saturday evening news bulletin. This prompted an even larger influx than before of enthusiastic dog-walkers to take a stroll in the vicinity of the old Ebenezer Chapel, who were also eager to see the now famous snow-policemen. The news team, however, did not focus purely on the old chapel; the whole village found itself in front of rolling cameras, especially the inn where the TV crew went for lunch and to chat to the locals, hoping to find out something the police may not have disclosed.

George and Rose, eager not to miss any more happenings, were also at the inn for lunch, where George got chatting to one of the news reporters, and both tried to wheedle any relative information from the other. But since neither knew any more than the next man, the reporter grumbled instead about the difficulties of finding interesting storylines.

"That's the problem with journalism, you get a bleedin' good story; it makes the headlines and then goes flat, dead, because no-one can tell us what's going on. I mean, look again at this wretched police car, it's gone missing, no-one it seems knows where to or why and we'll probably be the last to know when it does turn up."

"You think it will turn up then?" George asked.

"Well, of course, it's got to be somewhere, but God only knows where. I wouldn't even be surprised if it's not miles away. I mean, the coppers said they were by an Ebenezer Chapel, but there are loads of chapels in this part of Cornwall, so it could have been any one of them."

George frowned. "Well no, it couldn't have been any other because they were definitely coming to Trengillion, so it must have been our old Ebenezer Chapel they referred to on the radio."

"Right, so what makes you so sure they were coming out here?" asked the reporter, puzzled. "Have we missed something?"

George shrugged his shoulders. "Looks like it. You see, they were on their way to visit one of the farms here in the village. But surely you know that."

"What! But why? It's the first I've heard of this."

"Because somebody apparently saw someone who looked like one of the bank robbers on local farmland. Blimey, you are out of touch."

The reporter slapped his own forehead. "Bank robbers!"

"Yes, it was my wife who saw the man who she thought resembled one of the bank robbers," said Ian Ainsworth, leaving the side of the bar to join George, Rose and the news man. "I told her she was daft but she insisted it was him. She didn't tell me she'd already reported her stupidity though, at least not until the other day. I'm very annoyed with her. I hope her foolish mistake hasn't offended the farmers."

Rose smiled. "No, it hasn't. From what I've heard they were rather amused by the whole episode."

"Good, I'd hate to fall out with the natives in such a short space of time. My name's Ainsworth, by the way, Ian Ainsworth, and I recently moved into the Old Police House with my wife, Janet and family."

Rose shook the hand he proffered. "Yes, we know, we've heard all about you and I believe you're a dentist." Ian nodded. "I'm Rose Clarke and this is my husband, George. We live in Trengillion too, but unfortunately we were up-country when the snow arrived and the police car went missing so we dipped out on the excitement."

"I must go and join my colleagues and see if they've picked up on this latest development," said the news man. "It looks like they're making a move anyway." He thrust his hand in the inside pocket of his jacket. "Here's my card, if you should hear anything on the grapevine which you think might be of interest to us, please don't hesitate to give me a ring."

"We will," said Rose, scanning the card quickly.

"You must have one too," said the newsman to Ian, "for your observant wife."

Ian sheepishly took the card.

"Please join us," said George nodding towards the stool vacated by the reporter, "and then we can all get to know each other properly."

"Thank you," Ian replied, sitting down, "I should like that. We've not really had a chance to find our feet yet with the snow and so forth throwing things into turmoil."

"Of course, but you'll like it when you do," smiled Rose, warmly. "Trengillion is a very friendly place as long as you don't upset the natives, and believe me I speak from experience."

On Saturday evening, as prearranged, Lily was due to arrive at The Old Vicarage for dinner with Anne, John, Elizabeth, Greg, Susan and Steve, while Ned and Stella babysat Tally and Wills at Cove Cottage, and Gertie babysat Denzil and Demelza in Coronation Terrace; the reason for the gathering, Steve's birthday and a farewell dinner for Lily who was returning to work the following Monday.

Anne had planned to have a gathering earlier, but the disruption caused by the snow had preoccupied the minds of everyone and dictated different daily routines, hence the seven friends had not had a chance to meet as often as they would have done in more normal circumstances.

Anne and John had deliberated for several evenings as to what to feed their guests, but in the end, realising a glass of wine and a good chat was probably what most looked forward to, they decided John should make one of his authentic curries, hence Chicken Vindaloo was on the menu and Anne made a Lemon Meringue Pie for afters.

Elizabeth and Greg arrived first with two bottles of wine.

"Ugh, this slush is ghastly," Elizabeth grumbled, as she removed her coat and hat and hung them in the hallway of the Old Vicarage, "and everywhere looks so dirty. I really find it difficult to comprehend how something once so beautiful can deteriorate into something so hideous."

"You should see it in town," said John, closing the door behind them. "I popped in this afternoon for some poppadums and was appalled by the litter and dog's muck along the paths. I'm glad Anne didn't see it."

"Yes, but this has been rather an extraordinary week," said Greg, realistically, as he removed his Wellington boots. "Poor old Kerrier have had enough on their plate keeping the roads gritted."

"Well, actually, I wasn't blaming the Council," said John, "I was getting at the careless behaviour of people, but then I suppose the ice prevented them from walking their dogs in a normal way and the litter could have come from all sorts of different places. Anyway, that's enough about such unsavoury things otherwise we might all lose our appetites."

John showed Elizabeth and Greg into the big room and poured them each a drink. "Anne will be down in a minute, she's just gone up to change. She's a bit behind tonight because Ollie and Jess didn't want to go to bed in case they missed something."

"We didn't have that problem," said Elizabeth, smiling as she sat down on the settee. "Mum insisted that she would put Tally and Wills to bed so that she could read them a story and that's why we're here earlier than I thought we'd be."

As she spoke the doorbell rang and John went to let in Lily, who entered the house with a large bunch of flowers for Anne, who arrived at the foot of the stairs just as Lily crossed the threshold.

The two old friends gave each other a hug and then went to join Elizabeth and Greg in the big room, while John returned to the kitchen to stir the Vindaloo and put the flowers in a bucket of water until Anne could arrange them later.

"Did you walk down, Lil?" Greg asked, rising to embrace his sister. "I should have offered to pick you up but I never gave it a thought. Having said that, we didn't drive here anyway."

"No, Dad dropped me down and he's picking me up too. I just have to give him a ring when I'm ready."

The doorbell rang as John returned to the room. "Good, everybody's here now. Don't get up, Anne, I'll let them in."

Susan and Steve entered the room to a tuneful rendition of Happy Birthday. Steve grinned. "I can't believe I'm thirty eight," he sighed, "only two more years and I'll be forty. It's daft, I still feel like I'm a kid."

"I know what you mean," Elizabeth agreed, "and we'll none of us ever be as young again as we are today."

John laughed. "What time do you want to eat? I can have it ready for whatever time you say; I just need to cook the rice and fry the poppadums."

"Whenever it suits you," said Lily, and the others agreed.

John sat down. "In that case I'll just finish this drink and then I'll go back to the kitchen."

"Aren't Tony and Jean joining us?" Lily asked, noting their absence.

"They were meant to," said Anne, "but Tony's not feeling too good, so they've asked to be excused."

"I see, first symptoms of flu, I suppose."

Anne nodded. "It looks like it."

"Did any of you see Trengillion on the telly tonight?" Greg asked. "I thought it rather peculiar because the place looked so different through the eye of a camera and some bits I didn't even recognise."

"We said that too," said Anne. "The old chapel looked completely different from the angle they took it. The shot of the two snowmen was good though, so whoever built them must have been proud, not that I think they'll ever come forward and claim credit for their handiwork."

"It doesn't necessarily have to have been done by a local anyway," said Elizabeth. "We get all sorts of visitors in Trengillion, although admittedly not quite so many this time of year."

"Talking of visitors, I saw Danny Jarrams this afternoon," said Lily. "He didn't recognise me of course, but then I've never got to know him like you lot."

Susan grinned. "It was only Anne that really got to know him, wasn't it, Anne? I don't think he knew the rest of us existed."

Anne felt her face flush. "Excuse me, I'm sure I just heard one of the children calling."

"I didn't hear anything," said Greg, with a puzzled frown, "and I'm nearest the door." But Anne was gone, keen to get from the room and cool her burning cheeks.

After the meal, approved of by all, the seven friends left the dining room and returned to the big room where John topped up their glasses. As he sat down the telephone rang.

"I'll get it," said Anne, "jumping to her feet. "You deserve a rest after cooking that gorgeous curry."

She returned minutes later with an excited smile on her face.

"You'll never guess what? Well, actually you'll not be in the least bit surprised but that was Diane on the phone. It's Ginny's birthday today as well apparently and Graham has asked her to marry him. Naturally, she said yes. Isn't that brilliant?"

"Fantastic," Susan agreed, "and Ginny will be impressed when we remember the date of her birthday next year. Fancy it being the same day as you, Steve. And how romantic to propose on her birthday. I didn't realise Graham was such an old softie."

"I don't think I've ever met Ginny," said Lily. "Is she nice?"

"She's got gorgeous legs," smirked John, grinning at Anne's raised eyebrows, "and she's clever too."

Elizabeth sighed thoughtfully. "Well, that's most of us either married or engaged now. It sort of makes me feel quite old."

"Do you remember the Pact, Lily?" Anne asked, "Actually you probably don't because it was formed in your absence, although we did include you of course. I wish you were married or engaged. You've not mentioned a boyfriend since Paul, a couple of years ago. Are you happy? Not just with your job, but with life in general."

Lily sighed. "I love my job and I can't think of anything I'd rather have done, it's very gratifying."

"Yes, but what about your social life?" Anne persisted. "There must be someone you care about; I sense you're reluctant to tell us for some reason?"

To the surprise of the small gathering, Lily blushed and squirmed, her discomfort quite obvious.

"Well, actually there is someone, but…oh dear, if I tell you, do you promise that you'll not tell Mum or Dad?"

"Oh, my goodness!" Elizabeth gasped. "You're not in love with a woman are you?"

Lily smiled. "No, but I'm not saying anything more until you promise me that you'll say nothing to my parents."

"Mum's the word," said Anne, and all nodded in agreement.

"Well, I have a very good friend whom I love dearly. His name is Nick Ferguson, he's a doctor, is thirty nine years old, has light brown hair tinted with grey and is five feet eleven inches tall. There, so now you now."

"What's wrong with that?" Susan squealed, nonplussed, "he sounds dead gorgeous."

"He also has a wife," whispered Lily, hanging her head, "to whom he has been married for nineteen years and they have two teenage children."

"Oh Christ," hissed Greg, "I might have known; you idiot, Lil. How long's this been going on for?"

"Eighteen months," she sighed, "give or take a week."

"Eighteen months!" Greg spluttered. "What, so is it serious? Good gracious, no wonder you've kept so quiet."

"I think you're being a bit harsh, Greg," said Elizabeth, "you don't know this Nick or the circumstances. Is his marriage over, Lily, do you think?"

"Or are you just a bit on the side?" Greg snapped.

"Greg, stop it, please," Elizabeth shouted, "you're being unfair."

Lily promptly burst into tears. "That's the problem," she sobbed, "I wish I knew. He says he wants us to be together and talks of leaving his wife, but I don't think he ever will. He doesn't like conflict you see. He's very easy going and I think deep down he feels sorry for his wife. She's very shy and doesn't like going out and meeting people, whereas Nick's a bit of a party animal."

"Have you met her?" Anne asked.

"Not exactly, but I have seen her. I saw them both out shopping together some seven or eight months ago. I didn't get a very good look at her though because I hid in a shop doorway so that Nick didn't see me."

"Oh, poor you," said Elizabeth, "what a horrible situation to be in. For all of you, for that matter."

"Yes, it is, and I think if something doesn't happen soon I might seek a job in another hospital and end the whole thing. But I'd break my heart to do that. If I gave up the job I love and the man I love, then what would be left for me?"

CHAPTER EIGHTEEN

"I hear Graham and Ginny are engaged at last," said Giles Wilson, as he sat on the sofa in the flat above The Pickled Egg watching Jane pin up the hem on one of the new curtains, "and according to Diane they're going to have a do for close family and friends in the pub, to which we'll be invited."

"Hmm, that's right. Ginny rang this morning to say about it. Should be a good evening. You will be able to make it, won't you? I'll feel a right ninny if I have to go on my own."

"Of course, you can always count me in for a good booze up. Do you know when it is so that I can pop it in my diary?"

"They haven't decided yet because they need to have a chat with Cassie first." Jane looked up from her sewing. "I didn't know you had a diary. I thought Brendon did all the paperwork side of things."

"He does and I don't have a proper diary, just my head. I retain dates and so forth in the old grey matter: it's never let me down yet."

"I see," said Jane, as she glanced from the window where her brother Matthew was strolling across the beach throwing pebbles into the waves. She sighed. "I wish our Matthew would find himself a girlfriend and settle down. He's a smashing looking lad, but it doesn't seem to bother him one jot when he's on his own for all our social events."

"Bah, there's plenty of time yet before he needs to think of settling down," said Giles. "I mean, it's never really too late for a bloke, is it? We don't have biological clocks ticking away like you females."

"No, I suppose not, and I think he's inclined to think fishing is too unreliable an occupation to support a wife and family, even though Dad did it and quite successfully too."

"Yeah, but fishing isn't as profitable now as it was a few years back, is it? At least that's what they tell me. And no doubt your mum worked bloomin' hard as well cutting hair and so forth, so her earnings must have boosted their living standards considerably."

"Yes, but all the same, money, or lack of it, is no reason for Matthew to want to stay single."

Giles attempted to smother a yawn. "I dunno, I daresay it's nothing to do with dosh. I mean, I wasn't that smitten with girls when I was his age, not for a committed relationship anyway. In fact you're the first serious girlfriend I've ever had."

Jane felt flattered. "Really, tell me more. I mean, what were you like when you were young? You seldom mention your past."

"Humph, that's because I was an unambitious, lazy, beer swilling lout with a chip on both shoulders," laughed Giles. "I fooled around at school and never learned when to stop. I had all sorts of jobs but never stuck with any of them. I don't think you'd have liked the person I was before I came to Cornwall."

Jane lay down the curtain on the table. "So what changed you? I mean, you're not lazy now and you've stuck at farming since you've been here. You work hard too and are always up at the crack of dawn."

Giles grinned. "Not always, I get a lie in some days when Jim does the milking. Anyway, the answer to your question is money. Simple as that. I suddenly developed a desire to have nice things and realised to achieve such you have to work for it."

"Was Brendon as hopeless as you?"

"No, he was the exact opposite: that's how we got the farm, through Bren's hard work not mine and that's why I always genuflect to his whims and ideas. I owe him a lot; he saved me from wasting my life."

The snow continued to thaw after the initial rise in temperature and Ned was glad to re-open the school on Monday the nineteenth of January, although he was concerned over his mother's welfare during the working day in spite of both his daughters, his wife, and friends, Rose and George, all promising to see that she had everything she might possibly want.

The swelling around Molly's ankle had gone down considerably since her unfortunate fall and as Lily had handed over the case to Molly's own doctor, Lily was able to return to her work knowing her job was done and her erstwhile patient was in good hands. Molly, on the other hand, did not think she needed constant care and attention; she was able to potter around and do a certain amount of things for herself, she even contemplated moving her bedding back upstairs. But she rather liked watching television in bed by the fire and so decided to put off the move until the following weekend. Besides, she still had a cold which seemed in no hurry to leave and it was nice to have a bit of warmth and comfort. As for the frequent visits from her carers, it was wonderful to have their company, as long as they didn't fuss too much.

Danny Jarrams put down the telephone receiver in the Penwynton Hotel, cheered, and with a big beam on his face ran off to find his parents, he then returned to his room, packed his bags and threw them into the boot of his car. For once again he was on the move and returning to London for the bright lights. The phone call had been from his friend, Guy, and Guy wanted him to join and play bass in a new rock band he was forming.

Danny was very excited at the prospect of being a musician again, for although he had not once played an instrument since Gooseberry Pie had disbanded in 1974, he had always looked back on the Pie days as some of the happiest in his life.

Before he left Trengillion, however, he was conscious there was something he had to do and so after loading up his car he wandered down to the reception desk and helped himself to a wad of note paper; he then returned to his room.

After an hour of deliberation, chewing the end of his pen and drumming his fingers on the surface of the coffee table, he put a sheet of paper inside an envelope and scribbled Anne's name on the front. He then said goodbye to his aunt, uncle and parents and drove to Penwynton Crescent to find his cousin, Linda, before he set off for London.

Linda was surprised to hear of Danny's sudden departure, even though his behaviour had been unpredictable for many years. She was also saddened, for Danny's presence was always welcome; he made her laugh and she had dearly hoped that his current visit might result in his settling in the area once and for all and one day even taking over the running of the Hotel. However, her surprise and disappointment regarding his leaving shrank into insignificance compared with her curiosity as to the contents of the envelope for Anne. Danny had emphasised it must be given to Anne and Anne only and under no circumstances must she post it through the letter box at the Old Vicarage should Anne not be in when Linda called.

Linda looked at the clock after Danny's departure, it was only midday. She groaned, if Anne was home, she might not be alone for there was always the possibility John went home for lunch. Linda twiddled her thumbs while she contemplated what best to do, and eventually she decided to play it safe and wait until two o'clock, that way if John had been home he should have returned to work. She would also be able to pick up her three girls from school after leaving the Vicarage, which would save her making a second trip later in the day.

Linda left her home at five minutes to two and walked the short distance into the heart of the village, treading carefully to avoid slipping on any compressed snow in shaded areas where the sun's rays had not reached and which were a potential hazard to pedestrians.

When she reached the village she turned down the lane which led to the Old Vicarage. Once through the gates she kept to one side of the drive, where she was partly hidden by shrubbery in order to establish whether or not John was home before she made herself conspicuous. To her relief there were no vehicles in the driveway and so she approached the door and rang the bell, greatly relieved.

"Linda!" Anne exclaimed, much surprised, "what brings you here?"

"I, err, I've something for you," she whispered, hesitantly, pulling the envelope from her pocket. "Is John home?"

Anne shook her head. "No, why?"

Linda pushed the envelope into Anne's hands. "This is for you. It's from Danny and he said I was to make sure you got it in person."

"From Danny," said Anne, conscious of her colour rising. "But what is it?"

"You tell me," said Linda, her eyebrows raised. "I mean to say, what's going on? Why all the secrecy?"

"You'd better come in," said Anne, glancing around the garden to make sure there was no-one around.

Anne led Linda into the kitchen. "Please sit down." she casually said, dropping the envelope onto the table. "Tea or coffee?"

Linda pulled out a chair from beneath the table and sat down. "Tea, please. Milk but no sugar."

Anne attempted to smile. "Actually I remember the way you like your tea from back in our Hotel days, and you don't like it too strong either."

"Spot on," said Linda, watching closely as Anne poured boiling water from the kettle on top of the Rayburn into two mugs.

Anne placed the tea on the table and then sat down. "I actually don't know what's in that," she said, touching Danny's envelope. "In fact I've no idea at all. But I can tell by the look on your face that you think I've something to hide and for that reason I'd like you to open it to prove that I haven't."

"Oh, but I can't, Danny would be really cross if I did. Besides, what goes on between you and him really has absolutely nothing to do with me."

Anne shook her head. "But there is nothing going on between us and that's the truth. Please open it, Linda."

Linda did as she was asked. Inside was just one sheet of white paper.

"Read it," whispered Anne. "Read it out loud, please."

"Okay, it says:

Dearest Anne,

I can't go without saying goodbye and I can't see you to say goodbye because if I tried to I'd not be able to go. Does that make sense? Probably not. Anyway I'm going back to London.

Guy phoned me this morning and he wants me to join a new band he's forming and so I'm leaving today, right now, before I change my mind. It'll be good to play the bass again and hopefully I'll end up rich and famous, because although the Pie made us famous we never made much money from the venture and to be perfectly honest, I'm skint.

Before I go I have to apologise for my outspoken, foolish behaviour that day I bumped into you at the old chapel. I was totally out of order, Anne; I was stupid and very, very unfair to you and your family. Please forgive me.

I saw you the other day, out walking with John and the children. You didn't see me because I hid behind a hedge until you'd passed by. You've a lovely family and it was obvious even to a fool like me that you're very happy.

When next we meet perhaps it can be like old times, two old friends with lots in common, who enjoy each other's company and enjoy a laugh.

Take care, Anne. Please destroy this and have a wonderfully happy life.

Lots of love, Danny. X

Linda leaned forward and passed the sheet of paper to Anne, whose eyes were full of tears. "I don't know what Danny's referring to, Anne and I don't want to know, but I promise I shall never tell a living soul about that note."

"Thank you," croaked Anne, as she quietly read Danny's words through to herself. "Thank you." She then rose from her chair crossed to the Rayburn, lifted the lid and dropped the paper into the flames along with the envelope.

After dinner that evening, Anne asked John if he would put the children to bed so that she could walk down to Cove Cottage to see Elizabeth. John agreed, he thought Anne looked pale and hoped a chat and no doubt a hearty laugh with her sister would be a good tonic.

A fresh north westerly wind ruffled Anne's hair when she reached the top of the drive and stepped out into the lane. She pulled up her collar and tucked her gloved hands inside her pockets.

During her short stroll through the village she met no-one nor did she see any vehicles on the road. Everyone seemed tucked up snugly indoors with curtains closed to shut out the weather. In fact she saw no-one until she reached the inn and peeped through the condensation on the windows. Inside, several people sat around the fire and on stools alongside the bar. The idea of a bumper glass of wine appealed to Anne but she carried on walking.

The sea echoed wildly as Anne turned the corner and stepped onto the beach; its loud waves booming as they crashed onto the seashore, rattling pebbles and shingle before retreating back into the dark waters. She stopped to listen, wishing the night were lighter so that she might see the waves, but only a small patch of the beach was visible in the solitary light glowing from the lantern on her sister's front porch.

Elizabeth was surprised to see Anne, especially as she seemed to have called without reason.

"I just wanted to get out of the house," said Anne, kicking off her dirty boots in the porch. "I didn't even pick up the children today, you see, because Granny Gert collected them and gave them tea."

"Yes, I saw her. Is everything alright? You look awfully pale."

"I'm fine, must be lack of fresh air. I'm not disturbing you, am I?"

"No, no, I was just about to wash up," said Elizabeth, closing the front door, "and then watch Coronation Street."

"Oh."

"Come on in the kitchen with me and have a glass of wine; that should put a bit of colour back in your cheeks."

Elizabeth poured out two large glasses of wine and then quickly washed up.

"Where's Greg?" Anne asked, sitting back in the chair and raising her feet to warm on the towel rail on the front of the Aga.

"Reading to Tally and Wills. A work colleague of his was raving about some children's books featuring a cat and some mice who live in a church by someone called Graham Oakley and so Greg went to the library during his lunch break to borrow some of them. They must be good because I've heard lots of laughter."

"Really," said Anne, "I must have a browse through them then; we've just about exhausted the books on our shelves and could do with some more. Which reminds me, talking of mice, yesterday John found a poor mouse in one in the traps he'd set in our spare bedroom. So that explains your mysterious rustling noise."

Elizabeth's mouth turned upside-down. "I'm glad but poor mouse."

"That's what I said. I'm so glad the children didn't see it, especially Jess, she'd have been in tears for a week."

Elizabeth sat at the table on the opposite side to Anne. "Would you rather we went in the living room? It's a bit more comfortable than in here."

"Oh, sorry, I'd forgotten you wanted to watch Coronation Street," said Anne, putting down her feet.

"No, no, I don't, not really; I just watch it out of habit. In fact I watch most things on the telly out of habit. It's nice to be in here away from it, and I'd much rather chat to you any day."

"You sure?"

"Quite sure. Ah, here comes Greg," said Elizabeth, as the sound of footsteps descending the stairs echoed through the hall.

Greg peered around the kitchen door. "I thought I heard voices. Hello Anne, gosh you look pale, are you alright?"

Anne laughed and stood to look at her reflection in the mirror by the back door. "I don't," she said, rubbing her cheeks, "I'm always this colour."

"Must be the light then," said Greg. "Are there any beers left in the fridge, Liz? Seeing you two boozing makes me fancy a drink."

"One, I think," said Elizabeth, opening the fridge door, "but there's an unopened pack under the stairs, although they'll be warm of course."

"Okey dokey, I'll have the cold one for starters, but it doesn't matter about chilling the rest, they won't be that warm under the stairs because the hall radiator's only on low. Are you two staying in here?"

"I think so," said Elizabeth, passing the cold bottle to Greg, "Why?"

"Because if you are, I won't have to watch Coronation Street and can watch something on the other side instead."

"Yeah, go ahead," said Elizabeth, "but before you go and make yourself comfortable, pass another bottle of wine from under the stairs, please, because this one's nearly gone already."

Anne felt quite inebriated by the time she left Cove Cottage, but as she turned the corner to walk up the hill, the cold wind sobered her up and cleared her head. The evening had been enjoyable and all thoughts of Danny's brief letter were slowly fading in her mind. The evening therefore had served its purpose. Anne had wanted to prove to herself that she was happy with her life and even if given the chance so to do, she would not change it.

At the foot of the cliff path Anne climbed partway up the rugged track and then looked back down on the village. Lights twinkled from the houses, snow still thinly covered many lawns and nearby the sound of the sea crashing onto the rocks and shore warmed her heart. Trengillion was home and would always be home and nothing in the world would entice her away.

The Old Vicarage was silent when Anne crept in through the front door. Thinking John might have gone to bed she tiptoed through the hallway and into the kitchen where she made a mug of tea; with mug in hand she then crept into the big room.

To her surprise, John sat by the fire clutching his legs, rocking to and fro and gazing into the flames.

"A penny for your thoughts," said Anne, quietly closing the door.

He turned and gazed up into her face. "I was just thinking," he said, "thinking what I'd do if you went out and never came back. If you left me, that is. I mean, how would I cope? And now I've gone and depressed myself with my morbid thoughts."

Anne bit her lip as he lowered his head and then she stood her mug on the table. "I will never, ever leave you, John. I vowed till death do us part and I meant it. I love you, I love our children and I love Trengillion. In fact right now I love everything there is to love about life."

John reached up, took her hand and pulled her down by his side. "You wouldn't leave me then, not even for Danny Jarrams?"

Anne threw back her head and laughed. "No, not for him nor anyone else nor all the money in the world," she whispered.

CHAPTER NINETEEN

Molly had many visitors after her accident became common knowledge, so much so she abandoned trying to read her book as she kept reading the same passage over and over again. But she never tired of seeing people especially if they had news to convey, gossipy in nature. One such visitor was Dorothy Newton.

"You've no doubt heard about our Albert," laughed Dorothy, as she removed her coat and draped it over the back of the settee, "the incident with the two snowmen, that is. I mean to say, what a buffoon. God only knows how much rum he'd drunk with our dozy cousin to go and make a silly mistake like that. The crazy cretin is the laughing stock of the village now and serves him right."

Molly smiled. "Yes, I had heard. In fact I think everyone that's been in has told me about it. Shame really, I'd like to pass on some tittle-tattle myself but gossip seems to be doing the rounds pretty quickly at the moment. Would you like a coffee, Dot, and a cake? Ollie and Jess brought me some butterfly cakes round the other day which they'd made with Gertie; they're very nice but I'm never likely to eat them all."

"Yes, that'd be nice, but you stay put and I'll make the coffee. I take it you'd like one too."

"Yes please, but would you be a dear and make it with hot milk, it's so much nicer than plain old boiled water and cold milk."

"I couldn't agree with you more," said Dorothy, walking into the kitchen. "Frank and I often have it like that if we've a surplus of milk. Now, where do you keep your milk pan?"

"It's in the corner cupboard, top shelf on the left, you can't miss it. I seem to have a lot of milk at present; the family have all brought me some since supplies have got back to normal, they're afraid I might run short with my flow of visitors, you see, but I only use it in hot drinks and for my porridge."

"I've got Frank eating porridge at last," said Dorothy, placing the pan on the stove. "He'd never have it before, you see; in fact when we were at the Inn he wouldn't have breakfast at all. Since his retirement though he has at least started having Shredded Wheat, but I got him to try some porridge when the snow started and now he's hooked on it."

"The major liked porridge," said Molly, wistfully, watching Dorothy through the open kitchen door. "I always make too much now; I don't seem to be able to judge the right amount for just one."

Dorothy returned to the living room with two mugs of steaming coffee on a tray along with Molly's cake tin and two empty tea plates. "It's so easy to forget about your loss, Molly, with so much going on." She placed the tray on the coffee table. "And now on top of being a widow you've had this fall and you've got a cold. Things aren't going too well for you, are they?"

"There are a lot worse off than me," sniffed Molly, without self-pity, "and no-one could have a better and more loyal set of friends and family than I have."

As her words faded they heard someone entering the back porch followed by a sharp rap on the kitchen door.

"I'll go," said Dorothy, rising to her feet. In the porch she found Nettie Penrose wiping her feet on the doormat with a bunch of daffodils in her hand.

"Come in," said Dorothy, standing aside. "Oh, those flowers do smell nice."

"I thought so too," said Nettie, removing her boots. "They arrived at the post office from the Scillies while I was in there, so I had to get a bunch for Molly."

She entered the living room where Molly attempted to rise.

"No, don't get up," said Nettie, resting her hand on Molly's shoulder.

"I'll put the daffs in water," said Dorothy, taking the flowers from Nettie's hand after they had been shown to Molly. "Would you like a coffee, Nett, we've just had one?"

"Oh, yes please, it's still pretty nippy out there, although nothing like as bad as it was, of course."

"With hot milk?"

"Lovely, yes and a couple of sugars if that's alright."

"Thank you for the flowers," said Molly, as Nettie removed her coat. "It's very thoughtful of you."

"You're more than welcome."

Molly shuffled along the settee to make room for the latest visitor and Dorothy returned to the kitchen. "So how are things at the farm? I've not seen Tony and Jean since Christmas."

"Fine, now the thaw's set in, although Tony's got a bit of a cold but I don't think it's flu." Nettie sat down beside Molly. "It was tough going while the snow was around though, I must admit. Daily jobs took twice as long and I didn't dare go out in case I slipped. Wasn't it funny though for us to have a bad spell like that when we'd only been talking about snowy winters on New Year's Eve? And fancy old Elijah cropping up too. I must say I don't like the idea of those poor policemen being missing and in the very same area as well; it's a bit too close for comfort."

Molly sighed. "Yes and it must be awful for their poor families, not knowing, that is. I do feel so sorry for them."

"I think you ought to try and make contact with Elijah with one of your séances. You know, like you did all those years back and got hold of that Wagstaffe chap. Cyril and me had gone home by then, but we heard all about it and I've always regretted missing the fun."

"Now that is a good idea," giggled Dorothy, as she stood the vase of daffodils on the coffee table. "I missed out on that séance too because I had to take my drunken brother home, but I've heard many accounts of it over the years from various sources, and every one spoken with awe."

Molly smiled. "I don't think it would be a very good idea, ladies. Too many people dear to us all have passed over since those days and we must let them all rest in peace."

Nettie looked disappointed. "But couldn't you be specific and just ask for Elijah or even just enquire after the policemen? That way we'd not disturb our loved ones."

Molly laughed and her eyes twinkled. "It's not like making a phone call, Nett. There isn't someone on the end of a line answering queries."

"Well, no of course not, but surely the spirits must have some way of hearing the summons of spiritualists."

"But don't you think Elijah might have been gone for too long now," called Dorothy, back in the kitchen making coffee for Nettie. "After all, it's over a hundred years now since he went missing."

"It depends," said Molly, amused by the image of a telephone exchange run by celestial beings, "but I don't think it's a very wise thing to do, not in the current state of affairs. And as regards the policemen, it'd be awful if I did make contact with them. I mean, what on earth would we do? Dial 999 and tell them the poor souls are dead. No, I think it's best we leave things alone and don't meddle. Besides, we don't even know their names, so I'd have no idea who to ask for."

"Their names are in the paper," said Nettie, eyebrows twitching eagerly with hope and enthusiasm, "so that's not a problem. Please give it a go, Molly, we could all do with a bit of excitement to brighten these short, dull and dreary days."

"I would have thought you'd all had plenty of excitement lately," smiled Molly. "I know I have."

"Yes, but all any of it has done is raise questions," sighed Dorothy, handing a mug of coffee to Nettie. "It'd be nice to have a few answers for a change, and finding out what really happened to Elijah would be a very good start."

"Alright, but there's no rush after all this time, so let me think about it for a while. I'd have to see what Ned thought before I make a decision anyway, because I don't want to cause offence and that's so easily done in a close knit community such as ours."

"There must be plenty of money in dentistry," Giles Wilson laughed, as he walked into the kitchen of Higher Green Farm and warmed his hands on the Esse stove. "I've just seen that new Ainsworth bloke drive off to work in a gleaming brand new Jaguar Cabriolet; that must have cost him a few bob."

"Where have you been then? I thought you were feeding the cattle," queried Brendon, laying down an invoice and peering over the top of his reading glasses.

"Yeah well, I just popped down the shop for some fags. I meant to get some in the pub last night but got so engrossed in local gossip, I completely forgot." He sat down at the table. "Any tea in the pot, Candy? I'm parched."

"Should be but it's probably cold by now," said Candy, drying her hands having finished washing up. "I'll make some fresh."

"Lovely, ta." Giles laughed as he took a handful of custard creams from the biscuit tin on the table. "There's a new notice in the post office window. Twenty thousand grand's up for grabs to anyone who can come up with any information about the missing coppers."

"Bloody hell," snorted Brendon, "that'll get the locals out searching here, there and everywhere."

"Twenty thousand pounds," gasped Candy, pausing as she poured boiling water into the teapot. "That means, if I could find the policemen and the bank robbers whose reward if I remember correctly is twenty five thousand pounds, we'd have forty five grand and be able to pay off our mortgage and still have enough left for a new car."

Brendon threw back his head and laughed. "Dream on, Candy. You stand more chance of hitting the jackpot with your Premium Bonds than finding either. I mean to say, the bank robbers aren't going to be down here, are they? And I don't expect the coppers are anywhere around Trengillion either. Why should they be? They never got as far as here; that we do know, unless of course, someone kidnapped them en route."

"And if that's the case, I for one wouldn't want to try and hide anyone in this village," grinned Giles, "not with so many nosey buggers peeping out from behind their net curtains, like Fifi's mum."

"Why would anyone want to kidnap a couple of coppers anyway?" Brendon asked. "Especially while they're in a car."

"Ransom money?" suggested Candy.

Giles wrinkled his nose. "Blimey, that'd be a bit risky, wouldn't it? No-one would ever be able to get away with it. Besides, who'd pay up? The Government certainly wouldn't and I doubt that either of the coppers come from a wealthy family."

"Exactly, it'd be interesting to know what has happened to them though," said Brendon, rising from the table and taking his coat from a peg on the back of the door. "I've not heard any plausible theories from the any of the locals or the media either for that matter. In fact the most popular opinion with the locals is the poor sods have gone the same way as old Elijah Triggs, and that's plain daft."

"Hmm, I know, and that's why I shall definitely be at Molly Smith's séance," said Giles, nodding his head.

"Is it on then? I thought there was some doubt."

"Apparently so, at least that's the impression I got in the post office just now. Two old biddies were in there squeaking with excitement at the prospect."

Ned's initial reaction regarding the séance, was concern for his mother's mental well-being, especially as he was aware that pressure from many sources was purely to see if it was possible for Molly to contact the dead. In other words, more a test of her authenticity than curiosity regarding the solving of two similar mysteries which had dumbfounded everyone else. His response therefore was to put his foot down, claiming dabbling with the unknown was a risky pastime which could easily end in disaster. However, after discussing the subject with several of his closest friends, he was persuaded it would be just harmless fun, and as he was also keen to know what had happened to both the policemen and Elijah, he did, with a few misgivings, finally give the event his blessing.

After the Wilson brothers had returned outdoors, Candy quickly did the housework and then some baking. She liked to have a big bake up once a week to lighten the load for other days, and what was not needed for a day or two she froze down in the brothers' large chest freezer. Candy was a good cook; before she met and married Larry she had worked in the kitchens of a French restaurant where she had learned much from the two chefs, Pierre and Jean.

Giles and Brendon were pleased to sample her efforts, for unlike many other country-folk, they were not averse to trying something a little different and many of her concoctions proved a big hit.

However, her concentration was not entirely focused as she cooked that morning, for in spite of Giles' negative protestations regarding the reward money, her mind was thinking of likely places where the policemen might be hidden; because to her the possibility of kidnap for ransom money sounded the only plausible explanation for their disappearance. For when all was said and done, they had to be somewhere. She was also thinking about Larry and wondering how he was getting along at the dentists.

On Wednesday morning Larry Bingham had broken a tooth whilst eating muesli for breakfast. He thought little of it at the time, but by the end of the day his tongue was sore from rubbing against the jagged edge and so he decided he ought to visit the dentist. Hence that morning before she went to work, Candy rang the dentist's surgery and was told by the receptionist there was a vacancy at ten thirty due to a cancellation because a patient had come down with the flu.

Just before ten o'clock Larry left Trengillion for the drive into Helston, quite looking forward to the appointment, for the tooth was painless and it would give him a chance to meet Ian Ainsworth in the capacity as a dentist. For Ian had taken the place of the Bingham's usual dentist following his emigration to Australia.

Larry arrived at the surgery in good time and took a seat in the waiting room. When he was finally summoned to the dentist's room he put down the copy of the magazine he had been flicking through and walked down the corridor to the designated room. When he went inside, however, he was disappointed, for it was not Ian Ainsworth waiting beside the dental chair, but Ken Bradshaw.

"Oh," said Larry, "I was expecting to be seen by Mr Ainsworth."

"Were you indeed? Please take a seat. You're seeing me because it was one of my patients who cancelled. Mr Ainsworth is fully booked today. I hope that won't be a problem."

"No, no, it's not a problem, it's just that I live in Trengillion and I thought it would give me a chance to get to know him better."

Ken Bradshaw laughed. "From what I hear I reckon you'd be better off trying to meet him in your village pub. He seems to spend quite a bit of time in there judging by the amount of times its name crops up and he's only been here for two shakes of a lamb's tail."

The dental nurse present placed a bib around Larry's neck: he then opened up his mouth wide beneath the bright light of a lamp.

"Hmm," said Ken, "it's a nice clean break. I'll just patch it up for you today temporarily and then you can come and see Ian later to get it fixed more permanent. How did you manage to break it?"

"Muesli, I crunched on something hard, a nut, grain or something, I didn't get a chance to see though because whatever it was I swallowed it along with the bit of tooth."

During his treatment Larry was reminded why he had avoided seeing Ken Bradshaw before. Ken was rough, he pushed, pulled and poked around Larry's mouth in such a brutal way that Larry was thankful when the bib was removed and the chair raised to normal level. But for all the rough treatment, Larry had to confess the tooth was as smooth as silk and his mouth was devoid of pain.

The house was empty when Larry arrived home, Candy was still at work and their two boys, Charlie and Sam, were at school. Larry looked at the kitchen clock, it was a quarter to twelve, and so he decided to have a very early lunch thus enabling him to get in a long afternoon's work to make up for the lost morning. As he was finishing off a bowl of tomato soup, Candy arrived home with a cabbage given to her by Giles.

"Oh, I'm glad I caught you. How's the tooth?"

"Fine, have a look," said Larry, opening his mouth wide for his wife to see.

"Hmm, looks okay."

"It feels it. I didn't see our new bloke though because it wasn't his patient who had cancelled, I saw Ken Bradshaw. He's a rough so and so, but he's done a good job."

"I don't suppose you saw anything of Ian Ainsworth's car, did you?" Candy asked, placing the cabbage in the fridge. "Giles said he had a new one, a Jaguar something or other which he reckons must have cost a pretty penny."

Larry shook his head. "No, I didn't but then I don't know where they park their cars anyway, unless it's in the Gateway car park. I tell you what I did see though, Bradshaw's watch, a bloody great chunky Rolex, so they must both be earning well."

Candy wrinkled her nose. "Could be a fake. Anyway, you can have a Rolex soon because we're going to be rich."

Larry's eyebrows rose in a questioning manner.

"Yes," said Candy, "all we have to do is find the bank robbers and the two missing policemen and then we can reap the rewards. Shouldn't be too difficult, should it?"

CHAPTER TWENTY

Behind the Penwynton Hotel was the one-time stable block aptly named the Mews, providing accommodation for students who worked at the Hotel during the summer months. Each stable had been converted into a single self-contained bedsit, and the largest was the home of Jim Haynes, fishing crew to Matthew Williams during the summer crabbing season.

Jim, being relatively new to Trengillion, had moved around continuously from one short let to another during his first few years in the village. But when he heard of the bedsits, he boldly asked if he might rent one of them, as a winter let, when they would otherwise stand empty and he was permitted so to do.

At the end of his winter let, the proprietors of the Hotel, saddened that Jim was having difficulty finding a home for the summer, offered him the bedsit on a long let, for which he was very grateful. Hence since 1984 he had lived happily at the Mews, where not only did the Hotel provide him with accommodation, but also the opportunity of a few hours' work. Jim therefore had a varied lifestyle; in the summer he fished for crab with Matthew and in the winter he worked part time at Higher Green Farm and did useful maintenance work at the Hotel.

Because of the freezing weather the price of vegetables rocketed throughout the land during January, and the Wilson brothers, keen to capitalise on the inflated prices, gathered together as many willing hands as they could muster to get as much cabbage cut as possible before the price fell again.

After busy days cutting cabbage, Jim always looked forward to getting back to the Mews for dinner, and Monday was no exception. Before leaving for work at half past eight, he had prepared a hotpot to simmer throughout the day in his newly purchased slow cooker. Working in the cold fresh air, and continuously bending and carrying, built up his appetite, hence he was usually starving by the time he got home. However, when he reached the top of driveway leading to the Hotel, he suddenly had a desire to visit the old chapel; during the bad weather he had been busy much of the time at the Hotel, shovelling snow and helping in the kitchen because some of the staff were unable to get to work, hence he had never found the time to get up there.

Jim peddled his black Raleigh bicycle along the straight road towards the crossroads, and outside the chapel he stopped and leaned his bicycle against the open gate.

There was still a considerable amount of snow in and around the graveyard, but Jim was not really interested in the outside, he had seen it many times before. It was the inside that raised his curiosity and he had heard on the grapevine that it was always left unlocked. Jim was interested in architecture, churches and chapels in particular, and although he was familiar with the church and Methodist Chapel in the village, he had never actually been inside the Ebenezer Chapel.

As he approached the door he glanced at the two snow-policemen of which he had heard much in the Fox and Hounds. He grinned; it was difficult to imagine anyone could be daft enough to think them real, but then he supposed in the dark, when you had been out boozing, things would have looked a lot different. Besides, the thaw also meant their size had diminished considerably since Albert's frightening ordeal.

Still smiling, Jim reached out for the handle on the arched door and turned it; to his delight it opened and he stepped inside. He was not disappointed with what he saw. It was larger than it looked from the outside, but he put that down to the lack of seating which detracted a little from its original splendour. The pillars, however, which once had supported the upper seating still remained and the large archway where once the magnificent organ would have bellowed was intact and not damaged. Jim went further inside. He called out and his voice echoed through the empty shell. He wondered what was likely to happen to the building, for it was obvious if the hole in the roof went too long without repair then demolition would be the only viable option. Jim looked towards one of the large windows, the light was fast fading so he decided to go home and call again another day when the sun was shining.

Outside he gently pulled the door closed and walked back down the path towards the gate to collect his bicycle but to his surprise and dismay, his bicycle was no longer leaning on the gate. He walked out into the road, but it was nowhere to be seen along the entire length of the front wall. Jim was cross. He had only owned the bicycle for a month, having bought it just before Christmas when he had finally conceded his old one had seen better days. Annoyed and frustrated he walked around the perimeter of the graveyard, but in spite of his thorough search his efforts were fruitless. Determined not to give up he wandered across the scrubland behind the chapel, but there was nothing to see other than shimmering water in the old pond. Finally he gave up and walked back to the Mews cursing whoever had taken it.

The following morning Jim rode to the farm on his old bicycle and arrived just as Candy Bingham was about to enter the kitchen door.

"Where's your new bike, Jim? Don't say it's got a puncture already."

"No such luck," he growled, dismounting, "would you believe it? But somebody's nicked the sodding thing."

"Nicked it," Candy gasped, "oh no, but that's terrible, Jim. Have you reported it to the police?"

"No, I can't see the point; they'll never be able to find it, will they? Blimey, they can't even find their own bleedin' cop car."

Candy giggled. "But where did it get taken from? Surely not the Hotel?"

"No, it's safe enough up there. It was outside the Ebenezer Chapel, of all places. I only popped inside for about five minutes and there was no-one around at the time. I'm really fed up, I loved my new bike and it cost me a packet too."

"Phew, well thank goodness you weren't on it, that's all I can say. I reckon you had a close shave."

Jim frowned. "A close shave! What on earth do you mean? And how could anyone nick it if I was still on it?"

"Think about it, Jim. First Elijah and his cart went missing, then the two coppers and their car, and now your bike, but you weren't on it so it's not quite so bad. There's something odd about those crossroads though; something spooky. No wonder some are starting to call that area the Ebenezer Triangle."

Jim laughed and then his face dropped, "You're not serious are you?"

"Well, you come up with a better explanation if you don't think it's weird, but let's face it, people and things don't normally disappear without trace, forever, do they?"

Jim shrugged his shoulders. "No, I suppose not. Anyway, we might find out later at the séance. Are you going?"

"I'm not sure. Larry wants to go but I think it might be a bit too scary for me and we've not done anything about getting a baby sitter either." She laughed. "They might be a bit scarce tonight anyway if everyone's going to the inn."

"Yeah, I suppose so, anyway, whatever you decide I'm sure there'll be no shortage of people to fill you in with the details."

Originally it was proposed the séance would be held at Rose Cottage, but as word spread it soon became apparent the event had evoked a lot of interest and Molly's modest front room would be inadequate. The obvious choice therefore was the Fox and Hounds. At first Cassie and Gerald Godson were apprehensive about holding such a contentious happening on their premises, as by so doing it might offend anyone religious by nature. It was agreed therefore, the event must take place in the dining room behind closed doors and on a weekday evening. For even though the weather was still inhospitable and it was hardly likely there would be any strangers around to take offence, they opted to play safe, and in order to prevent any outsiders knowing the nature of the activity they would feign the dining room was in use for a private meeting regarding local issues, which to some extent was the truth.

On the evening of the séance, Stella helped Molly choose her outfit, for Ned had forbidden her to attempt climbing the stairs in order to rummage through her wardrobe. She had previously expressed her desire to wear a long floral gown which she had owned for many years, but finally bowed to pressure from the family who insisted that it would be impractical to wear a full length gown during the current weather conditions where the outside world was awash with slush and grime.

At half past seven Ned arrived to collect his mother, but to her absolute horror, he arrived with a wheelchair which he parked in the back porch.

"Ned, you surely don't expect me to go out in that," she spluttered in disgust. "I shall look like an invalid. Wherever did you get it from?"

"Oh, for heaven's sake, Mother, don't make such a fuss. I have it on loan from the Penwynton Hotel. Mary Cottingham suggested it when I saw her the other day and I think it's very kind and considerate of her. Furthermore, at present you *are* an invalid."

Molly scowled. "Why on earth does the Hotel have a wheelchair?"

"They keep it for emergencies."

"Ah, but I'm not an emergency, am I?" She shook her head and tutted. "You don't seem to realise, Ned that I'm very independent and more than capable of walking down the garden path to the car."

Ned looked heavenwards. "Mother, no-one knows more than me how independent you are. But as it happens I'm not taking the car, because if I do I won't be able to have a drink, will I? And I think on an occasion such as this I might require one."

"You mean I have to go all the way down the road in that?" said Molly, aghast.

Stella smiled sweetly. "Yes, but it's only to get you as far as the inn. Once there you can get out, walk, and sit at the table as you normally would. I don't expect anyone will even see you anyway as we're going down the road."

Molly sighed deeply. "Oh, alright then, I'll go in it if I must, but I insist on getting out of it well before we go inside, and I'm sure the Godsons wouldn't mind if you left it out of sight in the old toilet block."

To Molly's relief they arrived at the inn without being seen and Ned, as instructed, pushed the wheelchair into the old toilet block, no longer in use as a new extension, with modern indoor toilets, had

155

been added onto the back of the inn by the Withers family during their occupancy.

In the dining room the radiators had been turned down low, for Molly had asked beforehand that the room be neither too hot nor too cold. The curtains were drawn together and in the centre of the room, four tables had been pushed together to form a square, and around the square, twelve chairs were tucked. Ideally it should have been a circle, but that was out of the question at such short notice.

"Perfect," said Molly to Cassie who had asked if the room was satisfactory, "and if you'll light the twelve candles when everyone's here, then everything will be ready. I do hope we have enough people to form a circle."

"I think there may well be far more than the twelve we've allowed for," said Cassie. "Everyone's talking about it and they're expecting great things."

Molly groaned. "Oh dear, I've not done anything like this for donkey's years. I do hope I've not lost the knack."

With the aid of her stick, Molly left the dining room for the bar where Ned bought her a gin and tonic for Dutch courage. She would have liked a double, but Ned thought it unwise, as memories of a bungled séance from many years before flashed through his mind. It was common knowledge to all present back then, that his mother had been very drunk at the time, but to be fair to her, the same could be said for most witnesses that night, and Ned himself was certainly no exception.

The turnout for the séance was even higher than anticipated, hence, as Molly insisted the number of people sitting around the table be no more than twelve, it was decided all the men wishing to participate must put their names into a hat from which six be drawn, and then the same be done with the ladies, only in their case just five names as Molly was already one of the twelve. Those whose names were not selected, however, were not excluded, for it was agreed they should be able to witness any activity as standing spectators.

As instructed, Cassie lit the candles on the table shortly before the séance was due to take place and then once everyone was seated she switched off the lights, closed the door and returned to the bar. Molly felt very nervous, half afraid that nothing might happen and everyone would be disappointed, and half afraid that something would happen

156

which might cause panic and distress. Of the two options she was not sure which proffered the greatest fear.

"Thank you all for coming," she smiled, hoping apprehension was not detectable in her voice. "I hope you won't be disappointed, but please don't expect too much. Spirits are very temperamental and Elijah has been gone for a very long time, hence contact with him might be impossible. And as regards the two policemen, we don't even know that they have passed on, and for the sake of us all, I sincerely hope they have not. Are all of you around the table comfortable?" Eleven heads nodded. "Good, then if you're all ready, let's begin. All I ask is that you remain silent throughout: those standing as well as those of you around the table. Please don't whisper or make any noise that might disturb my concentration."

The collective rustle of shuffling feet from the spectators getting comfortable before things began to happen was the only sound other than the faint murmur of muffled voices emanating from the bar.

"Please join hands," said Molly, hoping no-one noticed her own hands were shaking.

Sid the sceptic, the expression on his face a cross between a smile and a smirk, eagerly took Molly's left hand and Betty's right. Betty, glad of the dim light, for it hid the terrified look she felt must be evident in her eyes, clasped her left hand with Ned's right. Ned, conscious of every slight sound, took the hand of Nettie Penrose. And Nettie, convinced the thuds of her thumping heart might disturb Molly's concentration, clasped hands with Larry Bingham. Larry, mentally noting everything so that he could report events faithfully to Candy, his wife, took Anne's hand. And Anne, noticing Molly's pale face, prayed the evening would not be too much for her elderly grandmother, as she reached out for the hand of Giles. The expression on the face of Giles told he was clearly enjoying every minute of what he hoped might be an extraordinary evening, and he squeezed Gertie's hand tightly as if to emphasise his delight. Gertie, took the hand of George, half wishing her name had not been drawn from the hat, and as George took the hand of Dorothy he recalled the weird events during the summer of 1953 and prayed, Daisy Rowe, the crazy aunt of his erstwhile girlfriend, Elsie Glazebrook, was not lurking on the astral plane or wherever it was that Molly might stumble across a spirit or two. Dorothy took George's hand with a feeling of unease, conscious that Molly might accidentally find the ghost of Frank's first wife, Sylvia. And finally, Pat Dickens took the unsteady hands of Dorothy on his right and Molly on his left.

"First," said Molly, once the circle was complete, "I shall try to make contact with Elijah." She cleared her throat, took a deep breath and closed her eyes. "Our beloved, Elijah Triggs, we bring you gifts from life to death. Commune with us, Elijah and move amongst us."

Inside the hushed dining room not a sound could be heard, even breathing was silent. Molly opened one eye and quickly glanced around the room for any sight of Elijah. Realising there was none she repeated her request.

As nothing continued to happen, Sid suppressed a desire to laugh. Anne thought about kicking the table leg to pretend Elijah was present but quickly decided it was a bad idea.

"Elijah has been gone from us too long," said Molly, sadly. "Instead I shall try and contact the policemen."

She closed her eyes and in turn repeated her plea, substituting the name of Elijah for each of the missing policeman. The room waited with bated breath, but again nothing happened.

Molly felt sick and wished she had refused the challenge of a séance. It was a silly thing to agree to after one hundred years, and as for the policemen, well, there was no evidence to even suggest they were dead. Molly sighed deeply; she could sense the feeling of disappointment emanating from every corner of the room. She closed her eyes tightly and began to repeat her request, but before her words were completed, her body temperature plummeted, her breathing quickened, her heart thumped loudly and she sensed a presence.

"Our beloved Elijah," Molly whispered, "we bring you gifts from life to death. Commune with us, Elijah and move amongst us."

The table shuddered. Anne's eyes darted around it convinced someone had done what she had contemplated. But all eyes were wide and staring; even Sid looked alarmed.

"Elijah, is it your presence we sense, here amongst us? Please tap once for yes, twice for no."

All remained quiet and then two muffled, distant taps broke the silence.

Betty hunched her back, convinced something or someone was behind her. Molly threw back her head.

"You answer no, you are not then Elijah?"

Two distinct taps echoed through the smoky atmosphere.

Sid frowned, where were the taps coming from? It was not the table and the floor was solid. He glanced around the room; it had to be the panelling. He smiled; Molly obviously had an accomplice in the room. It was not Ned because he was seated at the table, so it had to be Stella.

"If you are not Elijah, will you reveal your identity? Are you a man?" Again, two taps. "You are a woman then?" Two more taps followed by suppressed gasps of surprise from the bystanders.

Molly felt giddy and light-headed. "Are you a child?" She asked gently. One sharp tap sent shudders through the gathering.

Sid, who had been watching Stella, felt uneasy, Stella's hands were clasped and she had not moved, furthermore, Ian Ainsworth stood behind her so she could not reach the panelling without moving. Molly spoke again.

"Are you a little boy?" she asked.

Two soft taps.

"You are then a little girl?"

One sharp tap.

"Are you known to anyone in this room?"

There was a long pause and no taps, Molly was surprised.

"Did you live here at the inn?"

Two more taps.

"Did you live in the village?"

One loud tap.

Molly sighed, she had no idea who the girl might be and was unsure how to find out. Beneath her breath she quietly whispered, "I wonder how old you are and at what age you died."

All candles on the table began to flicker. "Twelve," said Molly. But as her voice trailed away the flames on seven of the candles grew smaller and went out.

"You are five," said Molly, watching as the smoke from the extinguished flames dispersed. "You are a little girl of five from Trengillion."

Ned and Sid simultaneously became aware that Betty's hands had gone from hot, to cold and clammy and her breathing was loud and irregular. Instinct caused Ned to glance behind her chair where something moved in the shadows. He cast his eyes back towards Betty. Her hair was moving but her head was perfectly still. Ned squeezed Betty's hand tightly, there was no response. He caught Molly's eye. She too was aware of Betty's delicate situation.

"Do you know Betty?" Molly gently asked.

Molly heard childlike sobbing. Ned heard it too. Betty's irregular breathing deepened, each breath interspersed with eerie high-pitched wheezing.

Molly alarmed, quickly withdrew her hands from the grasps of Sid and Pat to break the circle. "Thank you for joining us, spirit," she gabbled, "now please go in peace." She stood abruptly. "Quickly lights, and will someone please put out those damn candles."

With the room illuminated it was clear for all to see that Betty's face was grey and her eyes fixed into a terrified stare.

"Bet," Ned whispered, shaking her gently. "Bet, are you alright?"

"She, she, touched my hair," Betty whispered, "that little girl Molly spoke to; she touched my hair and stroked my face."

Sid laughed. "Oh, come on, Betty, it was your imagination. I was right beside you and there was definitely no-one there. I know that because I kept my eyes well and truly open."

"How can you say that, Sid, when we all heard tapping," Gertie snapped. She turned to Betty. "Would you like a brandy, Bet, you're still awfully pale?"

"No thank you, I'll be alright, but I think I'd like a bit of fresh air if someone will go outside with me, I don't fancy going on my own."

"I'll go with you," said Gertie, taking Betty's arm.

As the two women departed, others also left the dining room for the bar. Molly, still shaken, remained in her chair.

"Well, what do you think that was all about?" Ned asked. "There's no way Betty was putting on an act, she genuinely was scared stiff and what's more, I witnessed something touching her hair."

"You saw the little girl's ghost, Dad." whispered Anne. "Oh dear, I feel quite weak."

Rose shuddered and quickly glanced over her shoulder. "What did she look like, Ned? What sort of clothing was she wearing?"

Ned shook his head. "Regrettably, I didn't see her; I just saw Betty's hair being ruffled and it was obvious to me there was some sort of presence moving around behind her."

Anne sat down before her legs gave way. "This is really spooky. Have you any idea who the little girl might be, Grandma?"

Molly shook her head. "Sadly I know nothing more than anyone else and it'll be impossible to find out more with no name. We don't even know from which era she came. I should like to have another bash but I don't think that would be advisable for a while, besides, I'm mentally and emotionally drained."

"I bet you are," sympathised Ned, pulling back her chair. "Come on, let's go in the bar to join the others, it'll be interesting to hear what they have to say. Besides, it's damn freezing in here now that everyone's gone."

"Humph, I'm not sure I want to hear any more from doubting Sid," said Anne, picking up Molly's handbag. "I wanted to punch him earlier."

Stella laughed. "Don't mind Sid, Anne, he's just Sid. Remember how he poured scorn on our New Year's Eve ghost stories? Why, I don't think he'd believe in a ghost even if one sat by his side telling of his or her past life."

Back in the bar, Betty having recovered from her fright, found herself the centre of attention as she reiterated her experience in a surprisingly calm manner.

"Thank goodness she's recovered so quickly," said Molly, rummaging through her handbag. "I've seen people in similar circumstances that have been very badly affected and some even who've never been the same again. Damn it! Have you seen my cigarettes, Ned? I'm sure I put them in my handbag or maybe it was my coat pocket. Have a look please, love, it's hanging on the coat rack."

Ned returned, shaking his head. "Nothing there other than your lighter and a couple of crumpled hankies, that is. You must have left them at home."

"No, if the lighter's there then the cigarettes should be too because I always keep them together." She lowered her voice. "I know, they must have fallen out of my pocket into that beastly chair thingy, Ned. Pop out and have a look please, but don't let anyone see you."

"I'll go," giggled Rose, amused by Ned's exasperated expression, "it's a bit stuffy in here so I'll appreciate the fresh air."

"Fresh air," scoffed George, "it's bloody freezing out there; you'll need your coat or you'll die from hypothermia."

"Don't be daft, I'm not planning to linger, I'll be back in two ticks, you see."

The night air was cold and overhead the clear, dark sky was mottled with millions of twinkling stars. Rose paused briefly to admire the spectacle and then with folded arms walked briskly towards the old toilet block. Inside she switched on the light and approached the wheelchair with haste for the bitter night air was rapidly biting at her gloveless fingers and causing her teeth to chatter.

To the relief of Rose the cigarette packet lay tucked in the side of the chair; she retrieved it, switched off the light, left the building and closed the door. As she crossed the cobbles, a whisper, like a voice in the shadows caused her to pause. She stood still and listened for further mutterings, but all was silent, except for the murmur of distant waves tumbling onto the shore. Thinking it must have been her imagination playing tricks, Rose proceeded towards the door of the inn, but before she reached it something else caused her to turn, a shuffling noise, like dragging feet. Rose cast her eyes quickly in the direction of the noise but again there was nothing or no-one to be seen. She shivered, recalling the little girl in the séance and without wishing to witness any further activity dashed back inside the inn.

When Molly was ready to leave, Ned went to the old toilet block for the wheelchair but to his astonishment it was not there. He searched around stacked boxes and old furniture stored in the building assuming Gerald had moved it for some reason, but the chair was nowhere to be found. Completely dumbfounded, Ned returned to the inn and told those still present.

Rose frowned. "But it was there when I went out for Molly's fags and that was only a short while back."

George tutted. "Oh, for God's sake, this is getting daft. First Elijah and his cart, then the coppers and their car. The other day it was poor Jim's new bike and now a wheelchair, of all things, has gone AWOL. When is this disappearing phase going to end?"

"I expect the ghost-child took it," said Sid, flippantly, slipping on his sheepskin jacket. "She's probably knocking on a bit now if she's been dead for donkey's years and thought it'd help her get home quicker."

"Don't be such a prat, Sid. Ghosts don't age," snapped Ned.

Sid's eyes twinkled as he fastened his leather buttons. "Sez who?"

"I don't reckon it's got anything to do with the other missing things," said Gertie, thoughtfully, "because it hasn't disappeared near the chapel. What's more there's hardly any snow left now, and it seems to have been that that triggered off all these weird happenings."

"It must be there," said George, heading towards the door. "I'm not doubting you, Ned, but I'm going to take a look myself."

George returned shortly after as baffled as Ned.

Stella looked worried. "How are we going to explain this to the Cottinghams? They'll think us very careless."

Ned scratched his head. "I don't know, at the moment I'm more concerned with how we're going to get Mum home. She can't walk and we've all been drinking."

"It's only up the road so let's risk it," said Sid, pulling on a pair of gloves. "You all wait here and I'll go and get my car."

"No, Sid, it's not worth it, the police have been around a lot lately," said Landlord, Gerald, "and I'm sure they'd love to nick someone from Trengillion seeing as they seem to regard us all with suspicion. I suggest Molly stays here tonight, she can have our room on the ground floor and Cass and I can go upstairs. She'll be alright; we'll make sure of that."

"Of course, it's the obvious answer," Cassie agreed.

"But I don't want to be a nuisance," said Molly. "Won't it be putting you about?"

"No, not this time of year," said Cassie, offering her arm to escort her impromptu guest. "August might have been difficult, but not January."

"Would you be a dear and pop home for my nightie, Ned, if I'm going to stay the night I might as well be comfortable. Get me my nice pink one, please. You should find it in the airing cupboard all freshly laundered."

Ned did as instructed whilst Cassie walked Molly from the bar and down the passage to the bedroom. "It'll make a change for you staying here, won't it? Although there's not much of a view from the window; only the back courtyard."

"I have stayed here before," smiled Molly, as tears prickled her eyes. "This is where I met the major, you see. We were both staying here at the time as guests, but it was all a long time ago. A very long time ago."

CHAPTER TWENTY ONE

Elizabeth, who had not attended the séance because of a tickly cough was, in spite of trying hard to keep herself awake with numerous mugs of coffee, fast asleep when Greg arrived home, therefore it was seven o' clock the following morning before she learned what had taken place at the inn. Elizabeth listened to Greg's summary of the evening with interest, but asked no questions as she intended to save them for her grandmother.

After Greg had gone to work and she had dropped off Tally and Wills at school, she called in at Rose Cottage where Molly was making up the fire having just been driven home by Cassie Godson.

"Oh, Grandma, please let me do that for you, you're putting a lot of pressure on your ankle kneeling like that."

Molly smiled. "Since it's you, I'll do as I'm told, but had it been your dad bossing me about I'd be as stubborn as a mule and insist on doing it myself."

Elizabeth grinned. "I know what you mean. Dad seems to have that effect on me too, but I just think it's his didactic school teaching ways."

Molly stood with a helping hand from her granddaughter. "I expect you want to know what happened last night," she grinned, taking a seat on the settee.

"Well, yes. I've heard a little of it from Greg's point of view, but I'm sure your analysis would be far more enlightening."

Molly raised her eyebrows. "I daresay, but before I begin please tell me what Greg made of it?"

"He wasn't convinced," said Elizabeth, kneeling in front of the fireplace and laying coal on Molly's neatly piled kindling wood. "He said something wasn't right and he wouldn't be at all surprised if Betty didn't just let her imagination run away with her. Having said that, he's a bit miffed by the tapping and has no idea how that might have manifested itself."

Molly shook her head. "No, poor Betty didn't over react; your dad saw her hair moving and sensed something behind her. He was sitting next to her, you see, holding her hand in fact. He said she was in a genuine state of shock."

Elizabeth frowned. "So, who do you think the little girl was? I don't know of any children that have died in Trengillion during my lifetime."

"And I don't recall any since I've been here either. If it wasn't for this wretched ankle, I'd have been foraging through the churchyard at daybreak this morning looking for inspiration."

"Now that is a good idea," said Elizabeth, setting light to screwed up newspaper beneath the kindling wood. "I think when I leave here I'll go and call for Anne and then we can both have a good old nose round the graveyard on your behalf. The fresh air will do me good anyway because I think I've caught the cold everyone's talking about."

"Or the flu."

Elizabeth shook her head. "No, it's not the flu, I just have a tickly cough and a bunged up nose."

Molly leaned back on the settee and sighed deeply. "Oh, to be young again. Make the most of every day, Liz, because before you know it you'll be a useless, dithering old wreck like me."

"Now, now, Grandma," said Elizabeth, watching the wood crackle and smoke amidst the flames rapidly devouring the newspaper in the fireplace, "I won't let you undervalue yourself so; there's lots more life in you yet, so enough is enough."

Molly sat up straight. "Elizabeth Castor-Hunt," she bellowed, flabbergasted, "you're beginning to sound like your father."

Elizabeth found Anne sitting at the kitchen table, both cheeks flushed, mending the hem of Ollie's school trousers. She looked up as her sister entered the room. "I didn't hear you knock. Did John let you in?"

"Yes, I got to the door just as he was going out so I didn't need to knock." Elizabeth sat down at the table. "Are you alright? You look a bit grumpy."

"Yes, I'm fine, but where have you been? I've been trying to ring you all morning."

"I went to see Grandma after the children had gone to school. I thought I might bump into you but obviously didn't."

Anne looked up from her sewing. "John took Ollie and Jess to school this morning. He and Steve are beginning a new job today, you see, but they weren't able to make a start first thing because the blocks hadn't been delivered, but they have now. That's why John was only just leaving when you got here."

"I see, and I expect you were trying to ring me for the same reason I went to see Grandma."

Anne half-smiled. "Hmm and so you obviously know all about last night, but I guess you knew quite a bit anyway with Greg having been there too." She stopped sewing. "It was a funny old do, Liz, and I'm not sure that I can make much sense of it."

"Really? It seems pretty cut and dried to me, and so when you've finished your sewing perhaps you'd like to come with me to the churchyard to find the little girl's grave."

"What! It'll be like looking for a needle in a haystack, we don't know her name, when she died or even if she really existed. Believe me, it'd be a right wild goose chase."

"Does that mean you don't want to come then?" asked Elizabeth, her mouth upside-down.

Anne looked up. "I hate sewing, Liz, especially mending; you should know that, it always puts me in a bad mood. I just don't seem able to make a neat job."

"So you are grumpy. I knew it."

Anne scowled but said nothing

Elizabeth leaned across the table. "If I finish your mending, will you come with me then, please, sister dearest?"

"If you finish my mending I'll not only go with you but I'll make you a coffee and cut you a big fat slice of chocolate cake."

Elizabeth took Ollie's trousers from her sister's hands. "You're on," she said, standing to take off her coat and hang it on the back of her chair, "but don't make the slice too big and fat because I put on six beastly pounds over Christmas and I've not managed to shift even one yet."

The church tower looked bleak beneath the grey sky and the leafless trees stood lifeless and forlorn. The gravel path, however, cleaned and revitalised by the snow, crunched beneath the feet of the sisters as they made their way towards the church.

"So where do we start?" Anne asked, casting her eyes over the rows of graves.

"Well, obviously not in the new bit, that would be a waste of time. Why don't you start at this end and I'll start at the other and we'll meet in the middle somewhere. It shouldn't take long if we just look for the words *Aged 5*."

Anne nodded. "And *daughter* I suppose. After all she must have belonged to someone."

Anne began her search in the far corner near to the overgrown spot where Steve's father, Denzil, lay, but she thought it unlikely the little girl could be in that area as the graves were from the 1950s, hence her grandmother and other Trengillion residents, would be familiar with a child losing her life in that era.

Elizabeth began her search on the other side of the church where many graves were without memorial stones but those with them were dated in the 1700s. Elizabeth read each one with interest and built up images in her mind of the people from long ago who would have lived and worked in Trengillion when mining was big business in Cornwall.

"Any luck?" Anne called when her search reached the path and her sister was within earshot.

Elizabeth shook her head. "Sadly no, the only children I have come across are under the age of five, poor little mites. Life must have been very harsh back then."

"Which century are you in then? I'm in the present and currently the 1920s."

"Oh, I'm way further back in the eighteenth century, and the one I'm looking at right now is for a poor woman who passed away in 1752. Poor soul was only twenty and died of Scarlet Fever."

Anne crossed to her sister's side. "I don't think we'll ever find her, not without a name and she may not have a memorial stone anyway. Why don't we call it a day and come back when the weather is a little more hospitable. It looks very much like rain to me and you have a rotten cold."

Elizabeth sighed. "I'm inclined to agree. The grass is very wet and these tombstones are rather depressing even though they are really interesting."

Anne glanced in the direction of the Old Vicarage. "I was just thinking, Liz. I know it sounds daft, but could Grandma's little girl possibly be the child who you thought you heard singing *I had a Little Nut Tree* a while back? I mean, if she came from Trengillion it could well be her."

"The same idea had crossed my mind, but I don't even know that it was a girl. It could easily have been a boy." She laughed. "Or maybe just the wind."

Anne shuddered. "Oh dear, I really hope it was the wind otherwise her ghost might still be inside the Vicarage. That's creepy and not a very nice thought even if she is or was only a child."

Elizabeth tilted her head to one side. "Have you ever heard any unfamiliar noises?"

Anne shook her head. "No, I'm glad to say I haven't, and to be honest I really thought you must have been mistaken when you babysat the other evening, but after last night's bizarre happening, suddenly I'm not so sure and it's a little unnerving."

Elizabeth smiled. "Hmm, and sadly, it's unlikely we'll ever know for sure."

Anne glanced up at the church clock. "We've been here for nearly an hour now. Fancy coming back to the Vicarage for another coffee?"

"Yeah alright and I think I'd like another piece of your chocolate cake, calories and all."

CHAPTER TWENTY TWO

Janet Ainsworth was glad the children had returned to school for it meant she would have more time to dedicate to her current obsession, looking for the missing policemen. Her misjudged sighting of the bank robber had created a rub between herself and Ian, a situation which she was keen to rectify. She considered, therefore, that if she could locate the whereabouts of the two policemen, who had to be somewhere in West Cornwall, it would enhance her standing, not only in his eyes, but with the rest of the village also, for she was fully aware that people spoke about her behind her back and children whispered her name loudly behind their small hands. But she had to be cautious, Ian was keen to get along with the locals; they were after all, potential customers.

Janet considered whether or not it was possible for someone in Trengillion to have taken the policemen hostage. She knew the notion was a bit far-fetched, but the idea appealed to her sense of adventure. With pen in hand, she sat down and flippantly made a list of likely suspects, who in reality, she had to confess, were females to whom she had taken an instant dislike. Top of the list was Gertie Collins, whom Janet regarded as the dumpy middle aged woman with crooked teeth who was after her husband. The next name was Cassie Godson, landlady of the Fox and Hounds. Cassie was followed by Jane Williams who ran a ludicrously named café on the beach. Janet frowned. Her husband, Ian, had on several occasions expressed his admiration of the last two women saying he'd been told they were hard working achievers, but she thought his admiration might be a cover up for them having taken his fancy. Furthermore, Jane was to be mistrusted because she was the girlfriend of one of the dreadful farmers who had laughed at her beloved Glenda.

Janet tapped her teeth with the end of her pen. There was also some old biddy in the village called Molly whom she had not yet encountered but who was responsible for the ridiculous séance everyone was talking about. Janet laughed, even she as a newcomer could have told the silly locals that it was not possible to contact the spirits of people who were very much alive, and as for the over hyped twaddle about some illiterate farm worker called Elijah; she could not believe any human being could be so gullible in the twentieth century.

As Janet laid the fire ready to light on her return home, she thought about the little girl who Ian claimed had ruffled someone's hair the previous night. She laughed again. That claim was even more ridiculous than the other nonsense, and as for the tapping, it was obviously done by the devious Cassie Godson listening in the room above with a glass to her ear so that she knew when to tap on the floorboards.

Janet went into the kitchen to wash her hands. "In fact the longer I live here, the more convinced I am that this village is populated with eccentrics and oddities," she chuntered. "Ghosts indeed, they'll be looking for witches next."

Janet returned to the living room and looked at the names on her list. She laughed; to incriminate the three women was absurd but it made her feel better to fantasise they might be up to no good and she had on a couple of occasions seen them furtively chatting together. She sat down on the sofa, twiddled her fingers and sighed. It was all very well mulling over the names of possible villains but for what reason might someone have for abducting the two officers in the first place unless of course, it was to demand ransom money? She shook her head. It didn't make sense; if the officers were being held hostage somewhere, then surely their captors would have wasted no time before demanding ransom money; therefore, unless the police were keeping quiet on the subject, to date no such demand had been made. She flicked a piece of fluff from the knee of her jeans. Another possibility was the officers were abducted in order to receive the reward money, after all it was a substantial amount. In which case the kidnappers might intend, when they felt the time to be right, to fabricate a story about their finding of the officers which would make them eligible for the reward. Janet nodded. Her reasoning for the second option was more feasible than the first; furthermore, if Cassie Godson or Jane Williams were in any way involved, it would be wonderful publicity for the pub and the café.

She rose, crossed to the table and from the notebook tore out the page on which the three names were written. With a snigger she screwed up the paper and tossed it onto the unlit fire. She glanced at the watch; time to make a move; the children were having dinner at school and so she was free to pursue her investigation until three o'clock.

Janet put on her warm coat and fleecy lined boots, placed a dainty dish of food beside Glenda's basket and told her she must stay at home because her mission might be hindered by the poodle's presence. She then locked the door of the Old Police House and walked through the village towards the Ebenezer Chapel, for she considered that if that was where radio contact with the police was last heard, then that was obviously the first place to look.

When she arrived at the cross roads she looked in all directions. To carry straight on would lead to the main road to Helston. The left hand turn led to Polquillick and the road to her right, was a very narrow lane, which according to a map she had studied, was a dead end. She paused; the dead end lane was the obvious one to investigate, for if there were no reason for the police to go down there in the first place, then no-one would have checked it out. She turned down the lane which wound and twisted for half a mile down a steep hill. At the bottom, as she expected, it came to an abrupt end by a disintegrating gate which led into a yard where the remains of a tumbledown house stood alongside the stream which ran into the sea.

Janet walked for what seemed like miles around the site of the old house and the surrounding area. Eventually she decided the spot was too flat and devoid of trees and shrubs to provide a suitable hiding place for anything and certainly not something as large as a police car. Disappointed, she retraced her steps and returned to Trengillion.

By the time she reached the village she was frozen to the marrow and in desperate need of a drink and something hot to eat before she picked up the children from school. She looked at her watch, it was half past one and so she had plenty of time to reach the inn and buy a pasty before they closed.

The warmth from the open fire was very welcome as she entered the bar, but Janet's delight faded when she observed several men eying her as she waited to order her pasty. She glared angrily, convinced they were pointing at her, no doubt saying she was the batty woman who had informed the police that a bank robber look-alike was in the village. Janet tossed her head ordered her pasty and waited for Cassie to warm it in the microwave.

On a stool, with one elbow resting on the bar, sat a man whom Janet had seen once or twice before. She secretly called him Rudolph on account of his glowing red nose. He was talking to a man who Janet knew was Harry Richardson, a retired builder, for it was from him they had bought the Old Police House. The men were talking about someone who had vanished in the village many years before; someone called Jane. Janet edged a little closer, removed her knitted hat and pushed away a strand of hair covering her ear.

"Well, at least they won't find the coppers at the Broomstick like they did poor old Jane," muttered Rudolph.

"Why not?" asked Harry, "I mean, I know they'll not be there of course, but why are you so convinced."

"Well, nobody's likely to have taken a boat round there in a bloody blizzard, are they? Not without anyone seeing them, and it would've been far too dangerous anyway."

"Ah, but they could've gone through the tunnel," said Harry, with a laugh. "Not that it'd be very easy because I took the old ladder away years ago."

"Tunnel?" queried Rudolph, his face wrinkled in confusion.

"Oh, for heaven's sake, Albert, surely you've not forgotten the old tunnel that runs from the stables. We all had a poke around down there after Ned Stanley found it. Having said that, he were only a lad then and he's close to retiring now, so it must be a lot longer ago than I'd care to remember."

"One pasty," smiled Cassie, handing the warm paper bag to Janet.

"What, oh...oh, thank you," she mumbled, "thank you."

"No trouble, it's nice to see you in here. We often see your charming husband. He's a lovely man, so amicable and friendly."

Janet scowled. She was right in her assumption. Cassie Godson was after Ian. Janet left the inn without uttering another word.

CHAPTER TWENTY THREE

Ian Ainsworth drove home from work, singing along with the car radio and in a very happy frame of mind. He was settling in well at the new practice; he liked his partner, Ken, enormously, and all the attractive girls on reception and the dental nurses were fantastically efficient and friendly.

On arriving home he found the children sitting around the table in the dining room playing Ludo and Janet across the hallway in the lounge, curled up on the settee poring over a map of Trengillion, looking for the stables that housed the tunnel. She forced a smile as he peeped around the door. "Your dinner's in the oven. I hope it's not dried up too much."

"Okay, it smells good anyway. What is it?"

"Liver and onion."

Behind the door Ian scowled. Janet knew he was not partial to liver and onions.

"Why are you looking at the map?" he cheerfully asked, on entering the lounge with his dinner on a tray.

"No real reason, just thought I'd familiarise myself with the village and the surrounding area. I was also wondering if there were any stables around here. I thought the girls might like to take up horse riding when the weather improves."

Ian frowned. "Do you think so? I mean, have you asked them? I can't say that I've ever heard them express a desire for riding ponies and you've never been the horsey type either."

"No, but then they're not me, are they? And I'm sure they'd love a few lessons, after all it's what country folk do, isn't it? Anyway, do you know of any stables around here?"

Ian shrugged his shoulders. "No, can't say as I do. Cass and Gerald have horses of course, but I don't know if they give lessons or anything like that. I mean, I shouldn't think so as they're both far too busy running the inn."

"Humph," Janet grunted, "I suppose so,"

"I'll ask them if you like, I'm popping over there later."

"What again? You were in there last night and the night before," Janet snapped, flinging the map onto the floor. "What's the fascination?"

"I just like the company," he grinned, recalling the inn's friendly atmosphere. "It's also the ideal place to get to know everyone. We must look into babysitters so that you can come over with me some time. Anyway, I'm going tonight because Sid has asked me to join the darts team. The matches don't start until after Easter but I need to get in lots of practice and Monday is their practice night, so it should be a bit of fun."

"Who's Sid?"

"Sid Reynolds, he used to work on a local newspaper. You've probably not met him but you'll know his wife because she teaches at the school."

"Oh, yes, I know who you mean."

"Anyway, Sid's captain of the darts team and I'm really thrilled that he's asked me to join them."

"Does Cass play?" Janet asked through gritted teeth.

"What! Of course not, it's a men's team," Ian laughed, oblivious of the acerbic tone his wife used to utter the name of the inn's landlady.

As soon as Ian left for the inn, Janet, with the knowledge the Godsons had horses, sweetly asked her children if they knew where they might be kept. To her delight they did, for their school teacher, Mrs Reynolds, had mentioned when they had returned to school after the snow, how important it was to feed animals in the winter. This had caused Jess Collins to put up her hand to say she and her brother Ollie had helped their mum feed the horses for Mrs Godson in the stables near the Old Vicarage when it was snowy. Janet was delighted.

On her way home from the post office the following morning, with the daily newspapers the Godsons always placed in the bar for their patrons to read, Cassie met Gertie discussing with Jane, a delicious cake recipe with huge potential for inclusion on the Pickled

Egg's menu. Cassie greeted the ladies and joined in the chat, and as they spoke, Janet Ainsworth left the Old Police House armed with torch and a kitchen knife in the pocket of her coat.

As Janet walked past the three ladies, on her way through the village towards the lane leading to the stables, she felt her face redden. For to consider the female trio capable of serious crime seemed even more ludicrous when she encountered them face to face. She didn't acknowledge their presence even though they all smiled, instead she walked on, head held high, down the lane and into the field beyond, which she was surprised to discover was a recreational ground.

In the next field, just visible over the top of a wall, was the slate roof of a single storey building. Janet hurried on up the incline of the field. At the top she stopped. The building was obviously a stable, for in the paddock where it was situated, two horses ate hay scattered on the short grass. As she neared the gate they trotted towards her. She froze, they were much bigger than she had expected and their teeth were enormous. Janet decided that if she stood perfectly still they might go away and leave her alone. She was right. When they realised she had nothing for them they wandered back off into the middle of the field and continued to eat the hay.

With a cautious glance over her shoulder, Janet climbed the gate and jumped down on the other side; the horses ignored her and she was grateful. With haste she ran into the stables and closed the bottom half of the door to keep the animals out.

Pleased to be safe, she heaved a sigh of relief, and assuming the entrance to the tunnel would be through a trap door on the stable floor, she grabbed a rake leaning on the wall and prepared to push aside the scattered straw. But then suddenly, she heard a noise and the sound of heavy breathing; with heart in mouth she slowly turned around. In the corner was another horse, rising from the straw behind a wooden partition. Janet watched as he rose to his full height. He was huge.

"Nice horsey," she squeaked dropping the rake and backing away into a corner. "Nice horsey, oh, please don't hurt me."

The horse moved forward. Janet screamed in panic. Her head began to spin and she felt sick. In her ears she heard a whooshing sound; her vision blurred and the horse's head began to rotate. And then she fell, thud, onto the straw, away in a dead faint.

At half past eleven, Sid Reynolds entered the side door of the Fox and Hounds and hung up his sheepskin jacket on the coat rack; he then went into the bar and prepared to open up the inn for the lunchtime session. Tuesday was the Godsons' day off and Sid ran the bar for them at lunchtime and again in the evening, along with any other days when they needed a helping hand. On Tuesday mornings therefore, Gerald unwillingly tackled paperwork and Cassie did whatever she conceded needed doing.

On the Tuesday morning in question, once Gerald was settled in front of his desk, Cassie, as prearranged earlier that morning, met up with her friends, Gertie and Jane, to take the horses for a run. Cassie and Gerald were always grateful to villagers who helped take out the horses, for sadly Gerald could seldom spare the time.

The Godsons had three horses, one each, and another belonging to their daughter, Claire, who was in the Royal Navy and posted in Yeovil. Originally they had had four, but their other daughter, Clarissa, had taken her horse, Chestnut, to her new home in Kidderminster when she had married.

Janet came round from her faint, slumped in a heap and lying on her side. Confused, she opened her eyes; her vision was blurred, and through a muzzy haze she thought she could hear muffled voices whispering. Momentarily forgetting where she was, she reached out her hand and realised she was lying on straw. She blinked to adjust her eyes to the dim light. To her dismay, six feet, wearing boots, stood nearby and they were closing in. Before she had time to speak someone knelt by her side and gently pushed a strand of hair from her face.

"Are you alright?" asked Cassie Godson. "You're as white as a sheet. What on earth happened?"

Janet groaned as memories came flooding back. What ever could she say? She had never felt such a fool in her thirty eight years.

"I, um…I…um," to the surprise of the three women, Janet burst into tears. "The horse scared me," she sobbed, "I didn't know you had three. I'm sorry, I know I'm trespassing, but please don't tell Ian, he'll be so cross."

She sat up and attempted to stand, but her head began to spin again, partly through fear of the horse and partly through fear of her predicament.

"Here, grab my arm," said Cassie, kindly, "then we'll go outside, I think you need a bit of fresh air to get some colour back into your cheeks."

Janet obeyed and did feel better once outside, but when she looked at the three women it was clear that Gertie looked decidedly agitated. She was not surprised therefore when Gertie asked: "I have to know why you were in the stables if you don't like horses? It doesn't make sense."

Janet rapidly considered her options. Should she tell the truth, quickly think up a plausible story, or take the easiest way out and leg-it?

Cassie was still holding her arm, hence to run would be difficult. Anxiety prevented her brain to think straight, hence to invent a story was impossible. She sighed, knowing only the truth would suffice.

"I, I was looking for the tunnel. I heard Rudolph mention it when I was waiting for my pasty yesterday lunchtime, but the horse scared me before I'd had a chance to look for it. I must have fainted. I'm ever so sorry."

"Tunnel," spluttered Cassie.

"Rudolph," queried Gertie.

Jane laughed.

"But what's all this about a tunnel? Cassie asked, looking at Trengillion's two native women.

"Ah, the tunnel, it leads to the Witches Broomstick," giggled Gertie, "surely you know about it, after all it's on your land."

"I've no idea what you're talking about," said Cassie, shaking her head. "No-one's ever mentioned a tunnel to me and I've swept the floor hundreds of times. So where is it then?"

"Come with me and I'll show you."

The four women went back inside the stables where Gertie pointed to the back wall. "It's up there. There's a trap door on top of the wall, but of course you can't see it. There used to be a ladder in here, but Harry Richardson took it away years ago."

"You're joking," smiled Cassie, "how can there possibly be a tunnel inside a wall? It'd be too narrow for anyone to get down."

"There's a dead man at the back and so the tunnel goes straight into that, then it goes off down the hill towards the coast."

"A dead man," gasped Janet, finally finding her voice. "Whatever do you mean by that?"

"Not what it suggests. Come on and I'll show you."

Outside, Gertie led the other three women around the back of the stables. "See the back wall is built into the bank which nearly comes up to the roof, so when you're in the tunnel you're in the bank not the wall. A wall like that which acts to restrain the earth as well as form the back of a building is called a dead man."

"I wonder why," mused Cassie.

"No idea," Gertie replied, "and I only know because our John's a builder."

"Have you ever been inside it?" Jane asked. "Mum always told us to keep away from here when we were children and not to ask questions."

Gertie nodded. "Yes, Jane, I have. In fact I went in there with your mum back in 1952 when we first knew of it and the reason Betty, your mum, would never talk about it was because we knew of two girls who had died as a result of ending up in there. One was called Jane, your dad and mum named you after her. She was our friend, you see, but I don't really want to talk about it now even though it was a very long time ago."

"Who was the other girl?" Cassie asked.

"She was a holiday maker staying at the inn, so I knew her too because I was a waitress there then. Her name was Rosemary Howard. Poor kid, she was really sweet."

"I was going to suggest finding a ladder and taking a peep inside but I don't think I want to now," said Cassie.

"Me neither," Jane agreed. "I'd far rather we took out the horses, after all that's what we're here for."

"And I must be getting home," said Janet, her head spinning with information received.

"You sure you're okay now?" Cassie asked.

"Yes, thanks, I'm fine."

"Just one more thing," said Gertie, as Janet turned to leave. "Who on earth is Rudolph?"

CHAPTER TWENTY FOUR

Every day, weather permitting, Sam and Charlie Bingham took their dog, Copper, for a walk. Usually during the short days of winter when it was dark by half past four, they didn't go far, but now the nights were beginning to draw out a little it was still possible to see quite well past five o'clock, especially if the day had been bright and sunny. On one such day as they were about to take the usual route down the lane between their primary school and the Old School House, Charlie paused and nodded to the road ahead leading out of the village.

"Let's go this way and up as far as the old chapel, Sam, then we can see if old man Albert's dead snowmen have melted yet. If they have we can nick their hats."

Sam scowled. "But what do we want a couple of smelly old helmets for? They'll be all wet and soggy. Anyway, if we nick 'em people might think it was us who built the snowmen in the first place."

"Oh, don't be such a spoil sport. Come on, it's boring going the same way every day. Anyway, I bet the snowmen are still there cos ours hasn't gone completely yet and the helmets won't be soggy, dumbo, cos they're made of plastic."

Sam looked at his watch. "Alright, but we mustn't be too long, else Mum will start to worry; you know what she's like."

The two boys walked speedily along the road with Copper running and jumping close at their heels as if to show his approval of a different route. At the crossroads all three stopped; they had passed the chapel frequently in their dad's car and had never so much as given it a second glance, but now standing there before them in the fading light it looked rather sinister, almost threatening, although neither boy would admit to any feeling of intimidation.

Sam bent down to pick up a stick from the grass verge. "Come on, let's go for a run in that wasteland behind the chapel and give Copper some real exercise. I can't be bothered to see if there's anything left of the snowmen."

Sam ran off with Copper at his heels, Charlie followed, and when the chapel was a good distance behind, Sam threw the stick for Copper to retrieve.

"Humph, you're useless at throwing," said Charlie, mockingly, as the stick dropped just a few feet away, "you'll never make the junior cricket team. Here, let me have a go."

Sam picked up the stick and handed it to Charlie who hurled it three times the distance of his younger brother. Both watched as Copper ran after it, tail wagging, barking with delight. And then suddenly, he stopped. They heard a splash and Copper disappeared from view.

"Blummin' eck," shouted Charlie. "Where's the crazy dog gone?"

Fearing the worst, the boys ran towards the spot where Copper had vanished. Both were shocked, yet relieved, when they saw him frantically swimming through green slimy water towards the stick floating on the surface.

"I didn't know there was a pond here," said Charlie, scratching his head. "You can't see it from the road."

"You can't see it much from here either; it doesn't show up hidden among the grass."

Suddenly, Sam's face turned very pale.

"What's wrong?" Charlie asked. "You seen a ghost or summat."

"Don't joke about things like that cos I'm just thinking that this must be where the old farmer bloke fell in."

Charlie watched as Copper reached the stick. "What you talking about?"

Sam scowled. "For God's sake, Charlie, you must know who I mean; we heard Mum and Dad talking about him after the New Year's Eve party at the Vicarage. They think he either fell down a mine or into some water, so this must be the water, cos they said it was by the chapel."

Charlie laughed. "What! You mean Elijah Triggs! You idiot, surely you don't believe that old rubbish. I bet someone made it up at the party cos they didn't know any real ghost stories; you know what grown-ups are like." He turned to face the water. "Come on, Copper, it's time we went home, it'll be dark soon and I'm starving."

Copper stopped paddling and stood perfectly still, his head tilted to one side and all four paws resting on the surface of the water.

Sam's frowned. "Hey, how can he stay afloat if he's not swimming? I'd sink if I did that."

"I dunno," Charlie conceded. "I'd sink too. Hey, come back here, Copper."

But Copper remained where he rested, oblivious of the fact his buoyancy mystified his young owners.

"Hey, that's really spooky," Sam whispered, "he shouldn't be able to do that, it's not normal."

Both boys called to Copper repeatedly, but the dog remained still.

"Perhaps cos it's near the chapel it's holy water," whispered Sam. "You know, like what Jesus walked on. Remember, Mrs Reynolds told us that story."

"Don't be daft, it was Jesus who was holy, not the water. Anyway, Jesus didn't live in Trengillion and the water was the Sea of Galilee, not a tiny old pond."

"Yes, but…"

"Shut up, Sam," snapped Charlie, removing his shoes and socks. "It's no good, I'm gonna have to go and get him. Stupid dog!"

"But you can't go in there, it's filthy and Mum'll go berserk."

"I've got no choice, have I?" said Charlie, unzipping his coat. "Look at the sky, it's getting dark, so I've gotta get the daft dog and quick."

Charlie threw his coat onto the grass beside his shoes and slowly waded into the water. "Christ it's bloody freezing," he shouted, "and it stinks."

Sam watched from the side, biting his nails. He knew Charlie was a good swimmer, but that was in a pool of clean water or the sea, whereas the pond looked decidedly dicey - dirty to say the least and goodness only knew how deep it might be. Nevertheless, in spite of his young brother's misgivings, Charlie's swim was successful and as he approached Copper he reached out to seize the disobedient dog's collar. But then his legs hit something beneath the surface of the water, and he realised whatever it was; Copper was standing on it, and not floating as they had both believed. Charlie laughed through chattering teeth, relieved that nothing ominous had happened to Copper. However, with curiosity roused he felt around the object to try and establish its shape. It seemed to be solid and curved. Intrigued he held his breath and looked beneath the water. To his horror it was a wheel, a large wooden wheel. Charlie sprang up to the surface, grabbed Copper firmly by his collar and swam to the edge of the water gasping and screaming.

"Copper was standing on a wheel," he panted. "A bloody great wheel. You were right, Sam and this must be where old Elijah ended up and down there's what's left of his cart."

Hastily, Charlie put on his shoes, socks and coat. "Come on, let's get out of here; this place is giving me the creeps."

Sam giggled. "You cowardy-custard, it's only a wheel off an old cart. What are you scared of?"

"If the cart's down there, dummy, then so is dead Elijah, and his dead horse," shouted Charlie, "and I've just disturbed 'em. Dead things don't like being disturbed and I don't fancy seeing the ghosts of Elijah and his horse right now. In fact I don't want to see them, ever."

Sam burst into tears.

"Don't be a cry-baby, Sam. It's not you they'll be after, it'll be me."

They ran back across the wasteland towards the road, but before they reached it Charlie stopped.

"Hey, what's that?" he said, pointing towards a cluster of small trees.

"What, I can't see anything," croaked Sam, desperate to get home. "Come on."

"No, wait, I want to investigate. I can see a wheel, it might be Jim's bike. I heard Mum telling Dad that some miserable bugger had nicked it."

Charlie ran towards the trees. Sam reluctantly followed close behind.

"Wow, it's a wheelchair," said Charlie, amazed, as he eagerly stood it upright and dusting twigs from its seat.

"But what's it doing up here?"

"I dunno, but it'll get us home a lot quicker. Come on, Sam; help me get it down to the road."

Without too much effort, they dragged and pushed the cumbersome wheelchair over the coarse grass and onto the tarmac.

"We'll take it in turns to be pushed," said Charlie jumping onto the seat, and then we'll both ride it down the last bit where the road slopes into the village."

"But I want to go first, it's not fair, you're heavier than me."

"You want to get home, don't you? So do as you're told," ordered Charlie. "Anyway, it was my idea and I'm wet."

Sam obeyed his older brother and they took it in turns to push, but as they passed the entrance to the Penwynton Hotel, a flock of starlings flew from the branches of a tree and off towards the horizon. Both boys screamed. Sam leapt onto his brother's lap and then huddled together in the wheelchair, sobbing unashamedly, they flew down the incline and back to the village with a bewildered, wet Copper, following close behind.

CHAPTER TWENTY FIVE

During their frantic journey home, with teeth chattering through cold and fear, Charlie and Sam rapidly agreed that once they reached their home they must creep in quietly through the front door, unheard if possible, and then Sam must distract their mother and keep her talking in the kitchen, while Charlie slipped upstairs and changed before she had a chance to witness the wet and filthy state he was in. Their plan, however, was thwarted, for Candy, alarmed by the non-appearance of her sons after dusk, was anxiously waiting by the garden gate.

Candy was too shocked to speak when her boys arrived slumped in a runaway wheelchair. Without uttering a word, she pushed the chair onto the front lawn and ushered both boys into the house before asking any questions or even raising her voice. When the front door was closed, holding the hood of Charlie's jacket, she marched him into the kitchen and ordered him to remove his soggy, filthy clothes. Charlie obeyed, undressed and dropped his wet attire onto the tiled floor, he then, as ordered, went upstairs, with haste, to the bathroom for a shower.

In the absence of his older brother, Sam quietly dried Copper on an old towel, kept for that purpose in the cupboard beneath the kitchen sink, while Candy, although annoyed by the filth and foul smell, managed to keep her anger under control as she rammed Charlie's dirty clothes into the washing machine. Once done, she mopped up the patch of dirty water where her son's dripping clothes had been discarded, and put a pan of milk on the cooker to heat in order to make hot drinks for her young sons before Larry arrived home for dinner.

When Charlie returned downstairs, clean, dry and wearing his thick, warm dressing gown, she led both boys into the living room beside a blazing fire, where each sat side by side on the sofa, supping mugs of drinking chocolate and awaited their fate.

"Right, you first Charlie. What on earth have you been up to? How come you got wet through? Where did you get the wheelchair from and what happened to Copper?"

Sam cast a sympathetic glance at his big brother, anxiously biting his nails as he faced Candy's barrage of questions. Both boys knew she would be cross when she learned Charlie had risked his life just to save the dog, but at the same time they also knew they'd have been in even greater trouble if they had just let poor Copper drown. It was a no-win situation. Charlie looked from his brother to his mother and realised his only real option was to tell the truth. Hence, nervously he described how he went into the water purely to rescue Copper, who after retrieving a stick thrown for him, seemed reluctant to find his own way out. The wheelchair, they explained, was left abandoned in a hedge and they had taken it simply to hasten their journey home before darkness fell. Charlie made no mention of the cart, partly because he thought it irrelevant and partly because he thought by doing so it might anger Elijah's ghost still further.

The following day, Larry, who had a new bathroom suite to install at the Penwynton Hotel, put the wheelchair in the back of the van and returned it to its rightful owners, explaining his boys had found it on waste ground near to the Ebenezer Chapel.

Larry told of his day that evening, as the Bingham family sat at the kitchen table for dinner.

"Bob Jarrams was flabbergasted when I pulled the chair out of the van. I don't think he ever expected to see it again. Hmm, something smells good. But like us he's completely baffled as to how it could have got up there."

"Well someone obviously dumped it there," sighed Candy, dishing up plates of shepherd's pie and cauliflower, "but goodness only knows who or why. There are some daft folks about."

Larry poured everyone a glass of water from the jug on the table. "Well, we can rule out all the folks who was still inside the inn after the um, err, um, meeting the other night, because they've obviously all got good sound alibis."

"Yes, but anyone could have nipped out from the pub and quickly taken the chair from the old loos," said Candy, "it wouldn't have taken a minute."

"No, but it would have taken a while to get it all the way up to the chapel. Anyway, it's back now safe and sound, and it looked as good as new after young Jim had given it a wash. Pass the salt, please, Sam."

"I wonder if there's any connection between the Hotel's wheelchair, Jim's bike, the police car, and Elijah and his cart," said Candy, taking a seat once all four meals were dished up. "I mean, it does seem a little odd that they all went missing like they did. Even if there is a time lapse of one hundred years."

Larry shook his head. "No, I don't think so, I reckon the chair was taken by youngsters with nothing better to do and the same thing probably happened to Jim's bike. The police car, well, that's a complete mystery and as for Elijah and his cart, I guess we'll never know what happened to him, not after all these years."

This statement made the boys feel guilty and after brief consideration, knowing it was an offence to withhold evidence, Charlie decided to tell the whole truth regarding the previous day's happenings.

The following morning the village buzzed with excitement, for overnight it had become common knowledge that Larry Bingham had phoned the police to inform them of his two sons' extraordinary discovery, thus raising the probability that the police car may have met a similar fate to that of the unfortunate Elijah. The police, however, thought it an unlikely eventuality, for the roads were clearly defined in the present day, unlike back in 1881 when Elijah Triggs had gone missing on what was little more than a dirt track. Nevertheless, they felt obliged to leave no stone unturned, for pressure from both the Government and Scotland Yard was on the Devon and Cornwall Police Constabulary to find the missing men. Hence after lunch numerous police vehicles were parked on the grass verge near to the old Ebenezer Chapel and assembled frogmen prepared to search beneath the dirty water.

A considerable crowd gathered alongside the road to witness the search, for since the revival of the Elijah Triggs mystery on New Year's Eve, everyone in Trengillion was familiar with it, and each had their own opinion regarding his fate. The roadside spectators therefore, were a little disappointed with the outcome of the search, for although the cart wheels were recovered within the first thirty minutes, nothing else thereafter was brought to the surface. And as the police were not at all interested in the disappearance of a missing farm hand from the previous century, the search was called off when no trace of the police car or its drivers was evident. Before leaving, they did, however, inform Larry Bingham, that the remainder of the cart was in all probability still on the bottom of the pond, but not being as durable as the dense wheels, it was unlikely there would be very little of it left intact, and even less of poor Elijah and his horse.

Disappointed, the crowds began to drift away and only a few remained to examine the wheels once the police had also departed.

"Look at the size of 'em," said Giles Wilson, stooping to remove a piece of weed. "They're an impressive piece of engineering. And look, the iron tyres are still intact, though they're very rusty."

"I was hoping my bike might be in there," said Jim, wistfully, "not that it'd be in very good nick if it was. But the coppers said they didn't see it. I just wish I knew where the sodding thing was; I hate to think of it rusting away somewhere, so I'm hoping whoever nicked it did it because they needed something to ride."

"Rotten luck, mate," said Larry, patting his shoulder. "Cindy told me about it. I dunno, there are certainly some odd things happening round here lately."

"Yes, but at least things aren't disappearing into thin air like we originally thought," said Gertie. "I must admit I was quite relieved when I heard Elijah's cart had turned up because I was starting to believe in the Ebenezer Triangle theory."

"And the missing wheelchair's turned up too," said Larry, cheerfully, "and there was nothing spooky about its disappearance, after all. So it looks as though all the ghost stories were a complete fabrication."

Susan frowned. "No, no it doesn't, it's completely the opposite. Finding the cart at last actually confirms where Elijah died, and considering its close proximity to the milk churn stand, the cart wheels being in the pond actually backs up the ghost stories. I find that really exciting, although in future you won't find me walking around here on my own, not that I ever would have anyway."

"Blimey, yes, you're right," Jim laughed, "ghosts are alleged to haunt the spot where they died and as you say, Susan, the pond and the chapel are only a stone's throw apart."

"You dozy pair," laughed Sid. "No-one's actually ever seen Elijah, have they? So I still reckon it's a load of old cobblers."

"Well, whether the old timer's ghost is around here or not, I still like it up here," said Jim, wistfully. "In fact if I had pots of money I'd like to buy the old chapel and do it up to live in."

Susan gasped in amazement. "Are you serious? Rather you than me, it's so desolate and lonely up here."

"Better ask the boss for a pay rise then," smiled Larry, nodding in the direction of the Wilson brothers. "I've never met a poor farmer, yet, although they all plead poverty."

"Humph," grunted Brendon on hearing the comment, "and I've never met a rich one. I think you plumbers earn a damn sight more than we do."

Larry roared with laughter. "Actually, dentistry, that's the profession to be in if you want to make serious dosh, not plumbing. Although to be honest I've done alright this month, thanks to the freezing weather."

Susan ignored the banter, her thoughts clearly elsewhere but then she spoke, "I was just thinking; I wonder why no-one ever looked in the pond for Elijah when he first went missing."

Larry shrugged his shoulders. "I suppose because the weather was treacherous."

Giles shook his head. "No, I reckon it was because nobody really cared. After all, gossip has it that he was forced into a loveless marriage to the daughter of old man Richards, so I daresay once she had a ring on her finger and her baby had a name, they had no further use for him."

Larry nodded. "So you think they didn't give a toss whether he came back or not?"

"Yep."

Susan sighed. "That's really horrid. Poor, poor, Elijah."

Over the next few days, as the news of the cart wheels' discovery spread through the village, several wreaths made with winter foliage appeared alongside the water's edge of the old pond, and the bright yellow flowers of wild gorse were strewn over the slimy, green surface, to commemorate the demise of the unfortunate Elijah Triggs and his horse.

CHAPTER TWENTY SIX

On Thursday morning after the children had gone to school and Ian to work, and once the task of housework was finished, Janet Ainsworth, with time on her hands, left the house with Glenda for a walk to the beach where she hoped to find interesting shaped pebbles on which to paint pictures. For she had decided, since the incident at the stables, that looking for fame and kudos by seeking the whereabouts of missing policemen was not the way forward, although she still felt animosity towards her suspects, if for no other reason than that they had foiled her plans and made her look a fool.

She left the Old Police House with Glenda on her lead and walked down the garden path, pushing aside the wet, dripping branches of a leafless fuchsia dampened by a recent shower. The morning was grey and the street was empty. Janet sighed, lamenting the loss of her previous home where the hustle and bustle of suburban life was never dull.

On approaching the beach she became aware of a drilling noise emanating from The Pickled Egg and curiosity made her peer through the window. On a chair stood Jane fixing curtain pole brackets onto the wall. To Janet's embarrassment, Jane saw her, waved and beckoned her to enter the cafe.

"Come in," shouted Jane, leaping down from the chair and rushing to the door, "please, do come in, I'd like to ask your advice."

"What do you mean," said Janet, hesitating in the doorway, "advice about what? I know nothing about catering."

"No, no, it's not that, I don't have a problem there. It's colours that I'm uncertain about and I should value your opinion. I'd like to know which colours you think would complement my new curtains and cushions. You see, Meg Reynolds told me your oldest daughter, Lucy, said you're ever so good at decorating, and your old house was the most beautiful house in the world."

Janet dropped her hostility and smiled as she stepped over the threshold. "I used to design wallpaper during what seems like a lifetime ago, before I had the children, so decorating has always been close to my heart, and most of the papers I used were my own designs."

"Really, how fascinating," gasped Jane, closing the door. "So do you intend to go back into designing again when the children get older?"

"What from down here? I think the chances of doing so are nil. Besides things change and during my absence fashions have moved on. But it was good while it lasted, and at least I can claim to have a full and meaningful career, even if it was a while back."

"I see, so have you started to decorate the Old Police House yet? I would imagine it needs it badly after years of being rented out. I used to date one of the blokes who lived there for a time; he was a chef at the Penwynton Hotel."

"Really, what happened to him?"

"We drifted apart and since then he's moved to Bristol and opened his own restaurant. He was a nice bloke though and I learned a lot from him about catering. In fact if it wasn't for him I'd probably still be working in a shop."

Janet smiled. "Hmm, I should imagine shop work is not the most rewarding of jobs. But in answer to your question, no I've not begun decorating our house, although Lucy asked only yesterday when I was going to make a start because she hates the colour of her bedroom." Janet sighed. "But to be perfectly honest I've not really settled down properly yet and with the cold weather I've had no motivation at all. So I'll most likely leave it until the summer or perhaps the spring if the weather is good. Is it alright to have Glenda in here?"

"Yes, of course, I don't mind dogs as long as they're well behaved, but it doesn't matter at present anyway because it's a while yet before the new season starts." Jane bent down and stroked Glenda's back. "How often do you have her clipped? I see her coat's beginning to grow out now."

"That's because I'm letting it," sighed Janet, with a hint of sorrow. "Ian says clipped poodles don't suit country life, especially here in Cornwall, so I'm letting her coat revert back to normal. I suppose in reality it's phoney ever to have had her clipped, but it was my mother who got me into it and her poodles have won lots of prizes in shows over the years." She cast Glenda a loving glance. "What Mum doesn't know about poodles isn't worth knowing."

"I'm afraid my knowledge of dogs is zilch, in fact that goes for most animals and I think yours is the first poodle I've actually ever seen."

Janet laughed. "I expect you have seen some before, ones with coats as nature intended anyway. They're actually regarded as one of the most intelligent breed of dogs there is. They're useful as hunting dogs and other dog sports too and that's because they're obedient and agile. Isn't that right, Glenda, my darling?"

Glenda barked and wagged her tail which reminded Jane of the mop her mother used to wash dishes with when she was a girl.

"Where are your new curtains and cushions?" Janet asked, as she rose from tickling Glenda beneath her chin. "After all that was the reason you called me in."

"Yes, of course. They're upstairs, in my flat, come on up and I'll make us both a coffee. Please excuse the mess though, I've been very slack with housework these past few days, but that's probably because I find it so boring."

"Snap," said Janet, emphatically, "I find it a real drudge too, and I'm sick of mopping up the back porch where the Wellington boots get discarded. I must confess I'm not a bit sorry to see the back of the snow."

While Jane made the coffee Janet studied the curtain and cushion fabric and then wrote down a list of paint colours she recommended from which Jane could take her choice.

"You have a lovely view of the sea from up here," said Janet, as she laid down the pen and paper. "We have a sea view, but only from upstairs, but it must be wonderful to watch the sea whilst sitting on the sofa."

"It is. This used to be a fishermen's loft, it belongs to my dad and his fishing partner, Percy Collins. Percy is married to Gertie; you'll remember her, she was with Cassie and me when we found you in the stables."

Janet stiffened. "Yes I know who you mean, the chubby woman with crooked teeth."

Jane frowned. "Does Gert have crooked teeth? I can't say that I've ever noticed and I've known her for as long as I can remember,

192

but then I suppose with you being married to a dentist you observe such things."

"Well, no, not really, at least I don't think I do. I have very little time for dentistry and I'd hate to be one. I find the idea of looking into people's mouths abhorrent. It must be dreadful and I don't know how Ian does it."

"Hmm, I shouldn't like it either, nor would I like to be a chiropodist. What made your Ian take it up?"

Janet shrugged her shoulder. "No idea. He was already a qualified dentist when I met him and he was doing all right then too. We met in our local pub, you see, he'd just moved to the area in the same street as one of my friends." She laughed. "I used to think it was love at first sight."

"Used to think," queried Jane.

"Well, you know what I mean. Back then he could do no wrong in my eyes and we were extremely happy. We had a beautiful house in a wonderful location and I didn't really lament the fact I had to give up work when the kids came along."

Jane frowned. "So what made you all come down here?"

"Ken Bradshaw," spat Janet, with vehemence. "Ken sodding Bradshaw."

"Oh dear, I take it you don't like Ken, then?"

"Well actually I've nothing against Ken as a person; in fact I liked him when Ian first introduced us. But it's because of him we ended up moving down here and as I said, I was very happy in our old life."

"So, what exactly happened? Jane asked, sitting beside Janet on the sofa.

"Ian went to a dentists' convention a year back and Ken was there. They were pleased to see each other because they'd known each other since their student days. Anyway, Ken told Ian about his practice down here in Cornwall and the fact that his partner would be leaving at Christmas to start a new life in Australia because of some woman he was infatuated with. He then asked Ian if he'd like to be his new partner and began to extol the virtues of Cornwall. Ian thought it was a wonderful idea," she tutted, "and so here we are."

A sudden gust of wind rattled the window and caused Glenda to bark.

"Shush, Fifi," said Jane carelessly, "it's only the wind."

Janet promptly rose and laid her coffee cup on the table. "I must go," she said, coldly. "I've taken up enough of your time."

Jane also rose, her face reddening as she realised her blunder. "Sorry, I meant Glenda."

Janet's bottom lip quivered. "My mother, as I've already said, kept poodles; toy and miniature, and she won many shows with them over the years. The boys at school teased me tirelessly when I was young. They called me Fifi even though none of Mum's dogs were so called. I was an ugly child, Miss Williams. I had tight curly hair, and it's a name that hurts. It really hurts."

Before Jane could think up a response, Janet lifted Glenda, her moist eyes misted with sadness. Clutching the dog she then hastily descended the stairs and slammed shut the café door at the bottom as she left the building.

Molly sat by the window in her living room and looked out over her front lawn. She always found the depth of winter a depressing time for the garden, too early for the spring flowers and fresh green shoots of a new season's growth, and too late to relish the golds and reds of autumn. The back garden was more colourful as the camellia was in flower and hellebores in the bed shaded by the shed had been in bloom for a couple of weeks, but they could only be viewed from outside or through the kitchen window.

Molly gazed at the front garden where the borders looked lifeless and desolate, even the old rowan tree which she had planted nearly thirty five years before when she and the major had first moved to Rose Cottage, looked as dead as the dried broken twigs scattered on the grass below. And all was made worse by continuous light drizzle.

Molly sighed; still, perhaps it was for the best as she was not in good enough health to feel drawn outdoors to tend the garden, for even when she was feeling well, she lacked strength to dig and bend for weeding.

"Old age is a curse," she muttered, "but as daft as it sounds I don't really feel any different to when I was a girl; not in mind anyway, but in body, well, that's another story."

She leaned her grey head against the window pane and thought fondly of her family as she watched raindrops drip from the branches of her favourite potentilla. Ned and Stella had done her proud; two lovely granddaughters and four lovely great, grandchildren. There had been a time when she thought Ned might be the end of the Stanley line, and so he was in name, but at least by having children he had ensured the family genes carried on.

From the window sill she picked up a photograph of Elizabeth and Anne, sitting side by side, taken at Ned's sixtieth birthday party the previous year. Anne was a Hargreaves well and truly; she had many of Stella's features and mannerisms too, and like her mother, she was also very artistic. Elizabeth on the other hand was very much like her own side of the family, and time and time again Molly caught glimpses of herself as a young woman, not only in her granddaughter's looks but in her mode of expression and fascination with myth and mystique.

Molly put down the picture and thought about the mysterious little girl with whom she had made contact during the séance. No-one had been able to establish her identity or even take a wild guess as to who she might have been. Molly sighed; if she'd been twenty years younger she might well have attempted to make contact again, but as things were perhaps it was best to leave well alone.

Tired of the bleak view, Molly rose from the chair beside the window and crossed over to the settee; from beneath the cushion she picked up a glossy magazine dropped in earlier by Rose. She flicked through the pages and then put it back down, her eyes felt heavy. "I think I'll have a quick nap," she yawned, "my silly cough kept me awake last night and so I need to catch up with some sleep."

When Molly awoke it was dark. Surprised by the length of time she had slept, she scrambled up quickly to draw the curtains and switch on the light. She yelped as her ankle took her full weight and cursing hobbled towards the window. As she reached up to draw the curtains, she thought she saw something move in the garden by the hedge. Molly squinted and stared from the window; she could just make out the outline of her garden from the beam of a nearby streetlamp which cast shadows across the lawn, but there appeared to be nothing there that should not be there. Convinced it was a trick of the light and her half asleep state of mind, she drew the curtains, switched on the light and went into the kitchen to make a cup of tea before Ned arrived to make sure all was well.

The following morning Molly woke to find the sun shining brightly through the kitchen window. She rose from her make-shift bed on the settee and stretched her arms. If the sun was shining then the day would bring visitors, unlike the previous day when she had seen only Rose and Ned.

Molly crossed to the living room window and threw back the curtains to welcome in the new day, but instantly her eyes were drawn to something lying on the lawn. She tried to guess what it might be. It wasn't a leaf or a twig, nor was it a creature of any kind, and it had certainly not been there the day before. Molly glanced at the clock, it was ten minutes past eight. Rose would not be in to get her breakfast until half past and so she had time to slip outside before her neighbour's arrival. Molly picked up her walking stick, hobbled into the hallway and opened the front door which was inclined to stick through lack of use; to her surprise it opened with ease. Stepping outside she hobbled onto the lawn as quickly as possible in case Rose should arrive early, or worse still, Ned pop in before school.

The grass was wet and the morning smelled clean and pure. Molly drew in a deep breath; it was good to be outside in the fresh air. She crossed the wet lawn towards the spot where the mysterious article lay. As she got nearer she realised it was a handkerchief.

"So there was someone out here last night," she muttered, quickly glancing over her shoulder. She bent to pick up the handkerchief and laid it across the palm of her hand. It was small, dainty and white, with flowers embroidered around the edges, and in one corner, embroidered in blue, was the name, Viola.

CHAPTER TWENTY SEVEN

On Saturday morning, Stella and Rose changed the bedclothes on Molly's bed, for sleeping in the living room no longer appealed following the departure of the cold dry days and the arrival of rain and drizzle. Besides, Molly missed the view from the upstairs windows and the cosy feeling generated by the sound of raindrops falling on the slates when she was snuggly tucked up in her bed. Ned was a little apprehensive about her climbing the stairs, but she insisted her ankle was almost back to normal and Ned knew better than to argue with his mother over a subject which could not be proved either way. Molly, delighted at her triumph, gleefully tidied up her living room once the unsightly bedclothes had been removed by Stella and Rose. "See, I'm fine," she said to herself, "nothing wrong with my ankle that a bit of exercise won't cure." She was, however, a little concerned over her cold which refused to go away, but on reflection, considered that was probably due to the lack of ventilation in the living room and the constant heat of the fire which had burned freely both day and night.

"I'm baby-sitting tonight," said Stella, tucking the edge of a thick flannelette sheet beneath Molly's mattress. "The youngsters are going to the inn for Graham and Ginny's engagement do."

"Really, I heard they were engaged," said Rose. "It seems like only yesterday they were all at school."

"Yes, I don't know where the years have gone. I saw Meg yesterday and she said the same. Needless to say she and Sid are delighted that both their children are preparing to settle down."

"So whose nippers are you looking after, Anne's or Elizabeth's?"

"Anne's," said Stella, picking up four pillow cases and handing two to Rose. "Gertie's looking after Susan's two and Tabitha's looking after Tally and Wills. So we could all be feeling a bit weary tomorrow."

Rose smiled. "You're so lucky, Stell, having children and grandchildren, that is. I'd love to have been a mum like you."

"And a lovely mother you'd have made, but most of the children look upon you as an aunt, so in a funny way it's as though you do have family."

"I know, and I think of them all as family but it's not the same is it? I know George would have liked children, just as Reg did." She sighed deeply. "Oh, dear, life with Reg seems such a long time ago and he'd be retired now if he'd lived."

Later that evening, as arranged, former members of the Pact, their husbands, wives and sweethearts, met at the Fox and Hounds for a meal to celebrate Graham and Ginny's engagement. They ate in the dining room, originally used for the inn's paying guests to consume their breakfast and evening meals. But since Gerald and Cassie Godson had owned the inn, they had opened up the dining room for anyone wishing to eat, and dispensed with set evening meals for guests. For until their arrival, only basket meals had been available at the inn for non-residents, the consumption of which had taken place in either the bars or outside on picnic benches.

January being a quiet time of the year meant Cassie was quite happy to close the dining room to enable the engagement group to have a private party; hence the twenty guests were thrilled that their revelry would not be frowned upon by the inn's clientele.

Most of the guests were in couples, either married or engaged and only Matthew Williams, and Marigold, a friend of Ginny's, were unattached.

"There you are, Matt," whispered Jane to her brother, behind her cupped hand, "a nice girlfriend for you. Marigold looks right up your street."

"Get lost," Matthew hissed, "she looks half sharp and there's enough paint on her face to paint my sodding boat."

Jane giggled; she knew Marigold was hardly the type to take her brother's fancy, but then if the truth be known she was miffed as to just what type of girl might fall into the right category. For it bothered her that he seemed uninterested in girls, and other than a few brief dalliances with female holiday makers, he had not had a steady girlfriend since he had split up with Cissie Trevelyan a few years before.

Marigold on the other hand, realising Matthew was the only male not spoken for, made it quite plain through hand gestures and facial expressions that Matthew had taken her fancy, hence Matthew was thankful the party guests were seated around a collection of tables pushed together and she was not near enough for him to feel compelled to make conversation with.

After the meal, Graham proposed a toast to his future bride and all raised their glasses to ratify their approval.

After the toast, Susan, sitting beside Graham's sister, Diane turned to ask her a question. "When is it you and Mike get married? I should have written it on the calendar when you first got engaged but completely forgot, but then actually I didn't forget, I couldn't write it down because we hadn't got a new calendar for 1987 back then. Does that make sense?"

Diane giggled. "Sort of; anyway it's June the thirteenth and you're all invited of course, but we won't be sending out invites 'til after Easter. Will we Mike?"

Mike drained his glass of bubbly and pulled a face. "No idea, Di, that's your department. I'm not very au fait with wedding etiquette."

"Neither was I 'til December," said Diane, "but I'm learning fast and it's Mum and Dad's job to send out the invites, that I do know."

Elizabeth turned to the newly engaged couple. "Are you two planning to get wed this year as well?"

Ginny nodded. "Yes because we can't see the sense in my continuing to rent a place in Truro when my salary could be helping to run Graham's house, so we're thinking of a September wedding."

Elizabeth nodded her approval. "Lovely, September is one of my two favourite months; the other is October."

Susan gleefully rubbed her hands. "Brilliant! That's two weddings this year to look forward to. Will there be a third, I wonder?"

"It'll be a fair old way for you to drive to Truro from Trengillion every day, won't it?" said Anne, thoughtfully, "and it'll cost around a tenner a week in petrol too."

Ginny sighed. "I know, but I shall probably see if I can get a job a bit nearer here after the wedding. We'll see, I'm sure everything will sort itself out."

"Right, who's ready for another drink?" Graham asked, standing to go to the bar. Nineteen hands shot up in the air.

"Okay, so shall I order more wine or do you want to go onto something else?"

The unanimous vote was for more wine and so Graham went to the bar to ask Gerald for a dozen more bottles, six red and six white.

"You'll soon be the only one left on the shelf," Susan said, throwing a screwed up serviette at Matthew, "and that's daft because you're really quite good looking."

Marigold giggled and pouted her lips. "Yes, you are and I bet you're strong because your arms are very muscly."

The gathering laughed at Matthew's indignant face.

"Having said that I don't see a ring on big sister's finger either," said Susan, nodding across the table at Jane.

"Oy, now don't you go putting ideas into her head," Giles grinned, carefully folding his serviette into a paper aeroplane and sending it flying in Susan's direction, "we're quite happy with the way things are already, aren't we, Jane?"

Jane promptly nodded, but her smile lacked sincerity, and she slipped her hand with its ring-less finger from view beneath the table and rested it on her lap.

"And we mustn't forget Lily either," said Diane, as an afterthought, "she's still unattached, isn't she Greg?"

Greg scowled. His sister's love life was not a subject he wished to discuss, not even with his closest friends.

"Anyway," said Elizabeth, attempting to draw attention away from Greg mumbling by her side, "I think we should drink to the fact we've nearly all found partners, and that we're all still living here in Trengillion, just as we planned way back in 1976."

"Hear, hear," said Susan, "and long may we all stay friends."

"I think it's amazing," said Diane, looking lovingly at Mike, "amazing we're all still here, and amazing that we've nearly all found partners."

"There's nothing amazing about most of us getting snapped up," said Tony, jokingly standing to admire his reflection in the mirror, "after all we're a damn fine looking bunch."

On Sunday morning, Anne came in from the greenhouse with two trays of seeds which she had just sown, and placed them on the kitchen window sill in the warmth, each cosily wrapped in polythene bags.

"Gosh, it's cold out there this morning, it almost feels like we could be in for more snow and that's the last thing we want."

"Well there's none forecast," said John, taking an egg box from the fridge, "so it's probably just you feeling a bit fragile."

"No, it's definitely turned colder because the thermometer in the greenhouse is only just above freezing."

John grinned as he cracked an egg over a sizzling frying pan and dropped it alongside three rashers of bacon, four sausages and eight mushrooms. "What's in the seed trays?" No, let me guess, lobelia and geraniums."

"Oh dear," Anne sighed, "am I such a creature of habit? I'd like to prove you wrong and say they're something else, but they're not and you're right. Mind you, I will be sowing peppers soon and I want to get my tomatoes going nice and early this year too. I left it too late last year if you remember and they took forever to ripen."

"Hmm, tomatoes, that's a good idea, are there any in the fridge they'd go nicely with my fry up."

"No, but there are tinned ones in the pantry. But don't you think you've enough in the pan already?"

"Can't have too much after a night drinking and that wine was pretty strong stuff, I dread to think how bad I'd feel if we hadn't eaten."

Anne sat down at the table "Still, it was worth it, wasn't it? The hangover, I mean."

Before John had a chance to answer the phone rang in the kitchen, and as he was nearest to the dresser, he picked up the receiver. On hearing it was Lily he passed the phone to Anne whom he had beckoned to his side; he then went to the pantry in search of a tin of tomatoes.

As Anne put the receiver to her ear she immediately sensed a note of excitement in Lily's distant voice, an occurrence she had not heard for quite some time. Curious to hear what Lily had to say, she reached for a chair and pulled it towards the dresser. "Something tells me you're in a very happy frame of mind."

"Oh, yes I am," gabbled her friend, "I certainly am. Mind you, it's a little sad too, but in the long run it will be best for all. Anne, you'll never believe this, but I'm going to be married."

"What! Another wedding, this is crazy, but then things always go in threes. But who are you going to marry? I mean, it can't be your Nick cos he's married already, so what are you up to, and what do you mean?"

"Oh, but it is to Nick; my gorgeous, darling Nick. He's getting a divorce, Anne. In fact he and his wife have already set things rolling with their solicitors. Oh dear, I'm probably confusing you so I'd better start at the beginning."

Anne agreed. "I think you should as my head's spinning; mind you I did drink a bit too much wine last night."

"Really, why was that?"

"Graham and Ginny's engagement do at the inn. It was a really good night, quite like old times. We were all there; I wish you had been there too."

"Oh yes, so do I, it would have been great, we've had some brilliant times over the years haven't we, Anne?"

"Yes, and at present you're the only one to have left the area, and Roger and Colin Withers of course, but they were late arrivals so they don't really count and I believe they're still in Cornwall anyway. So, come on, spill the beans and explain your latest news."

Lily giggled. "Well, last Saturday Nick went home earlier than he had told his wife he would, that's because he swapped shifts with a colleague at the last minute so the colleague could go to the theatre with tickets his girlfriend had picked up at the last minute, at least it was something like that. Anyway, as he approached his house, he thought he saw an unfamiliar car come out of his driveway, but as he was some way off he supposed he must have been mistaken. When he got inside the house, however, he found his wife at the sink washing out two wine glasses and she was very surprised to see him and seemed really on edge. Nick thought it a bit odd but didn't say anything until he noticed four cigarette butts in the ashtray, and then his suspicion was aroused because his wife doesn't smoke and when he reflected on it he realised he'd got home several times in the past and the room had smelt of tobacco. Anyway, he confronted her and she broke down in tears and confessed she had another chap. Nick's first reaction was to be angry, but then he realised that would be hypocritical and in no way can that ever be said of him, so instead he told his wife all about me. He said at first she was shocked, but then they both had a good laugh and opened several bottles of wine and drank to their new futures."

"You jammy bugger," Anne laughed. "Only you could get away with it that easily. So naturally you'll tell your parents now."

"Yes, because now I can tell them he's married but not for much longer. They met in the Swinging Sixties you see, and it's the same old story, she got pregnant, so they got married to keep their parents happy and so forth."

"What about their children, how are they taking all this?"

"Fine it seems, they've been told over the phone. They're both away, you see, one at school the other at university, so it won't make a great deal of difference to them, except during the holidays. They're a very easy going family, in fact the girls already knew Nick's wife's new chap. He owns a nearby music shop, you see, to which they are frequent visitors when home and what's more they really like him. There's no animosity between Nick and his wife either, and they've vowed to stay friends for the sake of the girls."

"Well, this certainly is good news, so with you engaged now, and Graham and Ginny engaged too with plans for a September wedding, and Diane getting married to Mike in June, Matthew really is the only person left in the Pact unattached, because I reckon Giles will ask Jane to marry him soon. At least I hope so, because she's potty about him and they make a lovely couple."

In the afternoon, following a shower of rain, Susan took Denzil and Demelza to the recreation ground for a swing, partly for their benefit and partly for her own because she hoped a bit of fresh air might help shift the hangover which refused to go away.

After their departure, her husband, Steve, who had wisely not over indulged due to a slight headache and the first signs of a cold, decided, since the weather was brightening up, to honour his Christmas Day pledge and tidy his father's grave. After putting on his jacket he went to the shed for secateurs and shears and then walked the short distance to the churchyard, feeling pleased with himself for finally making the effort.

Once on the other side of the lichgate he walked through the long, wet grass to the neglected corner in the shadow of the ancient yew, and there proceeded to tear away encroaching ivy and cut into leafless brambles with the secateurs. When the area around the grave was clear, he knelt and neatly trimmed the long, dried grass with the shears. Once done, he carried the grass to the compost heap and threw it over discarded holly wreaths; he then returned to the grave to admire his handy work.

The inscription on the tombstone was legible, but only just. Being in the shade, moss and lichen covered much of the un-polished stone and partly obliterated some of the lettering. Steve stooped and attempted to remove some of the growth with the blades of the secateurs, but with little success. He was reluctant to scrape too hard for fear of doing damage; the memorial stone had after all been purchased with money donated by local people, saddened by the tragic loss which had left his mother a penniless widow.

Steve glanced at the surrounding graves, many of them also neglected, and since he was in no rush to get home, he set to pulling back ivy and cutting through brambles invading the final resting place of his father's neighbours.

Most of the ivy and brambles were sprouting from the badly overgrown wall which denoted the boundary of the churchyard and was part tumbledown in places. Steve pushed his way through the overgrowth, taking care not to tear his jacket on the thorny briars. He reasoned that if he could cut back the encroaching wilderness at source, then it might halt the invasion for a month or two.

The growth was dense in the gap between the wall and the trunk of the old yew, but Steve pushed his way through, cursing the fact everything was still wet yet determined to get to the root of the problem. In his final surge he at last broke through; but then something amongst the vegetation prevented him reaching the wall. Steve carefully plunged his hands into the damp foliage and parted ivy. He gasped with surprise. Hidden amongst the leaves was a black Raleigh bicycle.

CHAPTER TWENTY EIGHT

On Monday morning, Gertie walked down the lane by the school to visit her mother, Nettie Penrose, at Long Acre Farm; she found her alone in the farmhouse kitchen reading a Catherine Cookson novel.

"I hear young Jim's bike has turned up," said Nettie, before Gertie had even closed the door. "Who on earth do you think took it and why if they didn't want it for any purpose?"

Gertie hung her coat on the back of the door and reached for the kettle quietly boiling on the Cornish Range. "I expect it was kids and they did it for a laugh, like the wheelchair being nicked from the inn's loos. Coffee, Mum?"

"Yes, please. I suppose you could be right. They say the devil finds work for idle hands to do, and I reckon children these days have lost the art of playing." She frowned. "But then it couldn't have been young children that took the wheelchair from the inn, not at that time of night, so I expect it was teenagers."

"Hmm, probably. Where are Tony and Jean?"

Nettie lay down her book on the scrubbed pine kitchen table. "Tony's out in the fields, hedge laying, and Jean's popped into Helston for groceries. She's making a chicken and bacon lasagne tonight and needs to get some mushrooms as well as chicken and bacon."

"I see, very nice too." Gertie handed her mother a mug of coffee and then with a glance at the window sat down at the table. "Doesn't everywhere look dull now the snow's gone? I cursed it at the time, but at least it brought a bit of excitement to our lives."

"A bit of excitement and a few peculiar happenings too," sighed Nettie. "I don't know about you but I'm rather sorry we found out what happened to old Elijah. There was something kind of magical about not knowing, although we still have a mystery because it seems no-one has the foggiest idea of what's happened to the poor policemen. You never know, it might take a hundred years for that mystery to be solved."

Gertie stayed with her mother until Jean returned home from Helston, and then, to make a change, she walked back into the village by way of the coastal path. By the remains of the old mine she walked to the cliff's edge and looked along the coastline towards Polquillick. She sighed, her mother was right, for she too was sorry that the Elijah mystery had been solved. She was also a little disappointed that during the snow no-one had seen or heard his ghostly cart and the rattling milk churns nor witnessed a manifestation of the ghost ship on which all had perished as it ran aground by the Witches Broomstick.

Gertie returned to the coastal path and thought about the child with whom Molly had made contact during the séance. Even investigations there had been fruitless, and no-one had the slightest idea who she might have been or whether she had even existed at all.

Back in the village, as she passed the Fox and Hounds, a blue car slowed down, turned on the cobbled area in front of the inn and then pulled up alongside the kerb. From the driver's seat, a middle aged man wound down the window and asked Gertie where the Vicarage was. Gertie was intrigued. He spoke with a faint West Country twang; was casually dressed; had a handsome face and nicely manicured nails. As she lowered her head to speak, she noticed a young woman by his side and whilst trying to fathom out who they might be, she waved her arms in the direction of the Old Vicarage and gave clear directions. The driver thanked her and then drove off. Gertie watched as the car turned the corner and disappeared out of sight, she then hurriedly walked back to her home, trying hard with each determined step to think of a good enough reason to visit her daughter-in-law, Anne.

As she entered the front door of her house in Coronation Terrace, she hung up her coat on the pegs in the hallway and wandered into the kitchen concentrating on the task in hand. She was delighted, therefore, when she remembered Jess had left her umbrella whilst visiting the previous day, and as the present spell of unsettled, wet weather was set to continue, she reflected her granddaughter may well be in need of it. With umbrella hanging from her wrist, Gertie straightened her hair whilst looking in the hall mirror; she then put her coat back on. Delighted with her quick thinking, she left the house and set off for the Old Vicarage, eager to establish just who the strange visitors might be.

Anne was pleased to see Gertie when she answered the door, "Come in," she said, "what absolutely perfect timing, you can probably help us as you've lived in the village far longer than me."

"I've come to return Jess' umbrella, "Gertie mumbled feebly, as Anne led her into the kitchen where the man she had seen in the car sat with the young woman.

"Well I never, we meet again," said the stranger, nodding to Gertie as he stood.

Anne's eyebrows raised, as it occurred to her perhaps the arrival of her mother-in-law was by no means coincidental.

Gertie smiled smugly and hung the umbrella on the back of the door.

"This is Walter Bray," said Anne, waving her hand towards the stranger and the young woman, "and this is Rebecca, Walter's daughter."

"Pleased to meet you," said Gertie, warmly shaking the proffered hands. "Any relation to the Brays of Trengillion, by any chance?"

Walter sat down and smiled. "I'd like to think so. You see, some of our ancestors came from Trengillion and that's why we're here. I'm doing my family history and according to the 1881 census, my great grandmother, Cecily Bray, who in that year lived in Devon, has her place of birth stated as Trengillion, Cornwall."

"Really, how fascinating," said Gertie, removing her coat with every intention of staying as long as possible. "Your great granny must be related to our Brays then because I'm sure they've been here for yonks. I don't suppose you've any idea whereabouts in the village your ancestors lived, have you?"

Walter grinned. "Yes, I do actually, because if we go back a further ten years to the 1871 census for Trengillion, that clearly states Cicely Bray lived here, at the Vicarage, and was in fact the Vicar's daughter."

"Good Lor," said Gertie, taking a seat at the table. "I didn't know there was ever a vicar here named Bray. I must have a word with my friend, Betty, she was a Bray, you see, before she became a Williams. Better still we must have a word with her dad, Arthur; he'd be more likely to know family history than Bet, and even though he's a bit old and doddery, he still has his marbles."

Walter rubbed his hands together in anticipation. "Now that'd be brilliant. Does he live far from here? I'd love to meet him as soon as possible."

"No, he's only a stone's throw away in one of the bungalows at Penwynton Crescent," said Gertie, enjoying the enfolding drama. "This is really exciting, the prospect of Bet being the descendant of a vicar, that is. Come to think of it, Arthur, her dad, was a big church-goer a few years back when he was more agile; in fact when I was a youngster, he used to ring the bells all on his own, the dear of him."

"Did he?" said Anne, "I didn't know that." She stood up. "Why don't we go round there now while the children are still at school? He'd probably be thrilled to have a bit of company, especially from possible distant family members."

"We can go in my car," Walter said, also standing. "It'd save time, even if it's not far."

"Just give me a minute to scribble John a note in case he comes home for lunch," said Anne, "and then I'll be ready."

They found Arthur Bray at home doing the crossword in a daily newspaper. "Come in, come in," he said, after a brief introduction on the doorstep, "this is a turn up for the book. Now tell me exactly who you might be again so that it sinks in to my poor old brain."

They all took a seat in Arthur's sitting room.

"My name is Walter, Walter Bray, and I was born in 1943. My father was born in 1912 and my grandfather in 1882 and we were all born in Devon."

"Right," said Arthur, with a puzzled frown. "I think I've got that, but if you could write it down for me and include the names as well it'd make a bit more sense and I'd like it for reference anyway."

"Of course, do you have a pen and some paper?"

Arthur gave Walter the pen used for the crossword and then took a notepad from a drawer in the sideboard.

"Brilliant," said Walter, as he wrote down the family names and dates. He looked up before writing more. "It was actually my great grandmother, Cicely Bray, born in 1861 who came from Cornwall.

According to the 1871 Trengillion census, her parents were, Vicar Samuel Bray and his wife, Alice, who lived at the Vicarage."

"Good heavens," Arthur chuckled, his eyes twinkling as fond childhood memories flooded back. "I remember talk of an Aunt Cicely now I come to think of it; she was my dad's sister. He was one of five kids, you see, and he had two brothers and two sisters. I clearly remember his brothers because they both lived in Cornwall over Newlyn way and they were fishermen, so I believe. My dad stayed in Trengillion though and worked for the Penwynton Estate and I eventually worked there too. I never knew his sisters though, neither of 'em, but then one of 'em died long before I was born so that's hardly surprising, and you're right, the other was called Cicely. I'd forgotten all about her, and as you say she was living in Devon. I remember for some reason I never saw her. We never went up to visit her nor did she ever come down here. I believe she worked up there as a governess or something like that, but she was always persona non grata for some reason and was seldom spoken of in our house. Can you shed any light on that?"

"Probably," grinned Walter, "in fact definitely. You see my research reveals that she and my great grandfather weren't actually married and I suppose her being the daughter of a vicar didn't exactly go down very well, especially back then when illegitimacy was well and truly frowned upon."

Arthur threw back his head and laughed. "Well, that certainly makes sense. My poor, poor grandparents they must have been mortified. And fancy, I've lived in Trengillion all my life but I never knew my grandfather was the vicar here. It makes me feel sort of proud."

"Often men of the cloth run in families," said Walter, "but I suppose your grandfather felt the family name was tainted and so he didn't encourage your father or his brothers into the church."

Arthur laughed. "Well to be honest I couldn't imagine my dad as a vicar, nor my uncles either because they all swore like troupers, but then that was probably because they mixed with fishermen. So out of interest, how many illegitimate nippers did Aunt Cicely have then?"

"Six," said Walter, "the oldest was my grandfather and then there were four sisters and a younger brother who died in infancy."

"Six, Christ! That would have been a hard pill for a vicar to swallow," exclaimed Arthur, shaking his head. "I actually feel sorry for the poor bloke. No wonder my parents never told me anything about the family, although to be fair to my mother she often spoke of her family, but that's because they toed the line, so to speak. God, I'd love to be able to turn back the clock and meet them all, it'd be fascinating."

"I take it then, your great grandmother, Cicely, had the children all christened in her own name," Anne added, as she tried to figure out the details. "That's if they were christened."

"Oh, they were christened alright; I've seen the entry for myself written in the Baptisms records along with the dates and names of their parents. And if possible I'd like to see the Baptism records for Trengillion too. Genealogy is a fascinating hobby, everyone should do it."

Anne smiled. "I believe my mother attempted to find her ancestors many years ago, but I don't think she got very far."

"Hmm, so, out of interest, who was the fellow who Cicely had all the young uns with then?" Gertie asked. "I mean, was he a Devon bloke too?"

Walter laughed. "Oh, didn't I say? No, no, he also came from Trengillion. His name was Elijah Triggs."

CHAPTER TWENTY NINE

The arrival of Arthur's Meals on Wheels promptly curtailed the conversation, but as he was unable to shed any more light on the history of his father's estranged sister, they decided to leave him in peace to enjoy his meal, but promised if they found out more to let him know.

Outside Arthur's bungalow, Gertie, Anne, Walter and Rebecca agreed in order to pursue the subject further they must meet again, pool all evidence and try to establish the truth behind the new found mystery. It was decided therefore to meet again in the evening at the Fox and Hounds, where Walter and Rebecca planned to book themselves accommodation for a few days.

Inside Cove Cottage, later in the day, Elizabeth sat on the floor, telephone receiver in her hand, listening to Anne relay news of Walter and Rebecca's arrival and the subsequent information thereof. Elizabeth was enthralled, and asked if she too might join the gathering to discuss the findings further. Therefore, when Greg arrived home from work, Elizabeth excitedly conveyed to him the latest news, and requested, he stay in to look after the children so that she could join the planned meeting, where hopefully, they might finalise the mystery of Elijah Triggs once and for all.

Walter and Rebecca were already seated in the bar of the Fox and Hounds when Gertie arrived with her husband, Percy, and her best friend, Betty Williams, nee Bray. After greeting each other, Percy offered to buy a round of drinks and proceeded to the bar with his order.

"Pete's coming round later," said Betty, excitedly, "so is Jane and probably Giles." She turned to address Walter, "Pete's my husband, but I decided to come out without him because he was still in the bath when I was ready, and I didn't want to miss anything."

"I see," said Walter, "and who are Jane and Giles?"

"Oh, sorry, silly me, I'm so excited, I'm not thinking straight. Jane is my daughter and Giles is her boyfriend. He's a farmer up at Higher Green Farm."

"Farmer Giles," grinned Walter, "but I bet I'm not the first to make that observation."

Betty smiled. "No, and I daresay you'll not be the last either."

"I've been thinking," said Gertie, sitting quietly in contemplative mood, "and I know music's not my best subject, but isn't there a song about a Vicar called Bray?"

"Nearly right," chuckled Walter, "but actually it's The Vicar *of* Bray, Bray being a place in Berkshire."

Gertie blushed. "Oh dear, I'm such a dunce." To hide her embarrassment, she looked at her watch. "Anne's late, she's usually very punctual."

Inside the Old Vicarage, Anne was briefing Stella on the day's events, her mother having volunteered to baby-sit so that her daughter and son-in-law could both meet up with Walter, his daughter and several others at the inn.

"I wish I could help shed some light on the story," said Stella, taking a seat by the fire, "but not being a Trengillion native, I only know what I've picked up over the years from other people. Still, it'll be interesting to hear what conclusion you come to over all this."

"Hmm, but I don't think we'll be able to come up with many answers tonight, and I daresay most of what we do will be guess work anyway."

Stella looked at her daughter quizzically and frowned. "Anne, you're only wearing one earring, have you lost one or is it the latest fashion?"

Anne touched both of her ear lobes. "Damn, I must have dropped it in the bedroom. The stud on the back of these isn't a very good fit."

As she crossed to leave the room and search for the missing piece of jewellery, John entered rubbing his hands together. "All ready then?"

"Nearly, but I've lost a wretched earring, keep talking while I take a quick look upstairs. I'll be back in a jiffy."

Kneeling on her bedroom floor, Anne ran her hands over the dusky pink carpet and as she had hoped found the earring beneath the dressing table stool. Delighted with the speed of her find, she looked in the mirror and put the gold cross firmly back in her ear lobe and fastened it in place with a tighter fitting plastic stud. Pleased that very little time had been wasted, she crossed the room to leave, but as she reached for the door handle, a sudden distant memory flashed across her mind; a memory of when John was doing up the house. At the time it meant very little, but she decided in the current state of affairs it might prove a vital clue.

Anne walked to the corner of the room and dragged out the chest of drawers. On her hands and knees, she then pulled at the edge of the carpet. She cursed, it was tacked down well, but she was determined not to be beaten. With the aid of a shoe taken from its repose in the bottom of her wardrobe, she used the stiletto heel to lever up the carpet edge. Once loosened it was easy to pull back a large enough section to reveal the floorboards beneath. Anne squeaked with delight; she was in the right corner, and the initials they had first discovered several years before, neatly carved in the old floorboards, were as she had hoped, C B loves E T.

Inside the Fox and Hounds, Anne, who with John had called for Elizabeth en route, excitedly told of her find, and when that, and all other clues were added together they came up with the following surmise.

Cicely Bray, the Vicar's daughter, lived at the Vicarage in Trengillion with her family, and before she came of age she went to Devon where she took up the position of Governess to a well to do family. It was assumed by the next generation of Brays that she had gone of her own free will but in the light of Anne's discovery carved in the floorboards of the Vicarage, it seemed more likely she was sent away by her father to get her away from Elijah Triggs, who was after all, a mere farm hand. At some time, however, the couple must have been in contact; maybe Cecily came home to visit her family for Christmas in 1880 and she and Elijah had hatched up a plan to

213

stage his disappearance, for it was only two or three weeks later that he went off with the milk churns and was never seen again, at least not by the inhabitants of Trengillion, for Devon records show he was employed by the same family for whom Cicely worked, and he held the position of gardener. The couple never married because Elijah was already married to Henry Richards' daughter, Polly - that marriage having taken place after Cicely first left Trengillion when Elijah must have been feeling pretty low.

"So did Elijah and Polly have any children?" asked Walter, "if so they'd be our distant relatives too; like you Betty."

"They had just the one daughter who Elijah insisted wasn't his, but he married Polly all the same to keep the old man quiet and no doubt retain his job. She was pregnant before the marriage, you see."

"And I'm pretty sure there are no descendants of Triggs around now," said Gertie. "It's not a name I've ever come across, except in the legend of course."

"Well, at least that's one silly ghost story laid to rest," laughed Sid Reynolds, who had joined the gathering to hear the news as an interested bystander, "and no doubt all other such legends would have a similar outcome, if the truth be known."

"You ought to go and fetch Meg," said Gertie, ignoring his sceptical comments, "she'd be interested in our find since she was brought up in the Vicarage."

"You're right; if you keep an eye on my pint I'll go and get her, that's if I can drag her away from the goggle-box."

Jane, who had arrived with boyfriend Giles shortly after Anne, John and Elizabeth, was delighted to make the acquaintance of her long lost cousins, especially Rebecca with whom she felt instantly at ease.

"It's daft, but I feel as if I've known you for ever, I hope you're going to be around for a while."

"Sadly we're only here for a couple of nights. Dad has to be back at work on Thursday, don't you, Dad?"

Walter nodded. "Regrettably, yes. If I'd known we were going to find family down here I'd have taken the whole week off, but I'm afraid it's too late now."

"How about you, Rebecca, do you have to get back for anything special?" Jane asked.

"No, I've got the week off, so I don't go back to work 'til next Monday."

"Then you must stay here 'til the weekend," said Jane, gleefully, "you can stay with me and sleep in my spare room."

Betty cast Jane a puzzled look. "But you've got no bed in there, so you must stay with us, Rebecca, in Jane's old room at Fuchsia Cottage. It's just a few yards up the road from here, so you'll still be near everybody."

"That's very kind of you; I should love to stay a bit longer. You don't mind do you, Dad?"

"Of course not, and I'll drive down and pick you up on either Saturday or Sunday. I'll bring your mum too so she can meet everyone."

"So what do you do, Rebecca?" Jane asked. "For a job, I mean."

"I'm a hairdresser, and I love it."

Betty threw back her head and laughed. "Then you'll feel very much at home with us, because I have my own hair salon at the back of our house."

As they chatted they were joined by a few other locals keen to know the truth behind the legend of Elijah Triggs.

"I wonder if Cicely looked anything like any of us present Brays," pondered Betty. "I don't suppose you have any pictures of her, do you?"

Walter sighed. "Regrettably, only as an old lady. Photographs were rather rare in her younger days, unless you had plenty of money."

As his words faded, Sid returned with Meg, who was clutching an old suitcase.

"You off somewhere?" asked Betty, eying the case.

"No such luck, but judging by what Sid's just told me, I think you'll all be very interested in what's in here. I'd forgotten all about it until just now."

The case was small and made of brown leather. Brass reinforcements were attached to the eight corners and large brass clasps sat either side of the worn handle. Meg knelt, laid the case on the floor and opened up the lid. Inside, were a few items of old fashioned clothing, some jewellery and a few books."

"You been to a jumble sale?" asked Percy.

"Ha, ha. Listen. A few years back when Dad was in the throes of leaving the Vicarage, I found this case up in the attic. It meant absolutely nothing to me, and Dad said it was there when he and Mum had moved in, so I knew it wasn't anything to do with our family. Anyway, because I didn't know what was likely to happen to the house, I kept it, mainly because it seemed criminal to dispose of it and also because I've always had a keen sense of history. But, so that it didn't clutter up the house unnecessarily, I put it in the back of our shed out of the way, beneath an old chest of drawers."

She pushed aside the items visible on the surface and from the bottom pulled out an old wooden frame which she then laid on the table. "This I assume, is your Vicar Bray and his family. See, on the back it says Christmas 1880. I'd no idea who they were until now because the surname isn't included, but it has to be them because of the date."

They all leaned over the table to gaze at the gathered family.

"Blimey, Betty, now you've had your hair dyed you're the spitting image of the vicar's wife," said Gertie.

Everyone agreed.

Betty was thrilled. "Oh that's a wonderful compliment, it's really nice to think I look like my great grandmother, even though I never knew her."

"So which of the three lads do you think is your granddad, Betty?" asked Walter, studying the picture. "It's easy to see which of the two girls Cicely is because she's considerably older than her young sister. I know that because she was twenty in the 1881 census, but there's not much to choose between the boys, so they must all have been born in the years between the two girls."

"I've no idea which is Granddad," admitted Betty, shaking her head. "Dad will know of course, so I think we'll have to take this round to him tomorrow and see what he can make of it."

"Well, whichever he is, it looks as though we were right in our surmise," said Anne, cheerfully sipping her glass of Dry Martini. "And Cicely definitely did come home from Devon that Christmas." She sighed. "How sad: this must have been the last picture of the family ever taken together because the following year Cicely had her first child."

Walter nodded. "Yes, my grandfather."

216

"What else is in the case, Meg?" Gertie asked. "Anything interesting?"

"Items which I'd guess, belonged to your Cicely. See, they're very feminine."

She lifted out a silk shawl, magenta in colour and trimmed with a thick fringe, an emerald green plume, badly bent, a Chantilly lace and tortoise shell fan, several books by Jane Austen, a thimble and a few trinkets of jewellery.

Elizabeth picked up the fan and carefully unfolded it. "If these things belonged to Cicely, I wonder why she didn't take them to Devon with her"

Walter sighed. "Probably because she made use of them when she came home for a visit. It looks very much to me as if when Elijah joined her in Devon, the family disowned her and put these things in the loft to dispose of all memories of her existence."

"But if that's the case then the vicar and his wife must have known all along what happened to Elijah Triggs but didn't do anything to stop the rumours and ghost stories," said Gertie. "That was pretty harsh on the Triggs family. Assuming Elijah had any family members still living."

Elizabeth shook her head. "No, I would like to think the Triggs family knew exactly where Elijah was because I'm sure he would have told them of his plan and needless to say they would have kept very quiet."

Walter nodded. "Yes, and likewise the vicar and his wife would have realised it was either say nothing about Elijah's possible whereabouts or lose face. Morals were very strict back then and a vicar of all people would find it very hard to accept his daughter was living in sin with a married man."

"Well, the old adage certainly applies here," said Anne. "I refer to 'pride comes before the fall'. If the vicar had accepted Elijah in the first place then none of this would ever have happened."

Rebecca giggled. "Having said that, Dad and I wouldn't be here today if Elijah and Cicely had had the vicar's blessing and married here in Trengillion instead of running away. Because their son wouldn't have married a Devonian, and neither would his son. In fact, there wouldn't have been a son. There wouldn't have been any of us, if you see what I mean."

"In that case, it all turned out for the best," said Betty, patting Rebecca's hand.

While the large gathering chatted, Matthew reluctantly arrived at the inn having been prompted to do so earlier by his father, Peter.

"Matthew," said Betty, rising to her feet and grabbing her son's arm. "I'm so glad you're here. Now come and meet your cousins many times removed. "Walter, Rebecca, this is my son, Matthew."

Walter stood and shook hands firmly and enthusiastically with the late arrival. "Delighted to meet you, Matthew. I can see a family resemblance; you have my father's eyes."

"Do I? Cool."

Rebecca then took Matthew's hand. "Yes, you do," she smiled, "have my grandfather's eyes, I mean."

Bewitched by her gaze, Matthew was surprised to find himself reluctant to free her warm, slim hand. "I, err…um, it's nice to meet you," he whispered.

"Come and sit down, Matt," said Gertie, "and we'll tell you what we've come up with, and then you can tell us if it all makes sense. I bet you never realised you were related to Elijah Triggs."

"What!" Matthew muttered, conscious of Rebecca's presence. "But how?"

He listened intently to the group's theory regarding part of his family history, but when it was finished he frowned in a confused manner.

"Okay. So if Elijah never really went missing and never fell into the old pond by the chapel and drowned, then where did the old cart wheels come from that the Bingham boys found?

CHAPTER THIRTY

After dropping off their offspring at school the following morning, Elizabeth and Anne chatted excitedly outside the school gates, for at ten o'clock they were due to meet up with, Gertie, Betty, Walter, Rebecca and Jane, to visit Arthur Bray with the old family picture and they hoped the visit would prove to be very productive.

The group met, as pre-arranged, at Fuchsia Cottage, and then walked the short distance to Penwynton Crescent. Arthur, who knew of the proposed visit due to a phone call from his daughter, Betty, was waiting by the door to let them in.

"This is a real pleasure," he grinned, leading the small gathering into his sitting room. "Visitors two days running."

When everyone was in the room, Betty removed the large picture from a carrier bag and laid it on the dining table where the light was brightest, she then stepped to one side to enable her father to identify his family.

"Well, I never," he grinned, reading glasses perched on the end of his nose. "Fancy you finding this." He gently tapped the glass covering the old photograph. "That's my dad there," he said. "He's the middle one of the three boys, and the chap to his left is my Uncle Jack and the other my uncle George. I'd recognise them anywhere because they look much the same as I remember them when I was a lad."

Betty stood by her father's side and pointed to the vicar and his wife, Alice. "And they are obviously my great grandparents," she said, thoughtfully.

"Yes, that's right." Arthur chuckled. "You know, Bet, when I were a boy I was a bit scared of me grandmother, your great grandmother. She was ever so superstitious, you see. She had all sorts of lucky charms and suchlike. Of course me granddad didn't approve. He reckoned God was all as was needed to protect the family from evil. He weren't vicar then of course; he must have long since retired because as I say I didn't even know he'd been a vicar."

"So out of interest, where did they live when you were a boy?" Betty asked.

"They were in a little house called Holly Cottage. It were one of about six but they're all long gone. They were pulled down in the late nineteen forties and then Coronation Terrace was built on the land."

Gertie was surprised. "Oh, where I live."

Arthur nodded.

Betty looked puzzled. "Why on earth did they pull them down?"

Arthur grinned. "Because they were small, damp and all in a bad way. It would have cost a fortune to have modernised them so the land was sold, the houses demolished and nice new ones built in their place."

Jane looked down on the picture. "So where do you think this photograph would have been taken?"

"At a studio in Helston," said Gertie. "The photographer's name is on the back."

Betty sighed. "And to think it's been around all these years and we never knew of its existence. You must keep it, Dad, and hang it on your wall."

He nodded. "I'd like that. I'd like that very much."

Elizabeth and Anne waited until all family members had viewed the picture again before they took a second look, for the light the previous night in the Fox and Hounds had not really been good enough to see any fine detail.

Elizabeth sat in a chair and Anne looked over her shoulder. Central, at the back, stood the vicar, a proud upright man, and beside him his elegant wife, Alice, looking very much Betty's double. In front of them, seated on the floor, were the three boys, grinning cheekily. To their left, standing, was Cicely, and on the far right, stood her younger sister.

"What was Cicely's little sister called?" Elizabeth nervously asked.

"Viola," said Arthur, approaching the table. "I'd forgotten 'til Walter reminded me just now."

"Of course, she wasn't born when they did the 1871 census," said Walter, "but I sent away for a copy of her birth certificate. She was born in June 1875 but the poor kid must have died soon after this picture was taken because she wasn't on the 1881 census and they're done every ten years at the end of March."

Elizabeth turned cold, as she recollected the name on the handkerchief shown to her by Molly; the voice of a child singing *I had a Little Nut Tree* in the chimney of the Old Vicarage; the rustling sound on the bare floorboards and the shoe in the ginger jar. "Viola must have died in January," she whispered, "January 1881, when she was just five and a half years old. And it was she with whom Grandma made contact during the séance. See, it all makes sense. The snow fell on or around the anniversary of her death. She died at the Vicarage in what's now the spare bedroom, and that's why her spirit was present in Trengillion recently."

"But how do you know that?" Jane asked, in awe.

Elizabeth shook her head. "I can't give you a sensible answer, Jane. I just know."

Elizabeth didn't want to go into detail of her experience at the Old Vicarage. Due to the wine consumed and the fact she was half asleep at the time, she had until the arrival of Walter and Rebecca preferred to believe the voice may have been a figment of her imagination, therefore she had told no-one other than her sister, Anne.

She smiled and touched the glass which covered the little girl's image. Her manifestation in the Old Vicarage that night was something only her grandmother would understand but to date Molly knew nothing of it.

Anne clasped her hands together. "Well, if you're right, Liz, we should easily be able to find her grave in the churchyard now. It was impossible when we looked the day after the séance because we didn't have a name or a date, but now we have both, so it should be a doddle. And she's sure to have a headstone, being the vicar's daughter."

"Hang on, hang on," grinned Walter, "you've lost me a bit. What's all this about a séance?"

Gertie told him of the peculiar happenings at the inn.

"Phew" said Walter, his face a shade lighter, "so our arrival has put an end to your old ghost story about Elijah, but at the same time raised another, and I wonder, Betty, why she ruffled your hair."

"Obviously because you looked like her mother," said Rebecca. "We've all agreed there's a strong resemblance."

Betty shuddered. "Oh, don't, I'm getting all goose-pimply."

"Well, it seems to me that our next move must be a trip to the graveyard," said Gertie, dazed, "and since the weather's fine, I suggest we go now."

"No, stay for a coffee first," begged Arthur, raising his hands, "another half an hour won't make any difference after all these years. Not only do I like your company but you'll all be able to help me polish off my Christmas cake. I won the bloomin' thing in a raffle, you see, and at the rate I'm getting through it, it'll still be around next Christmas."

Later, as the small gathering began their search amongst the rows of graves, Gertie, on the left hand side and over by the wall, came across a tombstone for all the drowned seamen mentioned by Percy on New Year's Eve, who had perished in the blizzard of 1891. After reading the sad details, she called to the others, so they too might share her findings, they then separated to commence the search for little Viola Bray.

It was Betty who found the grave of the vicar's daughter. It lay amongst the ostentatious tombs on the right-hand side of the entrance porch, a spot passed many times over the years by all who entered the church. Betty recalled knowing there were Brays buried by the porch, for she had first spotted them as a girl, but having no reason to think people of such standing were her relatives, she took little notice of them, and had never thoroughly read the inscriptions.

Elizabeth's prediction regarding Viola's demise was correct, as they discovered from the inscription on her white marble headstone, which stated she was the beloved daughter of Vicar Samuel Bray and Alice, his wife, and she died on January 18th 1881, aged five. It also stated her death was caused by a fall from a pony and trap.

"If Viola died in January 1881," said Jane, thoughtfully, "well that sort of explains why the vicar and his family never said anything about Elijah's disappearance. I mean, they must have been devastated over her death, and that, coupled with Cicely's disgrace, would surely have over-shadowed any sympathy they might have felt for Elijah's family."

When Matthew went to sea, the morning after the gathering at the Fox and Hounds, he could think of little other than his cousin Rebecca, several times removed. Before her arrival he had secretly declared himself to be a confirmed bachelor, his true love being the sea; but suddenly everything, it seemed, had changed. Matthew did not believe in love at first sight, in fact he did not really believe in love at all. He thought it was just a weak state of mind, another word for lust and in spite of the obvious happiness of his married friends he did not think marriage was for him. Matthew therefore was a little annoyed that Rebecca's face was firmly imprinted in his mind, her voice repeatedly echoed in his ears and he could still feel the gentle warmth of her hand in his.

During the summer months, Matthew fished for crabs with his friend and colleague, Jim Hughes. In the winter he fished alone for mackerel, and Jim, prone to sea sickness hence not over-fond of choppy waters, worked for the Wilson brothers on their farm cutting winter vegetables. Mackerelling was a hard life, the weather was often inhospitable and it was possible to spend many hours at sea without catching a single fish. However, of the two options, fishing or farming, Matthew preferred the sea, for there was always the possibility of having an exceptionally good day, whereas cutting cauli and cabbage was very hard on the back, although Matthew conceded the money at least, was reliable.

The morning following Matthew's introduction to Rebecca was clear and mild with a gentle wind blowing from the south west, hence he left his oil skins in the wheelhouse and went to sea wearing fishing smock and jeans. His optimism was high as he chugged away from Trengillion towards Polquillick and the Witches Broomstick, for in the distance he could see a fleet of small boats, no doubt catching fish. With enthusiasm he turned the boat to join them, but as he headed into the breeze, something caused him to pause. Hopeful that his hunter instinct had sensed mackerel, he slowed down and trailed his hand line over the stern of the boat. When he had a bite he quickly knocked the rudder to the side, circled the spot and began to haul the line, shaking the fish into the boat as they came up. Delighted with his haul, he quickly repeated the process.

With a better than average catch, Matthew was exultant, and went about boxing up the fish with a song on his lips and a skip in his steps. But in doing so he became a little careless and through his high spirits, slipped, lost his footing, fell hard against the side of the boat and toppled, much to his disgust, awkwardly over the gunwale. Fortunately he was a very good swimmer, he regained control and pulled himself back up into the boat, but as he stood and retrieved his balance, his baccy tin slid from the pocket of his saturated smock and splashed into the swirling water. Matthew swore beneath his breath. Had it been any old tin he would have let it go, but it wasn't any old tin; it was silver and a twenty first birthday present from his parents, hence had sentimental value.

Already wet through, he considered a further soaking would not be detrimental to his health or well-being, and as he was not far from the shore there was a limit to how deep the tin could sink. And so without giving the task a second thought, he removed his boots and slipped back over the side to retrieve the tin before it disappeared out of vision.

Matthew was delighted when he caught sight of the tin glistening as it slowly sank beneath the waves. Holding his breath he followed it on its journey falling through the clear water. But then suddenly, it stopped and came to rest. Matthew swam closer, but as he did so, he realised it had not reached the sea bed, but was resting on a large solid surface. Assuming it had settled on a rock, he reached down, wishing the salt water did not sting his eyes and thus blur his vision.

As his hand grasped the tin, his foot tapped the surface of the object on which the tin had come to rest, and to his surprise he realised it was not rock, but metal. Thinking it might be a wreck his excitement rose. But then suddenly, it dawned on him, what it really was. Unable to shout, he swam back to the surface with baccy tin firmly in his hand and climbed back on board the *Betty Jane*. With water dripping from his clothing onto the deck he started the engine and headed back to Trengillion trembling with cold, shock and excitement. For on the sea bed, he had found something which had been much searched for during recent weeks; the missing police car.

CHAPTER THIRTY ONE

That same morning, Jim who had the day off work because the price of vegetables was falling rapidly, decided to take a walk, and because his initial look around the Ebenezer Chapel during the snow had been curtailed due to fading daylight, he proposed to seize the dawning of a bright new day and go to the chapel for a proper look at his leisure.

He left his home at the Mews, and crossed the driveway of the Hotel so that he could walk through Bluebell Woods. It was not the quickest way to the crossroads, but it was the most interesting, and as Jim had nothing else planned for the remainder of the day, time was of no importance.

Jim followed the contours of the stream through the woods until he reached the bridge at the foot of the hill, where small clusters of early snowdrops lay huddled amongst dead leaves and twigs. He stooped to admire them, recalling the churchyard near to his childhood home where they carpeted the grassy area alongside the path leading to the belfry door.

Jim straightened his back and kneaded his spine with his strong hands. Cutting cabbage and cauliflowers was all very well, but it was hard on the back. He left the stream, climbed the bank and slipped beneath the old wooden fence. As he stepped onto the road, a tractor emerged around the bend. Jim waved to the driver, Tony Collins, and then made his way slowly up the hill and into the village.

All trace of the snow had gone from the chapel graveyard; even the remains of the two snow men had vanished along with their police helmets. Jim laughed; someone no doubt had taken the helmets as souvenirs, memorabilia of something that would go down in Trengillion history as a very novel prank.

Jim walked up the chapel path and along the front of the building, marvelling at the neat stonework, admiring the architecture, especially the arches above the windows and door, for unlike most people who had visited the chapel during the first days the two policemen had gone missing, he did not feel afraid or threatened; in fact he felt very much at home.

Before he went inside, Jim scrambled onto a box tomb beside the muddy path and sat with legs dangling. He then rolled a cigarette and surveyed his surroundings. By the gate, the estate agent's For Sale board lay on top of the wall, having finally toppled from its vertical position following its brief use for the target practice of snowballers, young and old. Jim sighed; if only he had the money to buy the chapel, do it up and live there. It was a cherished dream, but he knew like everyone else, that dreams seldom, if ever, came true.

When his cigarette was finished, he stubbed out what was left on the tomb, threw it onto the grass, jumped down and then walked towards the door, but when he attempted to turn the handle he found it locked. Jim cursed, assuming the estate agents had locked it after taking people round to view, although if so, why: for it had been unlocked on his first visit.

Annoyed that his plans were thwarted, he walked around to the back of the chapel on the off-chance there might be a small back door. He was disappointed. There was no door, but several inches above his head was a broken window. Jim was puzzled, he recalled seeing a gaping hole in the chapel roof on his previous visit, but he felt sure the window had still been intact. Nevertheless, he concluded after a brief consideration, the act of vandalism was to his advantage, for with the aid of something to give him a leg-up, he should be able to reach the window and make his entrance through the substantial hole. He began to search amongst the overgrown shrubbery where various fly-tipped items were visible in the long grass, and eventually, much to his surprise, he found a perfectly sound ladder tucked behind a hedge.

He propped the ladder against the back wall of the chapel, grumbling beneath his breath about the immorality of disposing of an item with many years of life left in it; he then climbed the rungs until his waist was level with the base of the window. After checking there were no jagged edges of glass, he looked inside. A satisfied smile crossed his face, for a couple of feet beneath the window, a wide granite sill, littered with broken glass, offered its services as a safe platform on which to climb, once inside.

When his feet were firmly on the chapel floor, Jim crossed the large, empty space towards the front door. But when he saw it he stopped dead. Hairs on the back of his neck stood up and he knew something was wrong. For the old oak door was not locked in the conventional manner, with a key, but barricaded across with two large planks of wood, crudely nailed on either side of the door frame.

After the visit to the churchyard, Elizabeth walked home, deep in thought, saddened by the knowledge that Viola, the vicar's daughter, had died following a fall from a pony and trap. But as she neared her home, all thoughts of Viola slipped from her mind for she sensed something was amiss.

Calmly she stepped onto the beach and cast her eyes out to sea. In the distance she could hear the chugging of an approaching engine, and then suddenly Matthew's boat, the *Betty Jane* appeared from around the corner. When the boat hit the shore Matthew jumped onto the beach, his clothes dripping wet, the expression on his face a cross between anxiety and excitement. Elizabeth was surprised for it was obvious he was more concerned about attracting her attention than winching the boat up the beach as would be his usual routine. When she heard his news she understood why, and quickly led him into Cove Cottage to use the telephone and call the police.

Within an hour of Matthew's phone call, Trengillion was awash with police vehicles, officers and frogmen, while overhead two police helicopters circled over the village causing inhabitants to rush from their homes in order to establish the cause of their re-appearance. Matthew meanwhile, having dashed home before the arrival of the police, to shower and put on warm, dry clothing, found himself the centre of attention as he was asked to lead detectives in their dinghy to the spot where he had found the car.

Trengillion's inhabitants waited on the cliff tops overlooking the spot, with bated breath for news of the search, and all were both surprised and relieved, eventually to hear that the two policemen were not in the vehicle. However, it did not take long for either the police or the locals to realise that if the car had plunged into the sea without a driver then it must have been pushed, and the land above the spot where the vehicle was found belonged to Giles and Brendon Wilson at Higher Green Farm.

Candy Bingham was busy cleaning the bathroom at Higher Green Farm. She heard the helicopters hovering nearby but was unaware of the reason for their presence. However, as she turned off the cold tap after rinsing out the bath, she became aware of sudden raised voices, drawers slamming and doors banging, firstly from bedrooms across the landing upstairs and then down below. Intrigued by the activity, she left the bathroom and went in search of the noisy perpetrators. In the living room, she was surprised to find Giles and Brendon rushing around, gathering things together and pushing them into suitcases along with hurriedly packed clothing.

"What on earth's going on?" She asked, puzzled by their frantic actions. "Are you off somewhere and if so, what's the hurry?"

"We have to go away, Cand, and it's unlikely we'll ever be back," said Brendon. "It's a long, long story and there's no time to explain now. Sorry."

A sudden feeling of horror swept through Candy's body. "Not the police car," she whispered, recalling the sounds of hovering helicopters. "They've found the police car, haven't they? Oh, please, please don't tell me they did come here after all, and that you're both involved."

Brendon paused. "Yes, the coppers did come here, thanks to that bloody Ainsworth woman, and so now we have to go. She's ruined everything."

"But where will you go?" Candy asked, dazed and confused, "What'll happen to the farm and the animals and, and everything?"

"Don't know," said Giles, his face ashen and grey, "but I'm sure folks around here will make sure the livestock are all taken care of. As for our destination, we'd never incriminate you by telling you, even if we knew where we were going. But we have to get Ivan first and then it looks like we'll be fugitives for a while."

"Wait, just one thing," Candy muttered, as the brothers rushed to the door, "the policemen, are they, are they, I mean, are they dead?"

228

Giles shook his head vigorously. "No, Cand, they're alive. We're robbers, not murderers. We may be scum in the eyes of many, but we'd never take anyone's life. On that you have my word."

While Brendon dashed to the car and started the engine, Giles picked up his suitcase and two carrier bags and headed for the door. On the threshold he paused and his bottom lip quivering.

"Jane," muttered Candy. "Giles, what about Jane?"

"Oh God, she knows nothing of this, Cand, I promise you. She knows nothing at all and that's why I could never ask her to marry me. I knew there was always the chance we'd get caught one day and I couldn't expect her to understand."

In the farmyard Brendon tooted the car horn impatiently. Giles looked back pleadingly to Candy standing in the kitchen, his eyes brim-full of tears. "When you see Jane, Cand, tell her I'm sorry. I'm very, very sorry, and, and say, well, tell her, I love her; always did, and always will."

He ran from the house and leapt into the car. Candy watched from the doorstep as they left the farmyard with all wheels spinning and headed down the lane towards the village.

Dazed, Candy stumbled back into the kitchen and unsteadily sat down at the table, her hands were trembling; her legs felt weak and jelly-like. She thought of the half opened bottle of brandy on the pantry shelf; a drink might steady her nerves and stop her body from shaking, but she was too shocked to move; her limbs felt weak; her skin felt cold and clammy; her head was spinning and she felt sick.

Five minutes passed by and then Candy heard the sound of an approaching siren. It stopped outside in the farmyard. Several doors banged, and within minutes, eight policemen barged into the house demanding to know the whereabouts of the Wilson brothers. Candy sat feeling numb, her conscience torn between honesty and loyalty to two men she had regarded as friends. She wanted to cry and hung her head to hide her moist eyes, she then told the police she had no idea of their whereabouts, but said they had gone from the farm and did not intend to return.

When she was questioned further and asked if she had seen anything of the two missing policemen, she was able to answer honestly that she had not, but as she did so, reality suddenly dawned, and she recalled something which had frequently puzzled her. For since that snowy night, she had noticed food from the brothers' fridge had disappeared much faster than usual. At first she put down the excessive consumption to the cold weather, but when it continued she was less convinced. However, as she was unable to think of any other reason for its daily disappearance, she pushed it from her mind, concluding, what the brothers did with their own food was no business of hers.

"The policemen are not here, but they are alive," she whispered.

"How do you know that?" demanded a plain clothed officer, his gruff voice tinged with a Cornish accent.

"Giles and Brendon are not killers," she muttered, holding her head high. "They told me so and I believe them."

As her voice trailed away the telephone rang.

"Answer it," commanded the officer, "and if it's them keep them talking."

With hesitance Candy stood, crossed to the desk, took in a deep breath and lifted the receiver. A woman's voice was on the other end of the line. "Hi, Candy. Is Giles there please? It's me, Jane."

As Jim stared, with heart thumping, at the unsightly barricade in the old chapel, his eyes were drawn away towards a pile of old grey blankets bundled in the corner, for he sensed slight movement there. Thinking perhaps it might be wildlife which had made the chapel its home during the winter, he apprehensively walked towards the blankets. Momentarily he paused. He was, he believed, an animal lover, but his fondness of wild creatures did not stretch to rats and other vermin. He stepped backwards, casting his eyes around for a stick or something with which to prod the heap. And then it groaned; the pile of old grey blankets, groaned. Jim roared with fright at the top of his voice, ran towards the door and leaned his back against the barricade for protection. And then another sound filled the air. A familiar, comforting sound. A police siren, whining from a car as it sped by outside. And then suddenly it dawned on Jim, not what, but who, lay beneath the old blankets.

Over the next few days, villagers learned that the two Wilson brothers had been arrested along with their cousin Ivan, at Ivan's farm in Falmouth, and all had been charged, not only with bank robbery and the abduction of two police officers, but with three other bank robberies also. For although the brothers did not actually break into the banks, they were members of a gang of crooks and it was their job to receive the stolen money from Ivan and keep it hidden until the coast was clear. Their cousin Ivan, had of course, been questioned earlier in the month following the sighting at Higher Green Farm by Janet Ainsworth, but he had given the police, what seemed to be, a rock solid alibi for the day the bank robbery had taken place, hence no further action had been taken against him at the time.

In due course, three other men were also arrested in different locations up-country. However, in spite of the arrests and extensive searches over land at Higher Green Farm, the whereabouts of the money remained a mystery and it was supposed that unless one of the criminals talked, it was unlikely ever to be found.

Trengillion was shocked and saddened by the unfurling drama. Not just by the large media presence, but also seeing the faces of Giles and Brendon splashed across their television screens like common criminals. For other than Janet Ainsworth, the brothers had never given anyone in the village reason to dislike them; they had joined in with activities, helped with fund raising, and had always offered a willing hand to anyone that needed it.

"I feel as though they'd died," said Cassie Godson to Larry Bingham, following the latest news bulletin earlier that evening. "How's Candy? Young Jim said she was very upset and he's still in shock himself, poor lad. I'm so glad the poor policemen came out of this alive but goodness only knows what the brothers planned to do with them."

Larry thoughtfully shook his head. "She's coming round, but she's had a rough time, poor girl. At first the police thought she knew more than she did, so they were a bit hard on her. Not that that really bothered her as she's never been one to wallow in self-pity. Her concern is for poor Jane; she was the one who had to tell her what had happened, you see."

"So I've heard. I saw Betty yesterday and she said Jane's heart was broken. The family are all rallying round but apparently she just wants to be left alone. I wish there was something we could do, but I'm afraid it's one of those things that only time will heal."

On hearing the news of the Wilson brothers' arrest, Janet Ainsworth, at first, was cock-a-hoop. She felt she had revenge at last, and that, topped with the knowledge that her reported sighting of a bank robber, was correct all along, gave her great satisfaction. But when she heard of Jane's unhappiness the feeling of euphoria disappeared and her conscience began to prick. It was right of course, that the brothers be arrested, but had she never made that phone call and brought the police out to Trengillion, Giles and Brendon would never have been caught and Jane not hurt.

To dispel the feeling of guilt, and to occupy her mind with other thoughts, Janet decided it was time to start thinking of decorating the house, but she found that only made things worse, for it reminded her of the time Jane had asked for her advice and they had chatted in her little flat.

Janet looked from the window; the day looked fairly pleasant, so it seemed a good time to take a walk to the beach. She slipped on her jacket and boots, put Glenda on her lead and left the Old Police House without bothering to wash the dirty breakfast dishes.

The morning was chilly with a fresh north westerly wind blowing down towards the sea. Janet pulled up the hood of her jacket to protect her hair and then walked down the road, past the Fox and Hounds and on towards the beach. Outside the Pickled Egg she stopped. She wanted to knock on the door, but thought it unlikely that she of all people, would be welcome. Instead she continued until she reached the beach.

The beach was deserted and the tide was right out. Janet let Glenda off her lead and sat on a bench which she had noted on a previous visit was dedicated to the memory of a Denzil Penhaligon. Janet wondered who he might have been. The poor man had evidently drowned and the thought saddened her.

The cold wind was too strong for Janet to remain on the bench and so she stood and headed for the formation of rocks accessible only at low water. But when she reached the rocks and approached the sheltered, south side, facing the sea, she saw that the beach was not deserted for someone else was out and nestled in a tiny alcove, sheltering from the wind. Janet gasped as her heart skipped a beat. That someone was Jane.

Following the arrest of his part-time employers, Jim, downhearted and with no job, decided to walk up to Higher Green Farm to collect his Wellington boots and his oil skins from the barn where he always left them. On arrival the police were reluctant to let him onto the premises, but a senior officer gave him permission to enter on condition that he was quick.

"Not having much luck, are they," said Jim, nodding towards a field of half cut cabbage, where the police were looking for disturbed ground under which they thought the money might be hidden. "Bit like looking for a needle in a haystack."

Jim left the farmyard and walked back out onto the lane. On the roadside, an old glass dandelion and burdock bottle gleamed in the sunlight. Jim kicked it and watched as it rolled down the hill and into the grass verge. Suddenly, he stopped dead in his tracks. He felt dizzy, for the sight of the bottle jogged his memory of something he had heard the brothers say a few weeks earlier whilst he had herded the cows ready for afternoon milking. It meant nothing to him at the time and so he had dismissed it from his mind.

"Dandelions," muttered Jim, feeling his flesh creep. "Christ, why didn't I think of it before? A ring of five dandelions. That's got to be the answer."

It was Brendon who had uttered those strange words on the day Ivan had visited the farm and Giles had replied: "Perfect, Bren, Good thinking."

Feeling dizzy with excitement, Jim turned on his heels, ran back into the farmyard, rushed past the policeman standing by the house and flew into the field where officers were painstakingly searching.

"You're in the wrong field," he yelled, waving his arms and laughing wildly. "Oh, God, this is crazy, but I think you should be in the meadow where the cows graze and the coastal path runs through.

There are lots of dandelions there, you see, and that's where Brendon was when he said it and so it has to be the right place."

He then went on to explain what he had heard the brothers say and the logic behind his surmise.

In due course a search in the meadow began with officers looking for five dandelion plants in a circle, and to the delight and surprise of both the leading officer and Jim, five flowerless dandelions were found in the middle of the field, all planted close together and forming a near perfect ring.

Jim watched with thumping heart as a police officer dug up the dandelions and then began to dig a hole below. And no-one was more shocked than he, when, two feet down, the tops of two large metal caskets appeared through the dark earth.

Jim, down on his knees, looked on as the first casket was opened. The sight of all the money drew his breath, and then suddenly tears prickled the backs of his eyes.

"I say," he whispered, "it's just a thought, but do you think because it was me who directed you towards the right place to search for that dosh, that I might be in line for some of the reward money?"

CHAPTER THIRTY TWO

"I suppose the powers that be will seize the farm in order to recoup some of the stolen money from previous thefts," said Molly, when May and Dorothy called in to see her. "I really can't believe it. Giles and Brendon always struck me as being such a nice couple of lads. The major liked them too; he'd be horrified if he was still around to hear the truth."

May nodded. "Hmm, I liked them as well and so did Pat. We really thought the farm was in good hands but it looks like we've all been well and truly duped."

"Yes, but to be fair I believe they ran the farm well so we can't hold that against them," said Molly.

Dorothy leaned back on the settee and sighed. "No doubt it was them that made the ghostly cart wheel tracks and built the snowmen in the helmets. People will laugh about it for years to come but right now it doesn't seem very funny, does it?"

"But why would they have done it?" May asked. "That's what I don't understand. I mean, what was the purpose?"

Molly smiled. "To scare people away, I suppose. After all they didn't want anyone poking around the old chapel when the two poor policemen were hidden inside."

"Yes, but that's another thing, surely the police searched the old chapel when the bobbies first went missing. It was the obvious place since they last had radio contact with them around there."

Dorothy nodded. "I believe they did, in fact I know they did. Larry Bingham has been keeping everyone well informed at the inn and Frank had a long chat with him only yesterday. You see, they weren't there then, it turns out they were hidden in the cellar at the farm to begin with and the police didn't search it thoroughly because without the car they had no reason to think they'd even made it that far. It was sometime after that that the brothers moved the two policemen into the old chapel knowing it'd had already been searched and everyone was spooked by the place."

"I see, that sort of makes sense," May conceded, "but there's still the mystery of the cart tracks. I mean, how they could have done that without leaving any footprints."

Molly half-smiled. "Skis, quite simply, they did it with skis."

"Skis!" May exclaimed, "You'd better explain, I'm obviously not the sharpest knife in the drawer today."

"Well, I'm probably wrong but it's the only answer I've been able to come up with," said Molly, after clearing her throat, "and I have no proof, but they do have skis, Giles and Brendon, that is, because I asked Ned to find out. You see, I think they must have pushed the cart wheels that Candy's boys found in the pond down the lane and followed on close behind on skis, carefully keeping inside the same tracks, and then they'd have done the same thing going back. The tracks weren't visible on the main road because it had been gritted, so they only had to go the short distance from the junction to the old milk churn stand. That's my theory anyway, although as I say, I may well be wrong." She chuckled. "But they certainly weren't made by the ghost of Elijah Triggs; that we do know."

"Hmm, and I suppose once back on the main road they'd have loaded the wheels on the back of one of their vehicles and then dumped them in the pond." May laughed and patting Molly's back as she began to cough, "You're a right Miss Marple, aren't you? But then you always were. Well done."

"I've had more time to think than most," Molly croaked. "Lots of long lonely hours; still, in a funny sort of way I've enjoyed it."

"Sorry to go on but there's just one more thing that puzzles me," Dorothy said, "and that's that young lad, Jim and his bike. Why on earth do you think that went missing or do you suppose the brothers nicked that too?"

Molly shrugged her shoulders. "I can only assume they did and simply to fuel the talk of the Ebenezer Triangle. I suppose the more things that went missing the better."

"Ah well, at least some good has come out of all this," said Dorothy, "you'll no doubt have heard that Janet Ainsworth and poor Jane have struck up a friendship and that she's going to help Jane do up the cafe."

Molly nodded. "I did hear that. Poor, poor Jane, I hope she gets over Giles soon: she's such a lovely girl. As regards this Ainsworth woman, I can't really contribute much because I've never set eyes on her yet. What do you make of her?"

"She's alright," said May, "and when all's said and done, she was spot on with her identification of the Wilson's bank robbing cousin, so we must never hold that against her."

Dorothy smiled. "I think it'll be a while before Gertie likes her but then some people never will see eye to eye. Anyway, all's well that ends well."

"I expect you know Janet's going to get some of the reward money, don't you?" said May.

Molly's eyebrows rose. "Really?"

May nodded. "Yes, it's to be shared between her, Jim Haynes and young Matthew Williams but I'm not sure how it's to be split up."

"Ah, I know," said Dorothy, "because Frank found out at the inn last night. Apparently Jim will get two shares because he found the police officers and the money. Matthew will get one share for finding the police car and Janet one share for identifying the crooked cousin in the first place, even though it didn't lead to any arrests at that time."

"So how much will that be each?" May asked. "I don't even know how much the reward money is or was."

"Forty five thousand in total; twenty for finding the policemen and twenty five for information about the bank robbery. Which means twenty two and a half grand for Jim, and eleven thousand, two hundred and fifty pounds each for Janet and Matthew."

Molly blew out her cheeks. "Phew! Not a bad day's work. Good luck to them all but I do hope they'll spend it wisely."

May laughed. "Well, I don't know what Matthew or Janet's plans are but I've heard Jim is going to buy the old Ebenezer Chapel, do it up and live there. Rather him than me, I wouldn't be able to sleep at night surrounded by the dead."

Molly smiled. "Oh, May, you should never fear the dead for they are but sleeping souls."

May tried not to pull a face.

"My concern would be more about isolation," said practical Dorothy. "I mean, it'll be a bit lonely up there, won't it?"

May nodded. "Yes, I suppose it will, but looking on a brighter side, over the years the chapel will become a focal point for yet another story to add to Trengillion's folklore."

"And we were all here to witness its unfurling," said Dorothy, with glee. "I feel quite chuffed about that."

May sighed deeply. "We've had a few bits of excitement over the years, haven't we, ladies?" She patted Molly's hand. "And most of it started around the time you arrived in the village, Mrs Smith."

Molly smiled but her eyes were moist. "1952 it was when I first came here. It's the best thing I ever did. Trengillion's been good to me. The major and I had a wonderful marriage, I've a wonderful family and some wonderful friends. Who could ask for more?"

Jim, with the knowledge he had money due to him, made a very low offer for the Ebenezer Chapel which to his great surprise was accepted, for it was considered by the vendors, that a bird in the hand was worth two in the bush, and following the recent drama which had unfurled in the chapel it was unlikely there would be a rush of other prospective buyers to purchase the old place. Furthermore, it had already been on the market for over a year and during that time it had evoked very little interest.

Jim was delighted that after the purchase he would have a small amount of money to spare which would enable him to begin the refurbishment process.

Janet on the other hand felt uneasy about her surprise windfall. For in acquiring the money others had suffered, especially Jane Williams. For it was rumoured Jane had taken the loss of Giles Wilson very badly. She decided therefore, that as Ian was earning well, she would give some of the money to Jane, hoping in some small way, it might help ease the misery and heartache. Jane accepted Janet's offering with gratitude, for it would cover the cost of the café's refurbishment, and after it was all done, she decided to take out her old friends for a meal, along with her new found friend, Janet Ainsworth.

Matthew, like Janet, felt the reward money he received was tainted, for his discovery of the police car had led the arrest of his sister's boyfriend for which he felt very guilty. On the other hand, his discovery had probably saved his sister from getting any deeper emotionally than she already was with someone who could never give her the happiness she deserved. And so he invested the money in a building society, content with the knowledge it was there should he ever need it.

May and Dorothy's visit in the afternoon tired Molly far more than she would ever admit, the talking irritated her throat and made her cough, coughing made her chest feel tight; she also felt weak and ached from head to toe, but she would rather die than tell a living soul.

As the daylight began to fade, so did the therapeutic effect of the aspirins she had taken at lunch time instead of food because she had no appetite. Feeling hoarse, she went to the kitchen and made yet another cup of tea to ease her throat. As she took a seat by the fire, the telephone rang. It was Ned.

"Hello love," Molly croaked, "before you ask, I'm alright so you mustn't fuss."

"You don't sound alright to me," said Ned, "you sound awful and you should have shaken that cold off long ago. In fact, I reckon it's not a cold at all, it's the flu because you're definitely getting worse and your bloomin' fags aren't helping. Are you taking any medication for it?"

"Oh Ned, you know I dislike taking pills and potions, but actually I have had an aspirin or two today. There's no need for anything more, I'm just hoarse from talking a lot. May and Dorothy were round earlier, you see, and the three of us had a good old chin-wag."

"Is that the truth, Mother?"

"Ned, why would I lie about a visit from my closest friends?"

"I wasn't referring to their visit," Ned tutted, "I'm querying your hoarseness being caused by talking too much?"

Molly laughed and coughed at the same time. "You know me, Ned."

"I do," he said. "That's the trouble."

Molly sighed. "You must learn to fuss a little less, sweetheart. Now I must go, my tea's getting cold and you know I can't abide lukewarm tea."

"Okay, but I'll be round tomorrow morning since it's a Saturday, and be warned, if I don't like the look of you I shall call the doctor."

"Oh, Ned, look out of the window at the beautiful sunset, isn't it exquisite? If I were as talented as your Stella I'd have to paint that."

"I can't see it," said Ned, practically, "the curtains are drawn."

"Well you should see this one, it's spectacular. I shall sit by the window and watch it sink as I drink my tea. Goodbye, Ned."

"Bye, Mum, see you in the morning."

"Oh, and thank you, Ned."

"Thank you," Ned repeated, "for what?"

"Thank you for being you; for being my son, for caring and for giving me such a lovely family."

"You old softy," said Ned, with a laugh, "it must be the influence of your sunset."

Molly sat on her chair by the window and watched the sun sink behind the trees in a blaze of violet, rose, gold and apricot; she then drew her curtains with a deep sigh. For if the truth be known, she felt dreadful, but she had no intension of telling Ned or anyone else for that matter, and she certainly had no desire to bother the doctor.

She returned her mug to the kitchen and left it on the draining board; she thought about something for tea but still did not feel hungry. Molly held her aching head in her hands; her face burned beneath her fingers, she had a raging temperature and felt dizzy, hence she decided an early night might be the best possible remedy of all.

Back in the kitchen she boiled a kettle to fill her hot water bottle, for although she felt feverish and hot to the touch, inside she felt cold and shivery. With bottle clutched in her arms she locked the back door and placed the key beside the kettle. In the living room she leaned the guard in front of the fire, punched up the cushions on the settee and switched off the light; she then climbed the steep, straight stairs to her room, undressed, put on her thick, warm flannelette nightie and climbed into bed.

As soon as she lay down she began to cough again, and strong irregular palpitations thumped through her body. To distract her mind from her discomfort, she attempted to make plans for the following day, but all thoughts tumbling through her aching head became muddled, and the distant past tangled with the present, the improbable and the unknown.

After a while her eyelids felt heavy and eventually they closed. In her blurred dreams she saw her mother, her father and her first husband, Michael. And then, through a dark, swirling haze, she heard the major gently calling her name. A smile crossed her face; she was floating, drifting slowly away, like a cloud in the breeze, away from pain and on into another world.

The following morning, Elizabeth, having slept badly, slipped from her bed just before seven o'clock and silently crept down the stairs, eager to make a mug of tea. Moving quietly around in the kitchen, so as not to disturb Greg and the children, with mug in hand, she peeped through the heavy velvet curtains in the living room to view the new morning. It was still dark, but Elizabeth could hear the sea and felt compelled to go outside.

Quickly, she drank her tea and then crept back up the stairs and lifted her clothes from the chair in the bedroom. Downstairs, she wrote a note for Greg to say she was going for a walk; she then dressed, and from the pegs in the hallway reached for her coat and scarf, slipped them on and crept outside, softly closing the door behind as she left.

Elizabeth shivered in the cold morning air, and by the garden gate watched the white waves, visible in the first light, crashing onto the deserted beach. The air smelt fresh and good, scented with the pungent smell of seaweed washed ashore by recent heavy seas. Elizabeth took in a deep breath and then walked slowly up the incline towards the village. By the foot of the track which led to the coastal path, she stopped. Instinct told her to follow the path up onto the cliff tops. As she walked her mind sifted through recent events, the arrest of the Wilson brothers, the truth regarding Elijah Triggs and the ghost of little Viola Bray.

As she approached the Coastguard Cottages, Elizabeth looked eastwards. The sun was beginning to rise; a beautiful golden sun, glowing brilliant shades of orange and yellow, casting shimmering beams of dazzling light over the dark shadows of the bracken and the silhouette of the old mine. She watched, mesmerised by its beauty, until it dispersed into a bright silver sphere, heralding the breaking of a brand new day.

Elizabeth felt unusually composed and relaxed by the tranquil peace of the morning, yet as she turned and walked back towards Trengillion, she was a little puzzled as to what had drawn her out to view the wonderful sight of breaking day.

Near to the village, she gazed down on the houses nestled in the valley; proud and thankful that Trengillion was the place she could call home. But then she paused, and her heart fluttered, for the glow of the newly risen sun shone down onto the roof tiles of Rose Cottage and Rose Cottage alone, causing a beam of light to hover over the house like a brilliant golden halo. Elizabeth blinked and looked again, instantly the glow vanished like a puff of smoke. And then she knew what the glorious morning was about; why she had woken early and been drawn to the cliffs.

With a pitiful cry, Elizabeth ran along the remainder of the cliff path, slipping and sliding on muddy patches on her way down into the cove. At the bottom she turned right and ran up to the village, past the inn and along the main street. By the gate of Rose Cottage she stopped for breath. The house was in darkness. She ran up the garden path and round to the back door where from beneath a flower pot she retrieved the spare house key. She unlocked the door and let herself into the porch and then into the kitchen.

The house struck warm after the chill of the early morning, but no embers glowed in the living room's dark fireplace. Elizabeth quietly crossed the room, switched on the stairs light and gently called her grandmother's name. There was no reply. With heart in mouth, she tip-toed up towards her grandmother's room. On the landing she stopped; the house was deathly quiet except for the ticking of a wall clock at the top of the stairs. Slowly she opened the bedroom door. The room felt chilly in comparison with downstairs. Elizabeth crept towards the bed and reached out to touch her grandmother's face. It was cold. She pulled back the curtains to let in the daylight. A sunbeam fell across Molly's sleeping face. From the dressing table Elizabeth picked up a hand mirror and held it over her grandmother's mouth. No sign of breath misted the glass. Elizabeth switched on the light. Tears welled up in her eyes as she looked at the figure lying in the bed. Molly's head lay on the pillow with a smile on her face; she looked at peace, at rest, and just below the bedclothes, clutched in her arms, she held the picture she kept on the bedside cabinet; a picture of the major.

Ned vowed he would never forgive himself for not responding to his mother's last request, for he had not watched the sunset as she had suggested, instead he had picked up the daily paper and lectured Stella on the declining standards of society following an article about anti-social behaviour on an up-country housing estate.

"Don't be too hard on yourself, Dad. Grandma would have been amused by your lack of obedience," said Elizabeth, reassuringly, after the funeral, "and to be honest, I think she'd have been more surprised if you had watched the sunset than by the fact that you didn't."

"That's as maybe, Liz, but it was the last thing we should have shared together and I let her down."

"You didn't let her down, Dad. She knew you, and she loved you and the rest of us for who and what we are. But in future see sunsets as reminders of her."

Molly had always been very fond of April for it was the month in which she was born. It was uncanny therefore, that on the day which would have been her eighty third birthday, many inhabitants of Trengillion woke to find their gardens sprinkled with patches of blue shimmering amongst the late spring flowers.

At the Old Vicarage, John called Anne to look from the bedroom window to witness a sight that had not been there the previous day. Forget-me-nots in varying shades of blue dominated her flower beds and borders.

In the garden of Cove Cottage, Elizabeth and Greg too found a similar display, as did Ned and Stella at the Old School House. And in the garden of Rose Cottage where Molly had welcomed forget-me-nots for many years, they occupied every spare inch of soil.

Around the village phones rang as friends and family of Molly compared notes and marvelled at the unbelievable spectacle that had bewitched their gardens. But not only gardens benefited from the colourful display. Forget-me-nots bloomed in every corner of the graveyard and beneath the bench Ned had donated to commemorate the lives of his mother and the major. They bloomed on the cliff tops, on the grass verges, down the lanes and in the shade of Bluebell Woods.

"Must have been the freezing cold weather and snow that's brought this all on," said Albert Treloar, scratching his head, as he staggered outside the Fox and Hounds, where forget-me-nots had squeezed into the tubs by the front door amongst the tulips, "though for the life of me I've never seen the likes of it before."

From a drawer in her dressing table Elizabeth pulled out her jewellery box and from inside it she carefully took the necklace and earrings which Molly had bought her for Christmas. With shaky fingers she clasped the necklace around her neck and hung the earrings from her ears. From the card she then read her great grandmother's words:

Forget-me-nots, sweet conveyers of love
Tended by cherubs in Eden above,
Sprinkled by angels from heavenly skies
Reminders to mankind that love never dies.

So, when I am gone, I beg, please do not mourn,
I'll watch o'er you each day from sunrise at dawn,
'til stars fill the skies and daylight has gone
for I shall not be dead, but just passed on.

With wings I shall flutter and dance with the breeze,
I shall shout in a storm and rustle the trees,
I shall run with the wind and roar with the sea,
My pain shall be gone and my spirit be free.

Forget-me-nots, sweet conveyers of love
Tended by cherubs in Eden above,

Sprinkled by angels from heavenly skies
Reminders to mankind that love never dies.

THE END

20540987R00139

Printed in Great Britain
by Amazon